Ghost Fish
of Floating Bone Lake

Donna J. Hall Nobles

WestBow
PRESS
A DIVISION OF THOMAS NELSON

Copyright © 2011 Donna J. Hall Nobles

All rights reserved. No part of this book may be used or reproduced by any means, graphic, electronic, or mechanical, including photocopying, recording, taping or by any information storage retrieval system without the written permission of the publisher except in the case of brief quotations embodied in critical articles and reviews.

WestBow Press books may be ordered through booksellers or by contacting:

WestBow Press
A Division of Thomas Nelson
1663 Liberty Drive
Bloomington, IN 47403
www.westbowpress.com
1-(866) 928-1240

Because of the dynamic nature of the Internet, any web addresses or links contained in this book may have changed since publication and may no longer be valid. The views expressed in this work are solely those of the author and do not necessarily reflect the views of the publisher, and the publisher hereby disclaims any responsibility for them.

Any people depicted in stock imagery provided by Thinkstock are models, and such images are being used for illustrative purposes only.

Certain stock imagery © Thinkstock.

ISB:N 978-1-4497-2753-6 (sc)
ISBN: 978-1-4497-2754-3 (dj)
ISBN: 978-1-4497-2755-0 (e)

Library of Congress Control Number: 2011917012

Printed in the United States of America

WestBow Press rev. date: 10/25/2011

to

my real life granddaughter, Andrea

and her Floating Bone Lake

"For I know the plans I have for you," says the Lord. "They are plans for good and not for disaster, to give you a future and a hope." Jeremiah 29:11-12

Acknowledgements

Of my siblings who made publishing possible: Jim (Sharon) Hall, Diana (Wayne) Seaton, Elaine Tharp, Walt (Pam) Hall, and Terry (Ruth) Hall.

Of my readers, editors, and encouragers: Andrea and Kathy Loudermilk, Marsha Jones, Nancy Shuman, Barbara McPhearson, Dianna Mosedale, Joanne and Rev. Tom Malone, Linda Roberts, Dr. Richard Ruth, and Madison Park Church of God Writer's Group.

Thanks to Faith Saltsman, cover designer and to Tom Starland, info@ Carolinaarts.com for permission to use photo of lake on the cover.

Unless otherwise indicated, all Scripture quotations are taken from the Holy Bible, *New Living Translation*, copyright 1996, 2004. Used by permission of Tyndale House Publishers, Inc., P.O Box 80, Wheaton, Illinois 60189

This novel is fiction. Names, characters, places and plot are either the product of the author's imagination or are used fictitiously. Any resemblance to actual persons, living or dead, business, events, or locales is entirely coincidental.

Prologue

Russ and Carol had missed their turn. Neither spoke. Russ was focused on getting back on track and making up for lost time. Carol sat mannequin-like, stiff and unmoving, in the passenger seat. Her knuckles were white with tension as she clutched their prized possession.

Russ eased up on the gas pedal and turned to give Carol a brief faint smile. Then he refocused on the roadway and on the sheen reflected in the headlights. The weather had deteriorated, and the cold rain was now mixed with snow. The tires slipped on the icy pavement, but he still had control.

Suddenly headlights blinded Russ; on impact, he instinctively slammed the brakes. The car skidded through the guard rail and over the embankment.

Hours later when saving responders reached the smoldering auto at the bottom of the debris strewn hillside; they pronounced both Russ and Carol dead at the scene.

Chapter 1

Susan paused at a barbed-wire fence and shaded her eyes to see the little lake nestled among pines, budding oak, maple and sweet gum trees. The place seemed calm and innocent enough. As if shot from nature's paint gun, wildflowers, yellow jasmines and bluets were splashed into the dense undergrowth. Just how accurate were reports of exposed bones, unexplained noises, and wild dogs? She would undoubtedly have to refute any rumors or folktale to sell this property. Hopefully there wasn't more to contend with in order to make a sale. What secrets lay beneath the tranquility? She snickered at her own introduction of imaginary vultures.

Susan sighed. With a quick intake of warm, sweet, moist air, she shook her head and flipped her blond-streaked brown hair back over her shoulder. Had she had been paying attention; she would have noticed the ankle-deep mud much sooner.

"Oh, crap! My favorite shoes!" She lifted one foot. "Oh, they're ruined!"

Though it had rained for a day and night, Susan still felt she needed to view the area before she met with the sellers again.

"We would like you to begin the process of marketing our property," Iris Fenback and Melton Goldsmith, the heirs, had instructed. "Mother will not be with us for much longer, and we would like it sold as soon as possible after she passes."

The consultation with Iris and Melton had left a sour taste in Susan's mouth. Greed like this was out of her league, even with her grit and determination to make a sale. She had pictured the sister and brother as vultures circling over their mother's limp body and her property.

They notified Susan of Mrs. Goldsmith's death two weeks ago.

She sighed again. She couldn't help it.

"I wonder what Aunt Em and Uncle Owen would think about tramping through a muddy field?" A bitter grin creased her lovely face. Back in Columbia, Aunt Em and Uncle Owen had always been there, even after her move into her own apartment. She didn't need anyone looking over her shoulder, and she wasn't interested in their *God stuff*. She had discarded God when she was ten.

Then there was Jackson. He sure didn't come rushing after her when she moved to Plaincreek Crossroads. It had been six months and not even a call. Susan was beginning to realize she was not the least bit relevant to him.

Speaking to the barbed wire fence where she stood, Susan hesitated. "I had to go for the sales. The real estate market here is bustling, and I have the opportunity of a lifetime. I want the Sales Person of the Year award; I am going to get it. I'm even away from Aunt Em and Uncle Owen, too. This was a smart move … wasn't it?"

"Hey, lady, you can't...," called a blond-headed boy, pushing his bike toward her, "go-o fishing..." His voice trailed off as he stood staring open mouthed.

Hah! Go fishing. No way. Nearly twenty years of avoiding her most terrifying, and yet most cherished, experience had not dulled the pain. She brushed a strand of hair from across her eyes.

No wonder he stared; the designer dark blue skirt and matching jacket with blue-and-white-striped blouse she had worn to the office was not an outfit for a muddy tromp to the lake. She should have made a complete change of clothing instead of just switching from her high heels to her dress flats.

"Hey, lady, watch out for snakes!" The young boy had recovered.

Susan jumped! Given the authority by God, though she hadn't talked to Him in a while, snakes were at the top of her list of creatures she would un-create. Spiders were second.

"My mother saw you. We live there." He pointed toward the subdivision. "She sent me to warn you about the flooding and snakes. You don't look like fishin'. What are you doing out here?"

"Well, I wanted to see the lake, but I sure can't get near it today. I'll have to come back when it's a little drier. What can you tell me about this area back here? My name is Susan Walen, and you are--?"

"My name is Trevor. Why do you want to know?"

"Do you play back here? Do you kids fish in that lake? What do you call it? Are there wild animals? Did any of you kids ever get hurt?"

"Would you care to talk to my mom?"

"Well...sure, if your mother doesn't mind, and I won't be interrupting?"

"Naw, she's just watching my sister."

Trevor walked along with Susan, pushing his bike through the mucky, slippery spots in the saturated field. She could imagine the sucking, sliding and slipping in the South Carolina red clay she'd be doing if she'd still had on her three-inch navy heels. She chuckled. Trevor gave her a wry smile, as if she had grown a second nose.

Oh, good, he was taking her just down the street from the cul-de-sac where she had parked her Malibu. Trevor entered the back of a two-story house through sliding glass doors off a deck. Susan tiptoed right behind. He didn't call out. She paused to slip off her soggy shoes and then followed, looking around and behind, as if she were breaking and entering.

A fair curly-headed toddler brushed past them heading for the not-completely-closed deck doors.

"Mo-o-m, Gabi's going outside again!"

"Trevor, get her!" Trevor's mom ran in from another room but stopped short when she saw Susan. Trevor snagged his squiggling sister by the arm, and dragged her across the threshold.

Susan grinned.

"This is my mom. She wanted me to tell you about the rain." Trevor handed Gabi over to his mother and left the room.

With a quick glance, Susan noted the lived-in disarray and camera binoculars on a table next to a picture window.

"I'm Susan Walen. Thanks for sending Trevor to warn me." She extended her hand but offered no other explanation or information.

"Oh, please sit down--Susan. I saw you, and thought you were one of the kids going fishing. You can't tell how flooded it is until you're in the water, and there are snakes. I thought there could be a problem. By the way, I'm Maggie Riley."

"Maggie, I'm glad to meet you. I don't like admitting it, but I'm terrified of snakes. I'd panic just seeing one. I'm fairly new around here. Do you mind if I ask you about the woods and the lake?"

Susan followed Maggie's interest in her muddy feet. Susan was so embarrassed; the mud had painted the cut-out pattern of Susan's flats, stencil perfect, on her bare feet. What could she do but hold them up? "Beautiful, huh? Nature's artistry."

"I'd recognize the shoes those feet came from in a lineup, but I imagine those shoes are destined for the trash. It's too bad. Had they lived a long life?" Maggie chuckled when Susan pantomimed wiping tears. "Your favorites huh?"

"Yeah, well, it's my own fault for not putting on my scruffy tennis shoes, even if they wouldn't have matched." Susan shrugged.

Both of them leaned back laughing.

"About the lake, I can't tell you much, but because of some of the stories these kids tell, I've told Trevor he's not to go in the woods or to the lake by himself. When we bought this house, Mrs. Goldsmith told us not to worry about any development of the wooded area behind or in either direction. Her promise is one reason we settled on this property. Though neither David my husband, nor I claim to be a Tarzan or a Jane, we enjoy the untamed beauty of our miniature forest. We see deer in our backyard nearly every day."

"Yeah, and wild dogs too. Mama is as big as a horse, and you never hear her until she's breathing in your ear. You don't mess with her." Trevor had returned, munching on a peanut butter and jelly sandwich.

If she planned to talk to God, Susan could easily add wild dogs to her un-create list.

"Trevor! I've never seen Mama or any wild dog. I don't believe there are any wolves either."

As Maggie was explaining, Susan caught a movement out of the corner of her eye and turned to the window to watch a nice-looking man step up on the porch. When the doorbell rang, Trevor sprang to open the door before either woman could move a muscle. Maggie grabbed Gabi who was right behind Trevor.

"Come on in. Mom sent me to get her," referring to Susan, "'cause of the flooding. You should have seen her jump when I yelled about the snakes." Trevor stepped aside.

Susan stood as Maggie walked over to the tall, dark-haired man dressed in a business suit, "Hi, Garrett. This is Susan. I did send Trevor to rescue her. Susan, Garrett is a neighbor."

Maggie who was still balancing Gabi on her hip stepped back. Susan smiled and nodded but stood firm unable to say anything in response. She focused on the unruly lock of Garrett's hair on his forehead.

Garrett laid his right hand on the right side of his face, lowered the left side of his face to his left shoulder and raised his eyebrows. Slowly then, he surveyed Susan from her blue eyes to her immaculate suit and finally to her mud-painted bare feet. He focused on her muddy feet, shook his head, grinned and turned to leave.

Susan followed his gaze to her feet and without thinking curled her toes.

"Garrett, sit down and stay," but Maggie was too late. He was already out on the porch with Trevor close behind.

"I'll check with you later," Garrett called back.

"Heavens! Hum…I don't know what he was thinking." Maggie shook her head. "Do you feel as if you have gotten the once-over? What's the word I want—scrutinized? Never mind him. He probably stopped by to give me something for our monthly newsletter. I'm the editor for the Bone Brook Neighborhood Association. We've had some pretty hot topics lately. In fact, since you're asking about the wet lands back there, we've been discussing the possibility of developers purchasing the property for additional subdivisions. You can imagine we don't want it sold and more houses built. The owner, Clara Goldsmith, passed away recently, and her heirs are in a snit to get it sold."

Garrett's visual inspection of her and Maggie's negative feelings about the sale of the property made Susan feel off center. She saw the error of her ways in not exactly telling Maggie, the camera-binocular detective she was a realtor. Could she say now; *by the way, I'm the one who is going to sell the property the homeowners don't want sold?* No, it would be awkward and uncomfortable. She needed to leave. As if wearing a black trench coat, dark sunglasses, with a little notebook in hand, she now had insider information.

"Maggie, thank you so much again for the warning. Could you direct me to someone who knows the history of the property and the lake?"

"Susan, I'm trying to think."

Trevor, who had come back in from the front porch, interrupted, "Do you mean about *Floating Bone Lake* and all the weird noises? This ole' guy hangs out at the library. He's real old, and he knows some stories about the lake."

"Oh, thank you, Trevor. The library, huh? I'd better be going."

Susan sat in her Malibu collecting her thoughts. The kids named the lake, *Floating Bone Lake*. Floating bones? Well, with a name like *Floating Bone Lake* tales of wild dogs and strange noises seemed to fit. Then, too, there could be a problem with a restriction on the sale of the property because of Mrs. Goldsmith's promise. It was doubtful, of course, whether a oral agreement would stand up before a judge. This was becoming more of a challenge than she originally thought.

What tales would the storyteller spin?

Chapter 2

What was I thinking? Susan was at a loss. When she left Maggie's last week, she neglected to ask Trevor the name of the storyteller. All she knew was the storyteller was a man, and *he* was extremely old. "Now," she muttered to herself, "how am I supposed to find him?" She pictured a weathered gentleman with white hair and beard, a corn cob pipe between his teeth, a tattered book under his arm, leaning on a cane while he told his stories. If he showed up at all, she would consider herself fortunate.

Nevertheless, Susan pulled into the parking lot of the gazebo-like Plaincreek Crossroads Library. She craned her neck, awed by the floor-to-ceiling glass panels, ionic columns, cascading flowers in hanging pots, and a broad yellow brick sidewalk which encircled the entire building. Susan snickered. It fit; the yellow brick road, library path to wisdom or at least knowledge. Aunt Em's Wizard of Oz was forever with her. Plaincreek Crossroads Public Library was not plain as the name suggested; it was beautiful. This tourist attraction was also exceptionally busy.

Susan avoided even the appearance of helplessness. She would eventually need help and have to ask at the information desk about the storyteller. For the time being, she sat down to wait; she leaned back on the cushioned bench in the check out area and closed her eyes.

"Susan?"

She sat bolt upright, nearly butting heads with the gentleman leaning over her. His hand on her shoulder jolted her from her drowsiness. Out of the corner of her eye she caught a movement, and she thought for a moment she saw Garrett, Maggie's neighbor, leaving the library.

"Are you looking for me?" The man asked.

"I don't know. You are--?" Many adults and children in the checkout line turned to look.

"I'm Angus, the storyteller. I'm on my way up to the second floor to the South Carolina room. Care to join me?" With a sweeping motion of his arm, he invited everyone and extended his hand to Susan.

"Sure, yes. I do want to talk to you." Angus, the storyteller, had clear green eyes, short trimmed mustache, open smile and graying beard. A very old storyteller? Hardly. This Angus, in spite of grey in his beard, could only be a few years older than Maggie's neighbor Garrett. Well, Trevor was probably ten or so. Old is a different reality to youth.

Susan was willing to listen to his stories, but what she needed was to ask questions. Her interest lay with the Goldsmiths, their property, and what role they had played in founding the town. She wanted any details about the property or the lake, so she could formulate a sales angle.

She swallowed a yawn.

Angus began with some state history. On May 23, 1788, South Carolina was the eighth state to approve the Constitution of the United States. It was the first state to declare secession from the Union December 20, 1860, forming the Confederate States of America. In the early 1800's, a mercantile store and way station for a stage coach line were the beginnings of Plaincreek Crossroads.

Susan shifted in her chair; just maybe the mercantile was in some way connected to the great grandfather of Clara Goldsmith.

"Cotton was the first industry in the area, and slave labor built the plantations. The conscience of a young country, the United States of America, led to the formation of the Underground Railroad," Angus continued.

Susan nearly drifted off until Angus began to weave tales of slaves who tried to escape. If they were caught, the slaves could be shot, hung on any available tree or returned to their owners who chose their punishment. Angus described a journey often through swampy and out of the way haunts, enduring hunger and dangerously cramped, crowded conditions. Ultimately the slaves had to trust, not only their African brothers, but also whites whom they feared.

He finished.

Susan quickly scooted out of her seat to go speak with him, but Angus had vanished. Questions ran through her mind. How did he know her name? Had Garrett been in the library? Did Garrett know Angus? Susan had to admit Angus made the history of South Carolina come alive. She enjoyed this time in the South Carolina Room, only she wished Angus' stories related to the Goldsmiths and the lake. How was she ever going to have an advantage if she couldn't find some unique marketing strategy?

Surely the water had receded since last week; she could explore the lake. She would even think about possibly *going fishing*. Unfortunately she didn't have someone to bait her hook with the worm, another critter for her un-create list.

Susan would have stopped by Maggie's on her way to the lake, but she hadn't wanted to take time. As she walked, she swayed to the rhythmic swishing and rustling of the meadow. She inhaled the fragrance of the green Indian grass. It was so quiet she could hear her own breathing. When she came to the rusty barbed wire which had been bent and stomped to less than its original height, she had to remind herself; she had a perfect right to be there, even if on her own time.

"I look as if I'm going fishing now with old clothes, a fishing pole, bait, and bucket. Don't tell anyone, but I'm not sure about this. Is fishing like riding a bicycle? Is it something you don't forget?" Susan figured the old fence had heard many conversations on the way to the lake. "You know, it's been almost twenty years since I've been fishing. I used to go with my father, but I don't want to think about him right now." She took a deep breath and stepped over the fence to follow the meandering foot trail which appeared to lead to the lake.

The lake mirrored a late afternoon blue sky, wispy clouds and a leafy green framework of branches. She ventured closer down a slope, set her pail beside her and reached for her bait. She closed her eyes, squinting to skewer one worm, which she dropped, then another, before she finally was able to dip her baited line at the water's edge. As she followed the ripples, floating objects appeared in the middle of the lake.

"What are those?" She questioned the lake. "Trevor called this Floating Bone Lake. Then it is not just a story. No fishing today."

She backed up but caught her breath when she looked into the eyes of a dusty brown buck not more than a few yards from her. Could a young Indian brave have stared into eyes of a deer with his bow and arrow aimed for a kill? Had there been tepees close by, and a whiff of smoke wafting through the silent woods? How old was the lake? Susan shook her head and raised her hand. The buck darted.

As she turned, she stumbled and fell against Garrett. She screamed and jerked off of his supporting arm.

"Whoa, you ran into me, lady!"

Susan was skilled at regaining composure, except while straightening a totally crooked hat and pulling down an already stretched out shirt, she caught the hook from her fishing line in her finger.

"Oh ouch! Oh, it hurts!"

"Let me see." Garrett gently turned her left hand over to take a look. "Hum, oh, you're fortunate. It's not in far enough to have to be cut out. Be very still; I think I can get it." He extracted the hook from her finger and the fishing pole out of her grasp.

Susan looked at her cut.

"I recognized your car from last week, but I didn't recognize you from a distance. I met you last week at Maggie's. Are you really fishing?" Garrett offered his clean handkerchief. "Don't worry; the blood will wash out."

Susan winced as she wrapped her finger in the hanky. She was a little surprised at how much she was bleeding. She grabbed her pail.

"Yes, I'm Susan. You're Garrett, aren't you? I guess you probably wonder why I'm out here. When I heard Angus telling stories about South Carolina, I just thought I would try fishing again."

"Ah, yes, Angus. Trevor said you wanted to know about the lake. If you think Angus is a good storyteller, just wait until you hear my babysitter!"

"*Your* babysitter? Aren't you a little too big for a babysitter?"

Garrett cocked his head to the side and just stared at Susan. He shook his head. "Andy has been with us, me, since a freshman in high school. Next month is graduation. Andy is almost as good as, no, better than Angus at storytelling." While Garrett was talking, he ushered Susan toward his house in the subdivision, just down from Maggie's. They entered a mud room.

"This is Andrea Stokes, Andi, spelled A-n-d-i- not A-n-d-y, *my* babysitter." He grinned.

Garrett was becoming an enigma. He had led Susan to think Andy was a boy. He had not bothered to mention *his* babysitter, was an unusually pretty teenage girl. She was with two boys who were evidently Garrett's sons. If it weren't for their age difference, one about five and the other seven or eight, the boys looked enough alike to be twins.

"So you're Andi, spelled A-n-d-i! I'm Susan. You are not what I expected from your nickname. Garrett says you are quite a storyteller, and you can tell me about the property back there. I'm fairly new in the area. I'm interested in the history and stories about the lake and wet lands."

"Susan's been fishing down at the lake," Garrett explained.

"You've been fishing?" Andi looked at Garrett. "Did you catch anything?"

Garrett reached down and held up Susan's hand, still wrapped in his blood-stained handkerchief.

"Oh, you're hurt!"

"I'm not hurt; it is just a wormy-hook puncture. Yes, I planned to go fishing, but no, I didn't get to fish. Whatever was floating in the middle of the pond was not there at first. The buck was so big. Then Garrett came, and I'm rambling..." Susan paused, cocked her head sideways and squinted. "Garrett says you know about the lake."

"We named the lake Floating Bone Lake because of the floating bones you just described. Do you know about the vegetable house?"

Now the Goldsmith property was a valuable piece of real estate in itself. Because the area was growing rapidly, housing was at a premium; an undeveloped piece of land was highly desirable. Each time she discovered more about the property, selling it became more complicated. What was the vegetable house? Could there be some historical significance? Uninvited thoughts wiggled into her mind; perhaps it would be a shame to destroy this bit of wild loveliness; perhaps the property should not be sold to a developer. "I should go back to do more exploring and even try fishing again."

"I'll go with you, show you around, and I'll even bait your hook if you wish. Baiting a fishing line doesn't bother me at all," Andi offered.

Susan couldn't refuse; Andi would take her *un-create candidate*, the worm, and skewer the slimy, wiggling creature onto a hook. "I accept, and while we're going, I want to hear all about those floating bones and the vegetable house."

( )

One afternoon a couple of days later after school hours, Susan, at least wearing slacks and not a designer suit this time, met Andi at the cul-de-sac.

"Hey guys, this is Susan, the lady who wants to go fishing and to see the vegetable house. Susan, these are my friends, Jesse, Dan, and Matt. We are in the same class in high school, and we like to go to the lake together."

"Hey," they answered, grinned, and tipped their fishing hats to her.

The thought of Maggie with her camera binoculars was somehow comforting. The youths were friendly and excited about going, but they were too mischievous.

"We haven't been told not go to the vegetable house, but we usually don't tell anyone where we're really going. If you do want to see it, we'll begin to fish, but then go on," Andi was the spokesperson. The boys nodded in conspiratorial agreement and camaraderie.

Susan suppressed laughter at the cloak-and-dagger whispers of the teenagers. She was on her way to the lake for the third time. Fishing with her father had been off the end of the dock while they dangled their feet in the water. After her father had died, fishing was just a too-painful experience. Now she was a grownup, and this was different; she needed to find out more to market this Goldsmith land.

They had only gone a short distance when Dan brought her out of her thoughts. "Wow! You almost stepped on him!"

Susan stopped, and like a row of dominos Andi bumped her, and Matt bumped Andi. At Susan's feet was a straggly little puppy.

"That's one of Mama's. No, don't touch him! Mama is mean. She might be watching us right now. I, for one, don't want to hear her *growl*." While Dan emphasized *growl*, the others nodded and detoured around the puppy.

Susan was curious, but wasn't about to admit she was wary of any dog; unless it was small enough to carry in her purse, *or* any dog she did not know, *or* any dog, not on a leash *or* any dog, which growled. Aunt Em and Uncle Owen had given her a dog, but Susan stubbornly refused to share her space with a pet, again. They finally gave it away. She would gladly leave Mama's puppy alone.

At the lake, true to her word, Andi baited Susan's hook. The group settled down. Though they were all within an arm's reach of each other, all was hush, hush. The floating bones appeared.

"What do you know about those bones? When do they float? Do they sink again? How deep is this lake? Have you ever caught any fish?" Susan felt a tug on her line. "I've got a big one!" She held it away, so it wouldn't drip on her.

Andi turned in Susan's direction. The fish flashed like a piece of a rainbow, and all the bones and the entrails could be clearly seen through the skin. It was transparent!

Susan gasped and dropped her pole. She watched the fish flop off the hook and back into the water.

Without a word, Andi motioned to her friends. All four teenagers packed up their poles and started back through the woods and across the field.

It took Susan a moment to realize the fishing was over. They were done for the day. Andi had looked directly at her and the fish. Didn't she think the fish was unusual? Was that a stab of pain in Andi's eyes? About a fish? Susan didn't know whether to be more amazed about Andi seeming complacency or the strange fish.

She had to skip and hop to keep up with them. "Whoa, what about going to the vegetable house?" All four looked back and forth, smiling and nodding at each other; excitement was in the air.

"You still want to go?" Andi grinned. "The vegetable house is on the other side of the lake. No pretty clothes or good shoes. Well?"

"Let's go tomorrow after school. The three boys, dubbed the three musketeers by Susan, answered in unison. Then, they and Andi began chatting among themselves, making plans for the rest of the afternoon, without regard to Susan being there.

Susan scratched her head. She wasn't sure the boys had clearly seen the fish, but Andi had seen it. She asked herself again; *why didn't Andi react?* Then again, maybe the abrupt end to the fishing was Andi's response.

When Susan reminded them about going to the vegetable house, she couldn't avoid the glances and understood amusement. She had no idea what was in store for her. She did not trust Andi and the boys, even if they did appear innocent and responsible. Apprehension par excellence.

Susan caught up with the youths. "Andi, will Garrett's wife, be at home tomorrow? Do you have to baby-sit? You can come, can't you?"

"I'm pretty sure I can. You don't know? Garrett's wife, Carol, died in an auto accident over a year ago. She and my dad were on a trip together. My father died too. Instantly, they said. I think Garrett will be home early tomorrow, so I won't need to baby sit."

"No, I didn't know," Susan hung her head. "Oh, I'm sorry, Andi!"

Had Susan heard right, Andi's father and Garrett's wife both died in an accident? Andi would have been about sixteen when her father died; Susan was ten when her father drowned. Garrett lost his wife. Who was Garrett? What did he do? Was he at the library when Angus found her? How did he happen to be at the lake when she went the second time?

"See you tomorrow afternoon." Andi and her three friends crossed the street to Andi's house.

When Susan reached the Malibu, she pulled her map from the glove compartment to trace the outlines of the Goldsmith property. According to Andi and the boys, the vegetable house was on the other side of the lake. Why do they call it the vegetable house? Was there some history? Time for another trip to the library and perhaps to the South Carolina Room.

Susan was so engrossed in studying the map she wasn't aware of Garrett's presence. He leaned over with his elbows on the open window.

As if a child caught in a forbidden act, Susan closed the map and threw it down in the seat.

"What, no fish?" He glanced around.

She would have given anything to have been able to hold up an impressive string of fish. She would have been happy with a single fish. Why, she wondered, did she feel as if she were hiding something or caught in some compromising situation when he was around? Why do I care what he thinks? Well, I care what everyone thinks. Getting ahead in business isn't easy. I have to care what people think.

Garrett was still leaning on her open car window, his curious brown eyes searching her soft blue eyes.

"Well, I did catch a fish, but I dropped it. The kids will tell you."

"You went fishing all dressed up, and you caught a fish and then dropped it? Did I get that right? The one that got away. Typical topic for conversation. I'll catch you later." Garrett shook his head and stepped away from the car.

He sure believed her! Ha. Susan sat thinking about Garrett and his wife. It would have been difficult to express sympathy, since he hadn't been the one to tell her. According to Andi, the accident was over a year ago. Then, there was the fish. She wanted to explain about fish, but she wasn't sure if she was making too much of it. He might think she was foolish. As soon as she was clear about the fish, then it might be a topic for discussion.

$$\sim$$

Later Susan stumbled into her apartment with books on South Carolina history and geography. Determined to find out more, she also had one book on fish.

"I wonder who stood in this very spot almost one hundred years ago." Her cotton-mill-remodeled apartment sported high ceilings, a wall of windows, and hardwood floors. The lack of landscaping and lots of concrete didn't bother Susan when she had rented it six months before. Now, as she stood from her second story sun room, she longed for some green lawn and a place to plant flowers.

"Enough!" She had an appointment in the morning with Iris Fenback and Melton Goldsmith, her vultures, heirs of Floating Bone Lake. More background to enhance her marketing plan, not her imagination, was what she needed now.

Stories and the mystery of objects floating, disappearing and then reappearing on the lake intrigued Susan. Was there some deep, dark secret; was there special water or warm springs in the lake? Historically, Plaincreek Crossroads would have been Cherokee Indian territory. Could the bones be from an ancient Indian burial ground?

Along with Native Americans, several different groups, including Hispanics, Scots and Irish settled South Carolina. Ah, yes, that would explain Angus.

What about the fish? She had never seen any like it. What about the wild life? Had there been any research regarding this piece of property as a habitat for a variety of species of animals or even insects? What would life be without wilderness? What would life be without noise, concrete, businesses and houses with families and children?

Again Susan laughed; children will go where no adult would want to go. Tomorrow after work, she was going to be taken to the vegetable house, and she didn't know what it was.

Chapter 3

Glowing spike-covered fish leaped from red-murky water and flew at her from all sides. She broke off tree branches which immediately became poison tipped paper airplanes. When she struck the piercing eyes of what she named the *dinofish* with the poison planes, the fish fell back into the slimy depths. While fighting them off, a young girl who was standing next to Susan slipped into the watery darkness and disappeared.

Susan awoke and stumbled out of bed; she felt as if she had been hit by a Mack truck. She caught her breath in the middle of a sniffle and realized she had been crying. Now she would have to do something about her swollen eyes.

"I've got to pull myself together and get to the office!"

Later while waiting in her Malibu at a red light, the mounted policeman called down to her; "Is everything all right?"

She nodded and smiled, but she wondered if she had successfully erased evidence of her restless night. Did her make-up adequately cover her red, puffy eyes? Surely her brand new, lacy, green slacks suit was beautiful and would help her general appearance. She certainly needed confidence to face the challenges of the day despite the drama of the night.

When she arrived at the office, everyone was standing and watching. On her way to her own desk, she nodded as she passed each co-worker.

From all over the room, poison tipped paper airplanes missed their targets, and dinofish flew toward her. Was her nightmare because she was trying to fish again? She paused and then she knew; it was all about fishing with her dad. Now she understood all the tears. In the dream *she* was the small child who fell into the water.

It took her a moment to focus on the multicolored bouquet of spring flowers in a crystal vase on her desk. What was today? May 1ˢᵗ her birthday! She gasped while her colleagues sang *Happy Birthday* and applauded.

"Oh, they're beautiful! Thank you."

The Happy-Birthday-Susan cake was white with yellow trim and multicolored flowers, much like the bouquet on her desk. No candles, she noted. Good! She did not miss having twenty nine glowing, dripping candles anchored in little plastic roses all over the cake. She was gratefully spared all the huffing and puffing; remarks about needing a fire extinguisher or a smoke alarm going off; even questions about why she wasn't married and the mother of at least one, maybe two children.

From tears to laughter. Life can be good, and she was grateful for the change this morning.

"Let's put the cake in the lunch room!"

She hadn't quite read all the birthday cards when the owners of the Goldsmith property entered her office. Mrs. Iris Fenback had an air of distinction and nobility. Susan was jolted by the look Iris gave her; the look toward a troublesome, unworthy servant. Susan knew she didn't deserve Iris' disdain, but she passed it off. Mr. Melton Goldsmith, on the other hand, handsome in his dark suit, was neutral. The two resembled each other enough to be recognized as sister and brother.

"Is Garrett here yet?" Iris asked.

"Garrett?"

"Oh, of course, *you've already met him.*"

Garrett walked up and stood in the doorway. He stared at Susan's nameplate, the cards and the flowers. He looked from his sister-in-law to his brother-in-law, "What have I missed?"

"Nothing, Garrett. Clarissa said you knew Susan; the real estate agent Ron Keller in Columbia recommended. He said she would stop at nothing to make a sale. She has an exclusive listing for our property."

"Ah, yes, Susan, but I didn't know she was the real estate agent Clarissa was talking about." Garrett grinned at Susan as he answered Iris.

Susan tried not to look surprised, but she had no idea how Garrett was involved with the Goldsmith property. Then, too, who was Clarissa? "Come on in Garrett. Please everyone, have a seat."

Iris turned to Susan. "You moved to Plaincreek Crossroads from Columbia about six months ago, right? Surely you have already told Garrett all this, my dear." Iris, who had been studying her nails, continued. "Miss Walen, what have you done since our initial introduction? What progress do you have to tell us about the sale of our property?"

Susan gave herself a moment to think while she pulled her chair out from behind her desk and joined Iris, Melton and Garrett, already seated for their meeting. "I'm at a little bit of a disadvantage here. I understand you, Iris, and you, Melton, are both heirs of Clara Goldsmith and thus owners of the property, but I had no idea you, Garrett, were also an heir?"

"No he's not. His wife, Carol, was our niece. We just want his input. We still consider him family." Iris flashed another irritated look toward Susan.

Susan had to think for moment; Garrett's wife, Carol, was Mrs. Goldsmith's granddaughter. Andi said Garrett's wife and Andi's father died in the same auto accident.

For now, Susan had to confront the *promise problem*. "I've been out to the meadow and lake a couple of times. I do have to admit your property is an exceptional piece of real estate; however, I understand Mrs. Goldsmith had an agreement with current homeowners. To afford some degree of country living, this property would not be developed but would remain in its current state.

"Yes, we heard it. We are not our mother! We did not make any such agreement. Show us some proof. Both Melton and I have looked, and we cannot find anything, in writing, to substantiate these claims." Iris changed her sitting position. "Our attorney can fill you in."

Garrett lightly touched Iris on the shoulder. "As Susan said, Iris, several of the homeowners, who are my neighbors, would not have purchased their homes if they had not been promised the preservation of the wet lands. I don't think any of them thought it was necessary to get the agreement in writing as part of the terms of their purchase."

"What can I say? It is unfortunate. Miss Walen, I trust Ron's, Mr. Keller's opinion. I know you have your own reasons for selling the land, and you will do your best to expedite the sale of this property. Please keep in contact with me daily. Oh, just because Plaincreek Crossroads could be considered a *hick* little town, don't think we don't recognize your *city* ways." With a snicker, Iris checked her watch. She was ready to leave.

"I think we need to talk," Garrett whispered to Susan. As he was leaving he handed her a copy of the *Bone Brook Newsletter*.

After they had left, Susan began to read. The front page announced a meeting regarding the possible sale of the backwoods property. The article stated Mrs. Goldsmith had passed away, and Clarian Real Estate was the real estate agency. Discussion was to cover what could be done to insure the property would not be sold to a developer. Maggie had mentioned the opposition to the sale when she and Susan first met.

Didn't they understand the dynamics of a piece of property like this? Since the owners were intent upon selling the property, there weren't a lot of options. No one among the homeowners could afford to purchase the land themselves to prevent its development. The state would not identify it a wetland reserve due to its relative small acreage. Any developer would have to make a substantial investment. The lake, wild and lovely, was not large enough to be of value as a lake, and it would most likely be drained to make room for housing. The trees would be cut. Roads, lights, and sewers would also be a substantial cost. There was no other way.

All she could do for the homeowners was to make sure the property was sold to a legitimate, reputable company which would take these people into consideration where ever possible.

What bothered Susan was Clarissa. Who was she? How did she know Garrett? Most of all, what had Clarissa told Iris about Susan? Clarissa must have said something to Garrett also. How would this Clarissa know anything about her?

Susan had said nothing to Garrett about going to the vegetable house.

Later in the afternoon after she had changed out of her new slacks suit, Susan drove to Bone Lake Circle and parked in the same spot as always on the cul-de-sac. She had every intention of pausing to say "hi" to Maggie, complimenting her on the newsletter, and introducing herself as the real estate agent for the property. As she closed her car door, she could hear Andi and the boys on down the street.

"I don't want to keep them waiting," she muttered, as she ran to meet the gang.

Maggie who was standing on her front porch, put one hand over her mouth muffling her laughter, and waved as Susan ran by.

The kids bent double laughing when they saw Susan. So, maybe she did overdo the no-good-clothes bit. She was wearing faded, paint-covered and baggy bib overalls. She actually didn't know why she hadn't thrown them out, but they were perfect for this little trek. Her sneakers had reflective strips and lighted heels. So what! She had found a tattered plaid long sleeve shirt because, though it was spring and warm, Susan didn't want bugs all over her. To top off her ensemble, she had a straw hat with a wide fringe around the brim. At one time, it would have been the envy of even the most sophisticated scarecrow.

"Let's get going, *Huckleberry*," the boys giggled.

Later, as they all cut away from the fishing path taken previously to the lake, the kids were still making fun of Susan. She had to admit it wasn't easy keeping up with the teenagers, but there was no way she would let them know it. They were a couple of yards ahead of her, laughing and fooling around with each other, almost as if she weren't there.

After a moment or two, Susan realized she *was* alone. Where were those darn kids? She began to run, stumbled, and twisted her ankle. She stopped, leaned against a tree, and bent down to rub her throbbing leg. As she lifted her head, delicate gauze-like strands covered her face. She had forgotten to put on her hat, and now it was too late! What was all the screaming? She had to get the webs off! She clawed and slapped, but one web seemed to be attached to yet another. This time she did fall.

Susan blinked; there was one bright flash. Three eager faces focused on the trees. "Do it again," they shouted.

Susan turned in the direction of their amusement. Andi clicked a charcoal lighter, and in an instant, the web and its occupant flashed into arachnid oblivion.

"Sit still." Andi flicked the lighter above Susan's head, and there was another flash.

Susan could swear she heard the spider scream. Shaking and gasping, Susan had to wonder if it been her screams earlier? She stared at four poker-faced teenagers.

"Oh, wait," Susan was not going to be left behind again. On to the vegetable house. As she waded through the grass, she began to see the error of wearing baggy overalls. When she got home, she would remove the offending clothing and hurl them into the trash.

Susan limped along listening to the boys teasing each other.

"Matt, where'd you get that stupid hat?" Dan grabbed at it. "Is this a girl's hat? It makes your hair stick to your forehead."

Dan threw the hat to Jesse. "One of these days we're going to throw your hat in the lake, never to see it again."

"Hah! Never to see it again? It would just float along with those bones!"

Matt finally retrieved his hat. "Man, come on guys; don't talk about this veteran fishin' hat. It has character."

"Fishin', you don't go fishin'. Andi's our fisherman."

Susan caught up with Andi while the boys were naming other friends who had joined them on their trips to the lake and the vegetable house. Susan wished they would have elaborated on the details of their exploits, because they had a jolly good time referring to them. Teasing about the vegetable house bothered her. Susan hoped she would be laughing when they got there.

Andi came to a dead stop; Susan nearly rear ended her. What was this? Stretched between two trees was a rotting, crumbling, horizontal ladder covered with vines? Maybe if the area were searched, there would be evidences of fires or tepees. Had arrow heads been found around here? Huh? The kids were frowning and staring at Susan. Had she grown a second nose?

"Do you have any idea?"

Susan came back to the moment. They had been asking her if she knew what this contraption was. "No I'm sorry, I don't much about the history of this area. I'm reading and learning, but I don't have any idea."

On to the vegetable house then.

When Andi first mentioned the vegetable house, Susan thought it must either look like a vegetable or have vegetables growing around it. She visualized a neat little green house with cucumber vines on a trellis; window boxes of sweet peas; sidewalk borders of green beans; old tires full of tomato plants; gardens teeming with honey bees and flitting butterflies. In short, a Hansel and Gretel fantasy house secluded in the forest.

Susan hoped it was a historic building, such as a way station of the stage line or the first mercantile shop doubling as part of the Underground Railroad. Why if it were such a place, would the kids call it a vegetable house?

The group came to a silent halt.

The weathered specter, before them, had a face made of falling timbers and inner decay. Shadows laced in and out of broken rafters, and gaping shingles were hollow, cadaverous eye sockets. The mottled, sagging floor formed a toothless mouth. Flapping side walls resembled unkempt side-burns. The deteriorating porch and rotting blackened steps were like a scraggly chin. A gnarled tree of twisted branches was a grotesque arm, leaning to one side grabbing with fingered limbs. Add a rising mist, distant howling to a full moon outlining a bat or two, and it could compare to a scene in a spooky thriller movie. No one moved. This, then, was the vegetable house.

"There're some bags of stuff in the back. Let's see what's in them." The spell was broken. Andi led the way.

No way was Susan going to be deployed to go through some musty bags of unknown origin. On the other hand, if she didn't get closer, she'd miss what the kids were saying and doing. She carefully inched her way to the back of the remaining wall stacked with moldy hay bales.

As the kids paired off, they went to work struggling with rusty zippers, all the while talking about finding leather straps, pieces of harness, cords and jars of guck on their first visit. They had to pull and twist, but after nearly thirty minutes, they were able to open the bags to find what appeared to be simply rags. The kids had a terrific time and didn't seem to notice Susan did not explore with them. They teased one another about being courageous; about taking a risk; about who would last longer; about staying the night.

Stay the night caught Susan's attention. Here? Spend the night? She did not plan on hanging around. Now was her chance to ask some questions. "Can any of you tell me why you call this a vegetable house?"

Was it Susan's imagination or did the kids want her to ask them about the vegetable house? All four of them gathered around her.

"Did you know this place is haunted?" Jesse suggested, looking at Andi as he asked. When Susan didn't react, he continued in a hushed, secretive tone. "At night there are sounds like voices coming out of the walls and around the house. I don't think you could spend the night...."

"You're absolutely right. Count me *out*." The kids did seem disappointed, but they weren't surprised. "Why do you call this the vegetable house?"

"Did you see the cellar door?" Dan pointed to the decaying floor. The group stood quietly, as if one step would cause the floor to open and swallow them.

"Where?"

Matt nudged Susan to move. She looked closer and discerned the faint outline of a trap door in the dusty floor. She marveled that she had not seen it earlier.

She also made note the sun was much lower, and the shadows were getting longer. It would be getting dark before long.

She stepped back. The three boys, with Susan and Andi looking on, pried the trap door loose and raised it. Though very dark, Susan could see fragments of wood which would have been stairs below at one time.

"Would you like to see what's down there?" Andi was asking.

"How, we didn't bring a light? Surely you kids don't go down there, do you?"

"Naw, we go around back," Andi motioned for Susan to follow.

Erosion behind the house had exposed the walls of the basement. Then someone or something had broken one wall, and the cellar could be entered.

Andi went in first and stood aside for Susan to enter, as well.

"Don't make any fast moves. Just stand still," Andi instructed.

The boys made no attempt to go inside.

As her eyes became accustomed to the semi darkness, Susan could see the still open trap door. From light outside the broken wall, she could make out a large, coal black moving object. Susan froze.

Andi crooned "Come on Mama, we're not going to hurt you. Here, I brought you some food."

Susan saw then, Andi had a pouch of food around her waist and was extending her hand to the largest dog Susan had ever seen. Another smaller dog stood back in the corner.

Andi called him by name, "Come on Brownie, you too." Brownie growled.

Susan's instinct was to run and not stop until she got home. She saw there were puppies, too.

Andi motioned to Susan to back-step towards the broken wall where they had entered. Without a word, Susan turned, stepped out of the doggy basement, and ran double speed up the hill.

Andi and the boys sauntered back.

"Mama and Brownie don't like people. They always growl at the guys, but they seem to like me. Sometimes they let me pet them. They know I love them. I'm their friend," Andi explained.

What could she say? How nice! Well, it was, but Susan was more concerned with survival at the moment. The dogs had not followed them, so they returned to the porch and then up to the musty floor of the house.

From along the back wall Matt, Jesse and Dan pulled out some huge commercial-size cans, turned them upside down and dragged them together into a circle. As she looked around again, she wondered how she had missed seeing the cans stacked among the moldy hay bales.

The four teenagers were relaxed, and Susan didn't want to miss the opportunity to find out about Floating Bone Lake and the rest of the property. "What do you find to do out here?"

The boys just smiled. Andi spoke up. "We have made trails all around the lake, and we take turns hiking them, just for something to do. There are some caves on the other side, but we don't know what might be in there, so we have kinda stayed away from them."

"It is nice to get away from school and parents for awhile." Dan spoke softly.

"We have a place in the trees where we do target practice with bow and arrows. I have improved tons since I started. We did find some arrow heads, and we marked the spot, so we can dig around when we have time." Jesse fished in his pocket and handed Susan a broken arrow head.

"Sometimes we just sit and talk. Most of the time we're on our computers at home or at school, and so it's a change to swap jokes." Andi nudged Matt to get a can for her and Susan, too.

"Tell me about the cans." Susan sat down on one offered by Matt.

All four grimaced. "These we're using to sit on were empty. Some over there are still full, but we're not going to try to open any more. Ugh! The ones we opened were rotten and made us want to throw up. So we dumped the green-goop and the yellow-crud out back for animals to eat."

So now Susan understood. The vegetable house. How unassuming and un-conspiratorial of these kids to identify anything yucky, even vile as vegetables. How typical and even amusing. She wanted to laugh.

"Hey kids."

Shadows were long, and Susan was about to suggest time to start back, when she was interrupted by a screeching cacophony of black winged bombers, silhouettes against the soon-to-be setting sun. She was paralyzed, but only for a moment as they flapped and dove at her. She covered her hair and grabbed for her hat. Then, while kids yelled, cans clanged, dogs barked, and straw went flying, Susan took a desperate leap into the weeds beyond the shaky porch.

After a minute or two of ragged breathing, Susan brushed herself off and looked around for the others. "Another candidate for my ever growing un-create list. Bats!"

As the sunlight faded, Susan realized she was the lone person near the vegetable house. "No, I am not going to call out to them. I'm just going to catch up. I can do this." She ran from the vegetable house; she could see the outline of the trees around the back side and the edge of the lake; she mostly knew where she was.

A fine birthday! She wasn't as frightened as she was just tired and frustrated. Transparent fish, spiders, wild dogs and bats! "I'll process all this later, but for right now, I have to get out of here!"

She saw a shadowy shape in the grass coming toward her. Well, what now? She didn't know whether to run towards it or hide from it. The kids were long gone. Mama and Brownie, she hoped, were behind her at the vegetable house. If she walked slowly, her shoes wouldn't blink, and she might not be seen, at least until she knew who or what it was.

"Susan?"

She breathed easier and hurried to meet the shape coming toward her. She tripped and fell but scrambled to her feet.

She was a ten year old again; *she didn't need help; she could do it on her own.*

The tears came unbidden and did not have a turn off valve when Garrett reached her. Without a word, he put his arms around her; she laid her head on his shoulder and let the tears flow. Her frustration, anger and the uncertainty of what was going on inside her were more than she could handle for the moment. Garrett's arms were comforting. She relaxed and clung to him, reveling in his closeness and his tenderness.

Susan jerked free. What was she doing? Regaining her composure, however, could not erase her disheveled hair or tear streaked face. She was dirty. Her clothes were torn. Her shoes were grass-stained. Somewhere she had lost her pride-of-scarecrows straw hat.

What a wuss I am, she chided herself. She was embarrassed to be in such a vulnerable state. She turned to look at Garrett, "I think I'm just tired. I'm going to have to admit I am no longer a teenager."

"No, you're not." Garrett looked down at her, his brown eyes tender. "Come on," he took her arm. "It gets awfully dark out here when the sun goes down. No street lights you know." He chuckled. He pushed her a little ahead of him. "Well, look at you! You are lightning bugs!" He pointed to her blinking shoes. Now he laughed aloud. "Did you say you were no longer a teenager?"

Susan feigned a light punch to his shoulder and grinned when he ducked. Garrett, she sensed, was going to want to know why she had gone with the kids. As they headed for the road, she tried to think of what she was going to say. He seemed to have taken on the role of protector, but she certainly didn't want to present herself as a victim. She would need to find out about him.

As they neared the property line, Susan became aware of how she must look. How else, other than a damsel in distress, would he recognize her? First, barefoot with dirty feet, next the bleeding finger and now looking decidedly similar to a poster child for a third-world country. Well, this morning after her surprise at seeing him in her office, she was at her best. If she did the math, it was a 75 percent negative and 25 percent positive possible impression rate. Of course, the positive rate would decrease if Garrett had been at the library and had seen her when she nodded off, taking a wink or two in the lobby.

Garrett injected himself into her thoughts by taking her elbow and leading her towards Maggie's house and Susan's Malibu parked at the cul-de-sac. "My boys are at Maggie's, and I want to check on them. I'll see you home. Do you think you can drive? You seem a little dazed. I can take you home and then bring you back for your car tomorrow, or I can follow you home."

Susan breathed a little easier. As she gazed upward at the now starlit heavens, out of nowhere, she wanted to sing, "*… but the pavement's always stayed beneath my feet before. All at once am I several stories high, knowing I'm on the street where you live!*[1] Garrett was still talking. Susan shook herself.

"Are you cold?" The evening breeze was very comfortable.

Susan looked at him through those stubborn once-ten-year-old eyes and regained her composure for the nth time. "No, just tired. You don't have to follow me. I'm fine. I hope I haven't taken up too much of your time. I don't know why you came looking for me, but I'm glad you did. How can I thank you? I don't think I could have gotten lost, but who knows what I would have gotten into."

Garrett shrugged and let her go. "I'll call you tomorrow." Then, almost as an afterthought, he looked down at her and whispered, "Happy Birthday, for what's left of it. We really have several things to talk about; we need to get better acquainted; we should keep each other updated on the property, too."

He opened her unlocked auto door for her and walked away.

---

1   From 1956 Broadway Musical, *My Fair Lady*, On the Street Where You Live, by Alan Jay Lerner.

Chapter 4

Off with her dirty, grimy clothes. Her overalls and long sleeved shirt hung limply from under her trash can lid. Susan relaxed in a hot bath. Did the kids leave her on purpose? Why? What had the vegetable house been? Why had Garrett come looking for her?

She would have soaked longer, but she was hungry. No wonder, since she had not eaten since having birthday cake and punch in the lunch room at the office. After dressing, but too tired to go out, she turned to the refrigerator and found nothing appetizing. While she debated her dilemma, the doorbell rang. Susan could see Garrett illuminated by the outside light on her doorstep.

"I'm sorry, but being resourceful is not one of my strengths. I bring a monster pizza as a peace offering." He said as she opened the door.

"Peace offering? Whatever are you talking about?"

"You know it's pleasant out here tonight, but this pizza is still hot from the oven. Like I said, I'm not resourceful; there's no place to put it except here," he said, indicating the concrete slab which was the doorstep.

Susan stepped aside to let him in and motioned him towards the kitchen nook. "I guess I'm not on the same page, Garrett. What am I missing?"

"You mean you're not absolutely ready to skin 'em alive for what they did to you?"

"Oh, then they *did* leave me on purpose?"

Garrett put the pizza on the table and turned to face her. "I told those four I would come over tonight to make apologies, but they should come to you tomorrow. I'm not sure they will; those little *snots* could have gotten you hurt. They know every rock and trail of the lake, surrounding woods, and fields, but you don't."

Susan was ready to explain she could take care of herself, but the look of concern in Garrett's eyes stopped her. She wasn't sure if her feet were on the granite tile or floating somewhere above it. She leaned towards him.

"I got this monster pizza, and it's still your birthday," he said, seeming not to notice. "Since I didn't know what you liked, I got the largest with the works. I figured you can't put on what is not there, but you can take off what you don't want. Are you hungry? I know I am."

Here, she was ready to fall into his arms, but he was thinking about pizza. Her lips tingled as she began to eat the piece which he handed her.

"You look very tired." Garrett turned her face to him. "Now, I recognize you."

Susan grinned and stepped back.

"You have to admit most of my association with you has been with you as a damsel in distress," Garrett chuckled. "I've been by this apartment complex dozens of times, but I've never been inside. Show me the rest."

Susan turned on the light and directed him into the open living-family room and formal dining room. He caught his breath as he scanned the two-story high ceilings, the loft, and the railing along the windows. He sat down and motioned for her to sit beside him on the overstuffed sofa facing the fireplace.

"Why are you intent on going into the lake area, Susan? It's not something you have to do to sell it. You could tell this morning, Iris and Melton are motivated sellers, and I'm thinking your prospective buyers will be motivated, too."

"I don't know I'm up to anything, really." Susan laid her head back and felt Garrett's arm across her shoulder. He was close. She was sleepy.

⌒

Why was the alarm so loud? Wait, it was the phone. The phone? She sat up. The afghan slid to the floor. Everything was neat and quiet, and she was on the sofa. Time? The phone, again. She grabbed for it.

"This is your alarm calling. Are you awake? How are you this morning?"

"Garrett? Morning? What time is it? What happened? Why am I on the sofa? If I were a drinker, I would swear this is a hangover. But I'm not, and this isn't, so." She quit talking and glanced at the clock. Seven am. "Garrett, uh, thanks for calling. Uh, I didn't…uh, you didn't … I mean."

Garrett interrupted, "Susan, dear, I took the rest of the pizza home for Grant and Gary. I'll see you tonight for our talk. Bye for now."

Oh great! What now? The spell from last night was gone, and she had to face an entire day of uncertainty. She couldn't remember anything after relaxing on the sofa. She was going to have to find out from him what she might have said or done.

Despite her confusion, she felt refreshed. She felt incredible, in fact. Yesterday on her way to work, after a night of disturbing dreams, she had sponged at her eyes and blown her nose through half a box of tissues. Today, the faucet-works were off. Streaming instead were some of her favorite lyrics, "Who will buy this wonderful morning? Such a sky you never did see. Who will tie it up with a ribbon and put it in a box for me?"[2]

She inhaled the fresh, dewy morning mist and waved to the mounted officer who would ticket her if she were too relaxed and heavy on the pedal.

At the office, she immediately checked her email. Surprise. From Angus? He said he had something to show her at the lake and asked if she could meet him there around 4:30 pm. She replied to the email saying she could meet him. She asked him to call her if he changed his mind. She did want to ask him about the wetlands. One on one, this would be an excellent opportunity for her to ask him questions. What he would have to show her was a mystery. With nerves as taut as a violin string, Susan tried to keep her mind off both Angus and Garrett.

( )

By the end of the day, Susan had not heard from either Garrett or Angus. So now a veteran Floating-Bone-Lake-explorer, she stopped by her apartment to change out of her dress clothes to go to the lake to meet Angus. She donned a worn pair of jeans, a long-sleeve shirt over a short-sleeve shirt and walking shoes. Hopefully, these were not destined for the trash can, too.

---

2   From *Oliver*, music and lyrics by Lionel Bart based on Charles Dickens' <u>Oliver Twist</u>

She would just have to tell Angus she could only stay for a minute. Angus might not understand if he knew she was supposed to see Garrett, and she didn't want to miss Garrett when he came or called. After all, she did need to be on good terms with Garrett. Iris depended on him for advice, and Susan needed to keep him updated. It *was* necessary for her to be available for him. Right? Anything to expedite the sale of the property.

As before, she parked her Malibu at the cul-de-sac. When she reached the barbed-wire fence, she paused, looking for Angus. Floating Bone Lake and the woodlands were just ahead. She saw no sign of him, but she walked quietly on, absorbing the sun's warmth and enjoying the light breeze playing with her hair. If Angus didn't arrive within ten minutes, she'd have to leave. When she had called the library earlier, no one seemed to know much about his schedule. He was, she was told, a volunteer. Susan was sorry she had left her cell phone in the Malibu. She couldn't try again now.

Susan stood still at the top of the bank, just looking around. Some of the trees were aged, with a canopy of 70-plus feet. The underbrush was most likely full of living specimens she had no desire to encounter. The earth was red clay, so predominant in this area; the lake had a reddish hue she noted.

If the Indians had settled this area, they possibly used this exact kind of mud to make their clay pots. When she closed her eyes she could imagine tepees, and Indian hunters on the trail of squirrel, rabbit, deer, quail, or wild turkey. She would have to ask Angus about Plaincreek Crossroads and Indians.

He would also know if Plaincreek Crossroads had been used in the Underground Railroad when cotton plantations were culled out of the wilderness. Where *was* Angus?

Susan took a step toward the lake and began to slide down the slippery clay incline. She grabbed at the reeds, getting only handfuls of leaves. She dug her heels into the slimy path only to leave a muddy trail of desperation. All her attempts to turn around slowed her sliding, but not her tumbling backward into the water.

"Oh, God!"

Her splash-landing soaked her with stirred muddy water. She stood up and tried to grab at the reeds just outside her reach, but with each movement, she settled deeper into the silt and muck.

"Oh great, I'm sinking!" She didn't think it was quicksand, though she wouldn't know if it was or not. What she did know was she was afraid to move or step much for fear of being sucked deeper.

"Where are you, Angus?" Just wait till she got her hands on him. Maybe he had changed his mind or couldn't come. No one knew she was there. She had not stopped to see Maggie, because she thought she might miss Angus. Ha! Her car was at the cul-de-sac, but by now the neighbors were used to seeing it. Maybe they would think she went with the kids. Where were the kids?

"Oh, no!" she would be delayed, or not be available for Garrett and their talk if she didn't get out soon.

How many times on her trips to Floating Bone Lake did she end up bruised, stinky, dirty, or ... she just didn't know what? Was the Salesperson of the Year even worth a bloody finger, covered with spider webs, frightened by bats or soaked with fishy water in this bone-floating lake?

She had to admit Angus or no one else had pushed her into the water. She had managed it all by herself.

"How *did* I get here?" Looking up the bank, she could see where she had slid and dug her heels in to stop. Why was the little path wet at all? It hadn't rained since her last visit here. She hadn't splashed all the way to the top of the hill.

"How am I going to get out?"

"Oh, no!" What about her transparent fish? Was there something in the water? Was it safe for her to be standing in the lake? Could the bones be those of living animals who, falling into the lake, had the flesh eaten off them? Gross! Though the water was temperate, she shivered.

"Oh, no!" It was going to be getting dark in a little while. No way, no, no way, was she still going to be in the lake when the sun set. What was it Garrett had said to her, "after dark, no street lights out here?" Susan could imagine how black it would be. Worse than Susan seeing her un-create-candidate critters was for her to know they were there but not be able to see them.

"I am not going to panic."

The muddy bank was barely within her reach. Maybe she could slowly inch her way along until she could grab onto a limb or even a sizeable, strong weed to get some leverage. Not knowing how deep the lake might be, she realized one move either way might result in a drop off or more muck. If she could reach a stick to jam into the mud, or if one of those bones would float her way, she could use it to pull herself out. She shook off the goose bumps just thinking about touching the bones.

"O Lord, what do I do now?"

Susan looked around. "Angus," she called out. No answer.

She strained to see into the underbrush. "Anyone there?"

She was as helpless now as she had been when she was ten years old: she had the fish on her hook and almost had it reeled in when she lost her balance and fell off the pier. She had splashed into the lake and had gasped for breath as she fell deep in the water. She had felt strong arms around her as she had struggled, scratched, and clawed trying to get free to breathe. Then, she could breathe. She sat up on the pier. When she had screamed for her dad, everyone had come running; they weren't able to find him in time. They said he must have had a cramp and had gotten tangled in the weeds.

A tear rolled down her cheek. Why now, after nearly twenty years? She knew why. All this Floating Bone Lake stuff, because she had tried to go fishing, was stirring up memories of her dad, and when he drowned to save her.

She was lonely. "I am beginning to have new friends. If I'm going to be honest, I have no relationships at the center of my life. I didn't feel close enough to tell anyone I was coming here. No one is going to come looking for me because of my friendship with them. I have nothing."

No one was there to hear her confession. Then from out of her childhood, a verse, as if spoken aloud, came to mind;

> "I know the plans I have for you...plans for good and not disaster, to give you a future and a hope." (Jeremiah 29:11)

"Yeah, God, like I really believe that! Do You have a plan for me? It was your fault my mother left us. I heard her say my father loved You God, more than he loved her, his wife. The next day she was just gone. You let my father die. You could have saved him, so why should I want any of Your future or hope?"

Susan didn't know what her hope was. Other than achieving the Salesperson of the Year award and excellence on the job from day to day, she had no hope. True, Aunt Em and Uncle Owen had always been there, but wasn't part of her reason for moving to Plaincreek Crossroads to put distance between their God-stuff and her own life pursuits?

Captured in the muck of Floating Bone Lake, Susan had to ask herself if her way were better. She had always believed if she were successful, she would find happiness. Somehow after the parties and scheduled dinners, she would find some satisfaction. Somewhere out there was a reason for living.

Susan was in need of rescue. In more than more way, she decided.

A faint musty breeze drew her attention, and she craned her neck to look toward the middle of the lake. What if floating bones appeared? Again, she had to ask herself if there were unknown chemicals in the lake. Would the water do something to her, as it may have done to the fish?

Susan took in a deep, fresh breath. She needed another perspective. In spite of her predicament, the lake was calmness personified. For a moment, she consciously tried to relax the tight muscles in her neck and shoulders. It was so lovely; trees and flowers outlined the banks. Listening to the wind rustling the branches high above her, she closed her eyes, and she imagined the sound of marching as described in the Old Testament. No, the stirring high up in the tops of the pines was not like marching to war, but trees whispering in caressing breezes to each other, to God, and perhaps, even to her.

"Well, I ditched You, God, didn't I? Well, do you blame me? I was just a kid. The two people in the whole world I loved the most were snatched from me. You could have stopped it. Where were You? Where are You now?"

Was someone walking in the underbrush? "Anyone there?"

Nothing.

"Well, I guess I'd better figure out how I'm going to escape from becoming the transparent or even invisible woman." What an absurd thought. Susan tried to laugh, but perhaps in some ways, she was already invisible. She could see a new meaning to a *walking skeleton*. If she became transparent, anyone could see inside her. They could see her heart with a large, empty hole in it; maybe a heart broken into small pieces; maybe she didn't have a heart at all. Did she matter to anyone? Jackson? Finally, she had to stop and face the question actually bugging her; what was she doing with her life? It was as if she closed her eyes and blindly charged ahead each day to find meaning and purpose. What did she need to see? What was the utter emptiness she felt?"

"Oh, fine! I'm going over my life as if I'm on some counselor's couch, but I'd better get with the situation." Her moment of relaxation was over. Susan was afraid to move. She was standing up to her armpits in the waters of Floating Bone Lake, and she had been talking to God.

"Oh, Lord," her plea became more fervent. "Help me out of this mess." She took a slow breath.

Then, the answer came to her. Why hadn't she thought of it before? The kids would have laughed at her clothes again, but now she was glad, at the last minute, she had put on an old-long-sleeve shirt like a jacket over her short sleeve top. With as little movement as possible, Susan pulled her arms out of her shirt sleeves and threw her shirt within reach up on the mud bank. If she did it just right, she could lean forward without sinking deeper, grab hold of the shirt and mud under it, hold so it didn't slip, and begin to pull herself slowly out. She painstakingly held and pulled, inch by inch and was making progress when, out of the corner of her eye, she saw a movement. She lifted her head and saw a running shoe!

Garrett, much taller from her present viewpoint, was staring with a crooked slow spreading grin. How she must have looked. True, her hair was almost dry, but she knew it was a mess. She couldn't see her face, but she instinctively knew it was streaked with mud. Her arms were covered with red clay as was her shirt, and she was only slightly out of the water. She was thinking the maintenance man would probably wonder how and why she had so many wet, dirty, stinky, old clothes in her trash can. She had already, in her mind, written off her jeans and sneakers as unsalvageable. She didn't have a fishing rod or anything this time. What must Garrett be thinking?

"Oh, darn! Can you wait right there? Don't move! I forgot something..." Garrett made a motion to leave.

"Wait, Garrett, don't go... What did you forget?"

"Well, I forgot my white charger. You know, the shining knight in armor rides a white horse to rescue the fair damsel in distress? Yes, I forgot my steed, and I'm not gleaming in my jogging clothes either. Wait, I did bring my rescue rope," he bantered.

Susan gasped, but Garrett had indeed brought a rope which he proceeded to throw down to her. "Come on, I'll pull you up. It's really slippery, so take it slow. I don't want to join you."

She was so tempted to tell him to take his rope and lasso a tree. Truth be known she was grateful, and this was the quickest way out. When she finally reached the top of the bank and was on safe ground, she walked into Garrett's waiting arms. Then came the water works. Surely God had provided Garrett for her, but she didn't know if she genuinely believed it. She couldn't say anything about God to him just yet. She started to pull away. Despite the muck, mud, and clay, Garrett held her close. She could not see his expression, but she felt his tenderness and his strength.

For the first time in years, Susan actually allowed herself to be held. It was wondrous; she wanted the moment to go on. She did not pull away, but, instead, melted into Garrett's embrace. They both stood without saying a word.

"Look," Susan broke the silence. The lake shimmered and out in the middle were the unmistakable floating bones. "Ezekiel had his dry bones, but we have our floating bones. What a strange place this is."

"Ezekiel, huh?" Garrett looked down at Susan, "I guess I don't need a horse, just a lasso." She feigned a punch on his arm. "Let's get you home, Susan. What on earth were you doing? This neighborhood is going to think I tried to drown you or something. Come on."

"Where are we going?"

"We're going over to Maggie's. Andi has the boys for now. I've got a little favor to ask of Trevor."

Minutes later she found out what Garrett meant; "Who put ice in the water?" Susan's teeth chattered. "What did you do, Trevor, make an announcement?"

Every kid in the neighborhood begged Trevor for a turn at the nozzle. He had too much fun. All the children had too much fun. They did what children especially love to do; they love to make an adult miserable. Susan stuck her tongue out at Garrett who was bent over double laughing as the kids danced around her.

"Sorry, but it's about the only way to get rid of slime, muck, and clay. I'm afraid your clothes have had it." Maggie was right, but the water from the hose pipe was shivering-cold. "The air is warm but not warm enough for you to run around in those soaking clothes. So, what do you want to do? You're welcome to come in and shower. I'll bet I can find something for you to wear until you can get some of your own clothes, or if you just want to go home, you can take the beach towel with you and return it later." Maggie and Gabi handed her a bright-pink-Barbie beach towel.

"Trevor, turn off the water," Maggie instructed. The children, including Garrett's two sons Grant and Gary, were bored, and looking for other paths of excitement, began spraying each other.

"Thanks, Trevor. I knew I could count on you." Garrett winked. "Maggie, I'm going to take Susan on home and come back to change clothes myself. Andi, will you take Grant and Gary?"

Andi had been watching on the sidelines and now stepped up to take them. "Mom is grilling out tonight, and if any of you would like to come; I'm sure we have enough."

After we change, Susan and I have an appointment. Next time Andi."

"Andi, some other time for us too," Maggie said. "Why don't you bring Grant and Gary back here after they've had something to eat? They can stay here until Garrett comes home. Trevor has some new computer games, and he is anxious to have someone to play them with him."

Susan began to feel like the proverbial elephant in the room with everyone talking around her but not to her. She was about to express her frustration when the group seemed to break up. Andi took Grant and Gary by the hand, said she would call Maggie later, and then headed up the street. Trevor was saying goodbye to some of his friends and obediently putting up the hose, and Garrett had her by the arm maneuvering her to his auto in the driveway.

"Trevor and Maggie," Susan yelled, "thanks. I guess I'm heading home to get rid of this stench. I will feel and, hopefully, look fresh when I get cleaned up. I probably smell like some of those bones in the lake. Gabi honey thank you for loaning me your towel. Oh, Maggie, I almost forgot. How can I get in touch with Angus? Do you know his last name or where he lives? I thought I had an appointment with him this afternoon. I had just realized he wasn't coming when I fell into the lake."

Trevor had finished with winding the hose pipe and heard Susan question about Angus. "Oh, he's at some historical conference at University of South Carolina Upstate this weekend, and then he was going to visit some relative for almost two weeks." Trevor went into the house.

Susan looked from Maggie to Garrett. "You know, maybe I misunderstood."

Garrett frowned, "Angus keeps his word. I'll need to contact him to see if everything is all right." He didn't give Susan a chance to object, but drove her home and saw her to the door. "Susan while you're showering, I need to clean up, too. Somehow I've ended up with mud on my spiffy running outfit. Now I don't know how it could have happened, but I stink." He ducked at her imaginary swing at him. "I'll come back in about an hour for our little chat, okay?"

This was getting to be a habit. After she had peeled off her wet, smelly, clothes and shoes, she proceeded to the trash can, *again*! If any of these garments had been the good clothing hanging in her closet, she might have been angry, as it was she was just clearing out the old and worn. She could never be a nature girl. After her mother had left them, Susan and her father became close; they spent a lot of time together, but he never tried to make her into his buddy or a boy. He may have laughed at her idiosyncrasies, but he also respected her fear of dirt and bugs.

Oh, how she missed her father. As the water washed her tears away along with the remaining mud and grime, she realized Garrett, though much younger, reminded her of her wonderful, sensitive, loving, real dad. This day Uncle Owen flashed across her mind, too.

Garrett had said he would be back, so Susan hurried to get dressed and be ready. The revelation of her deep need for male attention gave her resolve to get her head on straight before he arrived. She had some, actually a lot, of questions. For one, why was he everywhere she turned? Thank God he was, but how and why?

Thinking over the afternoon, she began to feel chilled. She could admit now she had been scared. Being out there alone and helpless had been frightening. Susan was ashamed; she had not stopped to thank God for the answer He had given her on how to get out of the lake. She knew it came from outside herself. How marvelous it was, she began to believe; God had chosen Garrett to come to her rescue also.

Oops, wow, she needed to slow down; she was coming full circle. She had to get her head on straight before he arrived. Part of her just wanted to sit and feel, but the other part of her wanted to be with Garrett and maybe even tell him what she was thinking and feeling. She would see how her *talk* with him progressed.

The doorbell rang.

Though she felt like rushing to answer it, she squared her shoulders and opened the door. "Maggie?" Susan fell back. "What's wrong?"

Chapter 5

Maggie frowned, "Garrett sent me to explain why he would be delayed. He was changing clothes when Andi and Grant ran in to tell him Gary was missing. Andi said she went into the house for a minute, and when she came back out, she couldn't find him. Andi's mother thought he was with Andi, and Andi thought he was with Grant and her mother. After searching the house and the neighborhood, they began to think Gary might have overheard you say Angus was meeting you at the lake. Gary's new super-duper flashlight was missing as well."

"Oh, no, no! Not Gary, he's only five."

Even with daylight saving time, like last night, it was beginning to get dark, and Susan could not imagine a five year old out at the lake. What if he slipped into the water as Susan had?

"Maggie, my car is still on the cul-de-sac, may I ride with you?"

"Let's go. I could have called, but I figured coming was just as fast since you're not that far away, and I didn't have your number anyway. David has Gabi. I let Trevor go with Andi and her three friends. Those kids know every inch of that lake, and they will find Gary."

Every house in the subdivision was lit, and people were milling about in the street. As Maggie and Susan approached Garrett's back yard, Susan breathed a prayer. Gary was so young and innocent. Garrett had suffered the loss of his wife, and now this. It was as if they were walking in slow motion; in a parade with the whole neighborhood as bystanders. At last they found Garrett. He was kneeling in front of Gary and a drowsy brown puppy.

"Susan, Gary is fine. He found a puppy and forgot to go to the lake. I told Grant and Gary they could take care of the puppy tonight, and we'd talk about it in the morning. I was just getting ready to come for you. What do you think?" While he was talking, leaving Maggie and Gary, he took Susan by the elbow and ushered her into the mud room. Susan reached up without a word and brushed a stray strand of hair from his forehead. He stood and stared at her.

"Daddy, come look! The puppy is licking my hand!" Gary was unaware of the extent of the commotion he had created.

Andi and the boys came in, "That's Mama and Brownie's puppy, you know." Susan nodded her head in agreement.

Maggie crowded in, "Listen, Trevor and I are heading home. You know, Andi, it's not late for a Friday night, and Gary and Grant could still come to my house. The puppy can come too." She looked from Susan to Garrett for an answer.

Garrett came to life, "Maggie, I owe you. Andi tell your mom I'm sorry about not making the cookout this time. I know you and your friends were talking about going to a movie. It's not that late, and you still have time to go. Since Maggie will watch Grant and Gary, Susan and I have some business to discuss."

As they walked to Garrett's car, he leaned over and whispered. "Since it's not a good idea for us to end up on the couch together, let's go somewhere public to talk."

Oh, God, Susan thought for an unknown number of times this afternoon. She grinned. Praying without ceasing. As far as she and Garrett being together were concerned, prayer was unquestionably a smart idea.

"If it meets with your approval, let's go to the L & B. How about a sandwich, salad and dessert? We can talk. They'll be open for another couple of hours."

Perfect. The restaurant was close to her apartment, and she had planned to go for the last six months. With the Blue Ridge Mountains as a backdrop, the oversized billboard was a portrait of a servant, hands extended in giving. The L & B was in neon letters at the top. Smaller lettering advertised printed, audio and visual titles, plus a daily-bread menu. Adding interest as a tourist attraction, the lighted scroll of scriptures, along the bottom edge, could be changed by texting a request to the bookstore.

The L & B was in three sections; the restaurant, a lounging area with a panorama view of the mountains and the bookstore. Susan loved the laminated beams, high ceiling, stone fireplace and semi-circle of couches for groups to gather and fellowship. The adjacent bookstore sported a child's area, listening stations and monitors. The fully stocked shelves lived up to its reputation for an unparalleled collection of Bibles, Christian books and literature.

When they entered the restaurant side, they were each given a postcard-size copy of the bill board. It was owned by seven Christian brothers, and the name was L for Light and B for Bread.

In the Bible book of Acts, *seven* men, Stephen, Philip, Prochorus, Nicanor, Timon, Parmenas and Nicholas were chosen to distribute food to the early believers. The qualifications for those given the task were to be well respected, full of the Holy Spirit, and wise. Accordingly, those were the core values upon which the business was based, and those values defined their purpose to be in business. So, this was a Christian-owned business.

"I recognize the names of Stephen and Philip. This little card is full of information. Look at the number seven which is a perfect number. There are seven days of creation. In the Bible, it says we are to forgive70 X 7. Several scriptural references with the number seven are listed. I'll have to look them up."

"Well, *I've* learned something." Garrett rubbed his forehead.

After they had ordered, Susan asked her first question; "Garrett, this may sound ridiculous, but what is your last name? I know it's not Goldsmith, but you've only been introduced to me as Garrett. You're not a one name person are you?"

"How about that." He chuckled, leaned close, and looked around. Then in a husky voice he answered, "To think you don't even know my name. Tsk, tsk. Such a loose woman!" After winking, he replied, "Taylor."

"Garrett Taylor. Okay, thanks. I don't know why I hadn't heard it before."

"Does it touch your soul? It's such a good name."

Susan knew a tease when she heard it and tried to lighten up, but she was concerned about falling asleep on the couch the night before. Did she do or say something she did not remember? She wanted to know. How could she find out without actually asking him?

Garrett scooted close and looked around again. He seemed to be in a whimsical mood as he said, "It's not every night that I put a woman to bed, Susan."

Susan couldn't see her scarlet flush, but she felt her blood rushing to her face.

"I'm sorry, but I just have to do this." Garrett placed his hands on either side of her face, drew her to him, and ever so gently, kissed her on the lips.

She tingled from head to toe, but didn't know whether to protest, be vexed or just enjoy it.

"Well, do you think if anything had happened the other night, you would not remember?" He whispered.

How arrogant of him, but he had a point.

"I have to say it's not very flattering for me to admit I put you to sleep. I didn't think I was *that boring*. You were out like a light, Susan."

Susan breathed a little easier.

After the surprise kiss, Susan didn't know what to expect, but then Garrett became dead serious. "It seems to me, I've asked you before; why are you so interested in *experiencing* the property? I say *experiencing* it, because you don't ever seem to be just an observer or a bystander. You have been very involved; you even took a dunk in the lake. Now about pulling you out of the lake, do you mind telling me how you got in?" He had rescued her more than once, and he deserved to know.

"One minute I was standing at the top of an incline, and the next minute I was sliding down toward the water. I couldn't stop. I went to learn more about the history of the lake and the stories associated with it." She had fallen in love with its quiet beauty, and because she had been stirred to her soul, she had more questions.

In her desperation, she had cried out to God. Was it God's presence she sensed? Did it truly happen? Maybe it was just her imagination. She longed to tell Garrett, but she didn't know how much she could trust him.

"I have to be prepared, because there are going to be some upset people if the land is sold to a builder. Well, I'm new to the area, and I need to be comfortable with my knowledge, history, and stories of the properties I'm trying to move. I have to admit the excursions haven't quite turned out as I expected. I have to ask myself why those kids deliberately tried to set me on edge, Garrett. The boys hardly spoke a word except when they were acting goofy or talking about pranks they had played on classmates. Oh, Garrett, have you been to the vegetable house? It's in such terrible shape it won't change the status quo of the sale, but it does make me wonder if it has any historical significance. Andi seems to be the leader, and those boys would do just about anything for her. Am I off base?"

When their orders came, they ate in silence until Garrett picked up the conversation from where they left off. "Aside from everything else, what makes you think Andi is the ringleader of the group?"

"If you watch them, you'll see it's Andi who always makes a suggestion, and then *the three musketeers* usually agree and follow. Whatever Andi wants; Andi gets. I haven't gotten to know the boys very well. Matt, Jesse and Dan didn't pay much attention to me. When the four are together, they are in their own private little world."

"Interesting observation. Oh, I meant to ask you. How did Angus contact you about meeting at the lake this afternoon? Did you talk to him? Generally, if he says he's going to be somewhere, you can count on him. It worries me. I was just getting ready to call him when Gary went missing. I haven't tried again yet."

Susan needed more dressing for her salad, but there was no waitress in sight. "I'm going to go ask for some more dressing." Garrett rose to go. "No, I might just try another kind." She motioned for him to remain seated. "I'll come right back."

While searching for a waitress, Susan stopped at the cashier and looked over the desserts in their display case. "Cherry Cyclone? I've never had anything like it."

"It's unique to L & B; it has brandied cherries and pieces of cherry pie in a whipped cream cheese and cherry sauce swirl. We have chefs whose only job is to make these desserts. We have samples if you care to try it." The cashier was unusually friendly.

"No, we might get dessert later. For right now, I need to get more dressing from our waitress. I do love cherries. It does remind me of a white funnel cloud with swirling bits around in it. It is nearly too pretty to eat. I think I could manage it though."

"Just wait till you taste it. Heaven comes down at the L & B in more than one way! Is this your waitress coming this way?"

"Hum…yes," Susan finally chose raspberry vinaigrette for her salad. Returning to their booth, she was surprised to find another woman sitting at her place. Though she couldn't see her face, Susan was sure it was someone she did not know.

"What have we here?' she muttered under her breath.

As soon as Garrett saw her, he got up and had her scoot in next to him. He leaned his arm behind her on the top of the seat. "Susan this is Clarissa

Murray. Clarissa this is Susan Walen. She's the realtor for the Goldsmith property."

"Yes, I *know*." As if sensing a question, Clarissa continued, "Garrett and I are at the same school."

"We both work at Plaincreek Crossroads High School. Clarissa is a teacher, and I'm the Student Advisor/Counselor," Garrett added.

So, loving and caring were two of the hats he wore. His role was guiding, directing and rescuing. Most likely he was concerned about others and was naturally supportive. He was just being himself in her time of need, and she most likely had been reading far too much into all his actions.

So, this was *the* Clarissa, looking at Garrett as if he were a significant part of her world. Why, then, was Garrett's arm around Susan's shoulders? Maybe she considered, he was a *mansel-in-distress*. She got tickled at her own thoughts.

Garrett put a little pressure on her arm, making Susan realize she was grinning like a Cheshire cat.

"I'm *sorry*. I'm *interrupting*. Oh, this is *your* salad." Clarissa's smile did not match her words.

Susan smiled back. "I needed more dressing." She held up the little side dish and reached for her salad as Clarissa handed it across the table. "Don't worry, you're not interrupting."

Susan was ashamed because she was enjoying sitting close to Garrett and enjoying the bit of discomfort she sensed from Clarissa.

"Garrett, I wanted to talk to you. School business."

"Go ahead, Clarissa, if Susan doesn't mind?" He gave Clarissa a nod.

"Do you know what a promethean board is?" Clarissa directed the question to Susan.

"Yes, it's an electronic white board used for high tech video presentations, bullets, and movies. They are used in the seminars I attend." Susan was pleased, because she was able to answer. "So, you have one of those systems in your classroom?"

"Yes… Let me tell you about today. I was using the board in my senior, advanced world history class. It's a dynamic teaching tool, but I noticed the class was more attentive than usual. All of them seemed amused; they were all but laughing aloud when I didn't think anything was funny."

"Oh, no! Don't tell me that someone hacked into the system and took over your board?" Garrett leaned forward.

"Oh, yes. I've got to hand it to them. If it weren't so serious, I would applaud them. Their intelligence and skill are remarkable; whoever they are.

I was right in the middle of my lecture and lesson plan. Now, I sure am not technically savvy, so I had no idea what was going on until I looked back. When I raised my hand, suddenly I was holding the Lady Liberty torch, but I wasn't lecturing on Buddha or a Wild West show!"

Garrett exploded into laughter, so loud everyone turned to look. "You have to admit that's funny. I hadn't heard about it. The way the system is set up, it only is a matter of time until the administration narrows it down to the culprits."

"Yes, I know. Well, I thought I recognized your auto when I went by and just chanced you were here. I need to get on my way, and it's almost closing time. See you Monday." Clarissa looked at Garrett, then at Susan, and then turned and walked away.

Neither Garrett nor Susan moved away from each other after Clarissa left. "We still have time for dessert." Garrett gazed down at her.

Susan looked away quickly and understood he was just being who he was. She figured he meant food. "They have a *cherry cyclone* dessert. It has brandied cherries and bits of cherry pie in a whipped cream cheese and cherry juice glaze swirl, topped off with almond chunks and chocolate curls. I saw it up front in their refrigerated case; it looks tempting. I understand it's one of their specialties. Oh, by the way, e-mail."

"What?" Garrett paused. "Oh, you didn't actually talk to Angus about meeting him at the lake?" He rubbed the side of his cheek. "Let's try the *tempting* dessert you suggested. For next time you fall asleep on the sofa, let's see what other flavors; strawberry swizzle; raspberry rapture; peach perfection; yeah, pineapple pizzazz." Garrett improvised and read off the standing dessert menu on the table. "Enough for at least four more times and then we *could* repeat."

"As if all I do is fall asleep on the sofa and leave it to my guest(s) to cover me with an afghan." Susan just gave him a crooked smile.

After dessert, Garrett became serious, "Picking up where we had left off before Clarissa showed up, Susan. I didn't question you about who you were, or what you did, when I met you at Maggie's. I guess I just spaced it. When I saw you at your office, I just put two and two together; you were out on the property, because you wanted to know more about it. Does the sale of the property mean you even end up *in* the lake? Do you get this *involved* with all your listings?"

Garrett stopped to look directly at Susan. "You know what? You look exhausted. Let's get you home. We'll have to continue this some other time. Can we do this sometime when you are not recovering from a near-drowning? Oh, isn't your car still on the cul-de-sac? Do you want me just to take you home now and come by for you to get your car tomorrow?"

"You know Garrett, you're right. I am exhausted. We can continue this. I would like to some other time. Since my apartment is just around the corner, drop me off, and in the morning, I will walk to my car. The weather is perfect, and I could use the exercise."

Susan was suddenly overwhelmed at what had happened since the morning, and she had already decided she would not try to share her spiritual experience. She knew, too, she better not close her eyes before she arrived home.

Garrett walked her to her door. "What were you grinning about when Clarissa was at our table?"

"About a *mansel-in-distress*." She started to laugh, but when she saw Garrett frown, she stopped. "I'm so sorry, Garrett. Really, it's not like me to be catty. Clarissa, I imagine, is, in fact, an excellent teacher, and she did seem likeable. Is she the Clarissa Iris mentioned? I took it for granted she was a friend of Iris. I forgot to tell you, too; I am thrilled Gary is okay. You must have been frantic. I can only imagine. Have a good night Garrett. Thanks for pulling me out of the lake earlier this evening. I'd better let you go. I'm so tired I might forget my own name."

He stood holding the storm door while she pulled out her keys. "I still don't have my answers Susan, and one of these days we'll see what you will remember," he whispered and closed the door behind her.

⸺

"Oh what a beautiful morning, oh what a beautiful day, I've got a wonderful feeling everything's going my way."[3] It was a beautiful Saturday morning, but why Oklahoma was on her mind she had no idea. Susan hadn't seen it or heard any songs from the musical in a ton of Tuesdays. This morning she clearly remembered the challenges, especially the haystack, when her class presented it during her senior year of high school over ten years ago. She did have a decent memory.

What was it Garrett said when he brought her home last night? She heard it at the time, but she didn't actually pay much attention. He said it softly as he was leaving. Was she supposed to remember something? This was getting to be a habit. Now what? Similar to when she woke up on her couch and didn't remember what happened the night before, Susan might

---

3   O What a Beautiful Morning, Rodger and Hammerstein's *Oklahoma* musical.

have to ask him about what he said she should remember from last night. As it turned out, she didn't have to ask Garrett about the couch incident; he answered her unspoken question with a kiss. Oh, she remembered the kiss.

While walking to her car, which was still, at the subdivision, Susan was in a great mood. No one was about, but as she reached her Malibu, she thought she heard her name. Maggie was beckoning.

"Why are you whispering?"

"Gabi and Trevor are still asleep, and I'd like for them to be out a little longer this morning. They were up late with Grant and Gary here. The only reason I'm up is because David had to go to his second job, and I made him breakfast. I'm about to make some blueberry pancakes for the kids. Can you come in and keep me company? I don't get to have a real adult conversation very often. Did you know they say married couples only spend four minutes a day average in conversation with each other? Do you have time to come in?"

"I can come in for a couple of minutes. With all this fresh air, I'm awake now. Sorry, I didn't take time to launder Gabi's beach towel, so I don't have it with me. I'll bring it later. I've never tried to make blueberry pancakes."

"I'm afraid you won't learn much from me. This pancake mix is a gift from my uncle who lives in Vermont, and all I do is add milk. I put the blueberries in when I'm ready to flip them. I think I'll make a smiley face with the berries. Of course, I'll have to make a *T* and then a G. Aren't kids wonderful?" Maggie was still speaking in hushed tones.

"Maggie, my name is Susan Walen; I'm the real estate agent who has the listing for the Goldsmith property. There, I'm glad I told you. I hope we can be friends. I know you, and the rest of the owners in this subdivision don't want the wetlands sold, and all of you feel it's a broken promise if it is sold to a contractor. I've been out there a couple of times with Andi and her friends, and it really is fascinating. It's so quiet; it gives me a sense of relaxation for the most part. I've been trying to find out if there is any historical significance to the vegetable house or the lake. I do think the area is special. Actually, I hate to see it changed at all, but I don't think there is any way around it." Susan paused to take a breath.

"I know, Susan. By the way, a belated happy birthday! Garrett told me on Wednesday after the meeting in your office. Some investigator I am. I didn't question who you were or why you wanted to see and know about the lake."

"Thanks for the happy birthday wish. I think I've aged a year in just this last week."

Maggie reached into the refrigerator for the blueberries, "At our last Homeowners Association meeting, we concluded there was nothing we could do to prevent a sale, so it doesn't matter if you're the listing agent. I think most of us are resigned to the reality of the situation. In the next issue of the Bone Brook Newsletter, our attorney explains; without written or oral evidence of an agreement between the subdivision homeowners and Mrs. Goldsmith, we don't have a leg to stand on. The boys and Andi are going to be devastated, though. They either don't believe it going to be sold, or they're denying it can happen. They are hard to read, if you know what I mean." Maggie turned her attention to the pancakes.

"Your attorney is right, of course. I think I know a little bit of how you homeowners feel. I wish there were something I could do, really. I was afraid you would hate me. Oh, by the way, did Garrett talk to you and David last night when he picked up the boys? A teacher named Clarissa stopped by, but he didn't say much about her. Garrett had been very helpful and kind, except when he turned Trevor loose on me yesterday with the garden hose." Out of the corner of her eye, Susan could see Trevor coming down the stairs.

"Yeah, hosing off goopy mud was fun!"

"Yeah, is right! You did everything but sell tickets!" Susan grimaced.

"No, Mom wouldn't let me."

"Trevor! Stop it! Oh, I think I hear your sister waking up. Please get her, Trevor." Maggie turned to Susan, "Yesterday I thought I saw Andi go into the woods, but it must have been you. Anyway I don't know how you got so muddy, but I'm sure glad you weren't hurt. You wouldn't want to tell me, *would* you? I'm studying to be an investigator, but I'm not getting enough practice. I ordered the binoculars to help investigate and, of course, to keep an eye on this place."

"For real? So you thought I was Andi? It was yesterday, but it seems longer. A lot has happened. One of these days let's get together and recount my misadventures." Susan was talking to herself as much as to Maggie.

"Stay for pancakes." Maggie invited.

"You'd have to make an S. Thanks, but no, I'd better get my car out of the cul-de-sac and get home. I've enjoyed these few minutes." Susan started for the front door.

"Garrett did have something on his mind last night, but the boys were half asleep. He only stayed for a couple of minutes, but we could tell. You might be surprised one of these days, Susan. Yes, Gabi, I'm coming. Trevor!" Maggie set the griddle off the burner, opened the door for Susan and then headed up the stairs.

Chapter 6

"Susan dear, Aunt Em here. We're planning to come Sunday for a late birthday celebration. Hope you had a good day on Thursday. Seems like such a long time since we've talked, but you've been busy. Let's plan on church, out for dinner, and visiting for awhile before we head back. Call me back when you get in. You're not in Kansas anymore. Ha, ha. We can talk more tomorrow, but, please, call me back. Love ya." End of messages.

You're not in Kansas anymore was from the Wizard of Oz. When Susan watched the movie with Aunt Em and Uncle Owen, she felt sorry for Dorothy who was caught up in a tornado and landed in a strange place. Susan didn't like Toto, Dorothy's little dog. Well she didn't like dogs. Pets get hurt or sick and die. You're *not in Kansas* anymore meant Susan had different rules, new experiences and new forms of discipline. Plaincreek Crossroads would qualify as, *not in Kansas,* anymore for sure. She wondered if her Aunt Em knew how far Susan had strayed from her roots. She would know Susan had not followed the yellow brick road.

She should take them past the library. Then, she laughed at her comparison of the yellow brick road in the Wizard of Oz and the yellow brick sidewalk which encircled the library.

Susan sighed.

She had all the space she needed from Aunt Em and Uncle Owen. She savored the freedom, but now as she looked toward their visit, she realized she didn't have anything to show. Her listings and sales? She wished she had some friends to introduce. But who? Susan would be embarrassed, because Aunt Em, as sharp as she was, would know immediately church had not been a priority in Susan's life.

"I can at least take them to Community Church. It's close and very large, so it won't matter if I don't know anyone there. Well, I'm just going to try to enjoy them and my birthday celebration for tomorrow. I'll have time to share more with them later after I've figured out more for myself." She punched in Aunt Em's number.

⌣

After Aunt Em and Uncle Owen left, Susan slowly walked through the empty apartment. She sat down, at a loss of what to do for the rest of the evening. Her phone had not rung. She hadn't heard from Garrett since Friday night and chided herself for thinking he would call. He hadn't said he would call. So, why the disappointment? She knew why, because with each encounter she had bonded with him. She did have unfinished business; he was going to track down Angus about his no-show on Friday. If Angus had something to show her, what was it? If he didn't, why did he send the message? If not Angus, who could have sent the message? Lots of unfinished business. There was Mama's puppy and whether Garrett was going to let the boys keep it. This week, too, Susan was scheduled to meet with the Goldsmiths. Garrett might have some insight on how Susan could get along better with Iris. Nosy or not, she had to know about Clarissa. She sat next to her home phone with her cell phone in hand, willing for either to ring.

Susan reached for her Bible, a gift from Aunt Em and Uncle Owen when she earned her realtor's certification. She laid it aside when they gave it to her, but she always knew where she could get it. She opened to the maroon ribbon marker at Psalm 139. She began to read.

> "O Lord, you have examined my heart and know everything about me. ... I Never escape from your spirit! I can never get away from your presence! .You saw me before I was born. Every day of my life was recorded in your book. How precious are your thoughts about me, O God! ...they outnumber the grains of sand! ... Search me, O God, and know my heart; test me and know my thoughts. Point out anything in me that offends you, and lead me along the path of everlasting life."

Susan laid the Bible aside and mopped at the unending flood of tears.

In the quiet, she now reviewed not only the last 48 hours, but also the last twenty years; she blamed God for all her pain. She had not allowed anyone to come near her emotionally. Aunt Em and Uncle Owen loved her, met her needs, financed her college education, and encouraged her career choice. She not only took them for granted, but also often ignored them. She had to wonder if, while growing up, she showed any love at all. As a child, she could have been labeled as unresponsive; as an adult, she was just full of self pity. Not a pretty picture.

Like being stuck in the muck, in the lake, Susan had been stuck in her own selfish interests. She did not have any close relationships. All her contacts were business acquaintances or shallow friendships. She had disregarded her Christian heritage and rejected a relationship with Jesus, God's Son. All her sales meetings and trips; expensive designer clothes; seminars and education on sales and marketing techniques to be successful in the financial markets were for one reason only--to make herself respected and happy. Well she thought she was successful but to what avail? Jackson, in Columbia, was a prime example of her great choices. Ha. Happy? She wasn't trying to get away from just Aunt Em and Uncle Owen.

If God had a plan for Susan, she would have to let Him take control and would have to make Him her plan. As she again sensed the same Presence she felt in the lake, she knew God *was* the answer. She would have to have a close relationship with Him, to know Him. This was a path of faith she was now choosing.

"Lord, I guess you know I've been disappointed with You because You didn't do what I wanted You to do. I'm realizing getting my own way and having what I wanted was what I thought was love. So, I've been throwing a twenty-year temper tantrum, huh. I'm sorry. Forgive me. I don't have any excuses, because I was taught about Your love and Your gift of Jesus. I have known Jesus died on the cross to cover my sins. Thank you for your love and patience. I don't quite know what I want, but what I've been putting first in my life has been futile and meaningless. I just read you knew me even before I was born and you will not give up on me. I need You, Lord."

Susan fell asleep praying.

Aunt Em always said morning brings new chances. Susan knew it was going to be a beautiful day when the early dawn rays began to chart a path to her balcony. She tripped over the earth boxes, her birthday gift from Aunt Em and Uncle Owen. Today she would fill them with soil, put the tomato plants in them, and put them out on the patio. She also planned to buy a potted tree that afternoon.

"One breath at a time," she whispered to the morning. Somewhere, she had some books of meditations. Today, as she drank her coffee and ate her cereal, she just wanted to say, *thank you,* and listen.

> *"It is good to give thanks to the Lord, to sing praises to the Most High. It is good to proclaim your unfailing love in the morning, your faithfulness in the evening..."* (Psalm 92:1, 2)

She remembered part of what she learned as a child.

At the office, Susan had a message from Garrett on her answering machine: "Susan, this is Garrett. Iris wants me to go over some details with you. Would you mind coming over to the house this evening? I'll have the boys, so if you can't come, I'll try to get Andi or her mother, Joycelyn or even Maggie to watch them. If today is too soon to get records together or is inconvenient for you, then could you make it tomorrow night? I'll wait to hear from you. Don't worry about interrupting me. Call anytime convenient for you."

Susan stood unmoving, shocked at how his voice affected her. She welcomed the chance to become better acquainted with Grant and Gary. She also knew she'd better let God open and close doors for her regarding Garrett. So, holding off a bit and allowing more time to get ready, she called Garrett to say she could come the next evening.

Her second surprise of the day was a call from Maggie. She actually grabbed to answer the phone as she was clearing her desk at the end of the day.

"Susan, this is Maggie. Trevor and his friends were out in the meadow. He said there were men looking at the lake, checking the trees, and doing some measuring. Can you tell me if the property has been sold?"

"The contractors have permission to enter the property, so it is no surprise they're out there. The land has been surveyed, but these companies often have some of their own surveyors checking the lay of the land first hand for themselves. To answer your question; no it's not sold yet."

"Just what I thought. Listen, Susan, David's taking the kids out. I think they're doing some shopping for Mother's Day, but I'm playing dumb and not asking any questions. They're going to eat at the mall, so I was wondering if you could you join me for some C.O.R.?"

"C.O.R.? I'm sorry, what's that?"

"*Clean out refrigerator.* Actually, I have some left over bar-b-cue ribs from our cookout yesterday. They're pretty good."

"Terrific! I'll hurry home to change, okay?" Since her meeting with Garrett was not until the next evening, except for planting the earth boxes, her schedule was clear.

As she drove up, David was backing out of the drive. Trevor waved, and Gabi, even though restrained in her car seat, bounced around and waved until the car was out of sight. How long could David handle a toddler and a ten year old? Well, maybe she and Maggie would have a little time.

"David's a brave man."

"Yes, he is, but don't give him too much credit. He's picking up his aunt to go with them."

Susan had perfected her, according to Aunt Em, award-winning vegetable soup but not taken the time to learn to cook anything else. Beside making the soup and trying a couple of casseroles, she generally had just been collecting recipes. Some day she would need them. "These ribs are especially tender and juicy. Thanks for thinking of me."

"I've wanted to get to know you better, Susan, and I confess I don't relish eating alone. I'm glad you could make it even if it is just for leftovers. You'll find out we have a lot of *cook outs* during the warm months."

Susan was reminded of Andi's *spider cook out*. Someday she might tell Maggie. Susan chuckled to herself. "I plan to begin cooking out, too. You know what, do you mind telling me about this subdivision? Your house is not very old, is it?"

"We've lived here for about a year and a half. The neighborhood is like a small community. Jeff, next door on the left, works nights, but we seldom see him. The Warner's live across the street; they're a family with girls a little older than Gabi. A young divorcee lives a couple of houses over on the cul-de-sac. Some of Trevor's friends live across the street and down a couple of houses. David and I don't know everyone yet. The first houses, I believe, were built five years ago. Garrett's house was one of the last to be built. He halted all construction when his wife, Carol, died in an auto accident a year ago last December. When you go to Garrett's, you will see a lot of specific details because Carol designed it. To get exactly what she wanted, she worked with the builders. Clara Goldsmith was her grandmother, and she gifted the house to Carol and Garrett."

"I was not aware until just the other day that Garrett is related, by marriage anyway, to Iris Fenback and Melton Goldsmith. So, this is a fairly new subdivision, and Garrett's house is just a couple years old. Andi lives across the street from Garrett, doesn't she?" Susan knew a little.

"Yes, and Andi's father, Russ, was one of the contractors. He died in the same auto accident as Carol. That was just before we moved in, but it's a well known story of the neighborhood. No one knew why Russ and Carol were together the night of the ice storm on the road near Spartanburg."

Maggie paused to pour some iced tea. "Isn't Andi a beautiful girl? It's been difficult for her and her mother, Joycelyn. It's too bad she's not as nice to her mother as she is to any stray in the neighborhood. I've never seen her cry."

Susan had more to digest than just the C.O.R.: Garrett and Andi's mother Joycelyn, possibly thought their spouses were secretly seeing each other? At least their neighbors had suspicions. Susan could only imagine the grief, anger, hurt, disappointment, and even shame they felt or were even still experiencing. "I guess Carol and her grandmother were unusually close."

"Clara, Mrs. Goldsmith, was not the same after Carol died. Carol's father was Clara's oldest son; I don't know his name, and he died of cancer just before Carol and Garrett married. In fact, Carol's mother died of complications of cancer when Carol was just a teenager. Clara was most likely more of a mother figure than a grandmother. I don't want to gossip. It's just… I'm curious, and I love to investigate."

"What a story Maggie; Carol lost her parents at a comparatively young age, and then Carol died far too young. Garrett has to raise those boys by himself. It would be difficult for any man. What about Andi's mother? No one says much about her. She has sole responsibility for Andi, although it seems as if Garrett has been helpful."

"Joycelyn pretty much stays in the background. Imagine believing everyone thought your husband and your best friend had an affair. If it were me, I would be devastated."

Susan was mildly surprised when she heard the car drive in. Trevor ran in, slamming the door behind him.

"Gabi made Dad mad. She spilled her juice all over. She's asleep now. We saw Andi at the mall. She is supposed to be studying. Mr. Taylor is trying to make sure they all graduate. I heard him say it was going to be close. Is Andi in trouble again, Mom?"

"No, Trevor, I'm sure not. With only two more weeks of school, I'm sure everything will be okay. Don't you worry about Andi."

"The teachers were hopping mad at school, Mom, because of what the seniors did."

"Yes, I remember what you told me. Trevor, now you go get ready for bed. I'm sure we'll hear about what has happened." Trevor took the stairs two at a time. He didn't seem too worried.

"My, time is gone. I feel drowsy and content, like a cat stretched out in front of a glowing fireplace. I'd better move, or you might have another house guest for the night. By the way, I collect recipes. Someday I will cook. I don't suppose you'd give me some tips on preparation for ribs on the grill. What spices and so on?"

I honestly just go by cookbook instructions, although I do have a couple of secret ingredients. I'll be more than happy to share my secrets with you; just yell when you're ready to try 'em."

"I'll get back with you, but first I'll need to buy a grill. Don't laugh, I've been planning on it since I moved in, and I do have a small patio under the second-story balcony."

"After you get your grill then, just give a holler."

Susan leaned over and whispered to Maggie, "I'm grateful you reminded me Sunday is Mother's Day. I have some special plans to make. Since this is the first Mother's Day away from my parents, I need to be more creative and do something extraordinary." As she was leaving, she held the door open for David who carried a sleepy little Gabi. He did not acknowledge Susan or speak. Susan thought that a little strange but just closed the door as she stepped onto the porch.

Back at her apartment, Susan began to think about Mother's Day.

Aunt Em was very much a career housewife and didn't care for jewelry, flashy clothes, stylish shoes, and purses. There was one exception, dressing for the Goldie's Club monthly meeting. Behind her back, Susan referred to Aunt Em's transformation as the *fairy godmother syndrome*. Aunt Em went into the bedroom wearing a flour-dusted apron and came out wearing feathers and sequins. Each month her colors seemed busier and brighter making a statement in rainbow hues of her creativity. Each next-morning after her meeting, Aunt Em was back making biscuits with the flour-of-love captivating her spirit as well as her apron. As Susan thought back, one article never matched. Strange how she'd never thought it odd before. This gave her an idea for the perfect gift. She'd have to make some phone calls for some help....

"Yep, Aunt Em, I'm not in Kansas anymore and neither are you."

Chapter 7

"Dear Lord, here I am. I don't know what I need, but I'm so glad You do. Looking back, I thank You for helping me find a way out of the lake, and thank You for Garrett. Lord, I don't want to lose what I'm just beginning to find. I'm just beginning to sense how wonderful You really are. Help me make good and right decisions and care for those You put in my path today. In Jesus' name, Amen."

Susan took a couple of minutes to write down the names of people who came to mind, Aunt Em, Uncle Owen, Garrett, Gary, Grant, Andi, Maggie, Trevor and Gabi... the beginning of a prayer list. Next she turned to the first book of the New Testament, Matthew;

> Keep on asking, and you will be given what you ask for. ... Everyone who seeks finds. And the door is opened to everyone who knocks.... Or if they ask for a fish, do you give them a snake..... (Matt. 7:7 ff)

The fish. Susan had to remember to make Garrett understand not only did she catch a fish, but it was also a transparent fish. Had he known about the fish or had he seen one? Was there just this one? Were there others? What was the scripture saying about fish? A fish is a good thing. A snake is... Oh, she had forgotten about snakes. She hadn't seen one. What if there had been snakes when she tumbled into the water? Fish, oh, yeah, she remembered the story of Jesus helping the disciples to catch fish. One hundred and fifty three fish exactly. I wonder why it was so important they counted them. Was it unusual?

"My attention span is almost as long as a two year old Gabi! Now about fish Lord, you won't short change me. What I just read was You won't give me second best—like a snake instead of a fish."

Susan was excited and energized and desperately wanted to share with Garrett, but would he understand or even care? Immediately before the asking and knocking part, was not to *give pearls to swine*. She didn't mean Garrett was swine, but she just didn't know if she could share anything spiritual and precious with him. How spiritual was he? He took her to L & B, a restaurant operated by Christians. He made some remark about her being interested in scripture. He seemed to know Ezekiel. Maybe....

That evening when Garrett came to the door, Susan purposefully put her free hand behind her back briefly to keep from brushing back the stray strand of hair always falling down on his forehead. Garrett was on his cell phone shadowed by the youngest, Gary. He took a moment to accompany her to a sofa while he finished up his call. "I'm sorry, I'm a little behind schedule. I should have called to tell you to come a half hour later. Grant is finishing up his bath. When he's ready to say goodnight, I'll get them tucked into bed."

Gary had already transferred his attentions to Susan. "Do you tell stories? Me and my brother like stories before we go to bed."

"It's *my brother and I*," corrected Garrett. The phone rang, and when he answered, from his side of the conversation, Susan figured it was Iris.

Grant came down the stairs dressed in his pajamas. He, too, sidled up to Susan. "Do you tell stories?" Grant seemed to have the same preoccupation with stories as Gary.

Before she could answer, Gary spoke up, "Andi told us stories about when she was a little girl. If you don't know her stories, I'll tell one to you. Have you heard about the Monster Tree?"

"No, I haven't." Susan was going to enjoy this.

"Well, once upon a time. All good stories begin with Once upon a time, you know. This beautiful little girl named Andrea was afraid of the Monster Tree. Well, Andi didn't say Andrea was beautiful 'cause that's my idea! Andrea is Andi's real name you know. Well, Andrea knew her grandmother loved her a lot and took her on walks, only she didn't want to go because she was scared of the tree."

"Yeah," Grant chimed in, "Andi showed us a tree. It wasn't the Monster Tree, but it was almost like it. We looked up at the top of the tree. Boy was it big! We could see the monster; it had big eyes and a mouth opening to gobble little boys and girls and make them disappear."

"So you really saw a monster tree? Did Andrea's grandmother know about the monster tree?"

"No. Andrea said she was real scared and tried to pull away when they got close to the tree. So Andrea told her grandmother the monster tree was going to come get her, take her away, and make her disappear." Gary made a scowling face at Susan and Grant.

"What did her grandmother do?"

"Well she didn't make Andrea go any closer to the monster tree. Then she showed her pictures of all kinds of trees. Andi's real smart you know. Andi told us about the General Sherman and General Grant, giant Se-qu-oi-as in California. They are over two hundred feet high. Andi said they were so tall you couldn't see the tops. I know she was kidding, but Andi said they named the General Grant tree after me." When Gary reached to cover Grant's mouth, Grant slid to the floor

"Andrea told her grandmother she liked trees when they had flowers on them because they were so pretty. Andrea especially liked Christmas trees. Andi, Grant, and me don't like Christmas trees." Gary spouted that little bit of treasured info.

Oh, it took Susan a minute; Gary and Grant's mother, Carol, and Andi's father, Russ, died in an accident sometime in December. "What else did the grandmother do? Was Andrea still afraid of the monster tree?"

"Guess what? Andrea's grandmother drew a picture. Here, I'll show you." Both boys ran over to a desk and bought back some paper and crayons. Garrett was still on the phone.

The boys worked on the same picture, a towering pine tree with an odd shaped top. It looked like a witch with a hat, a crooked nose and a large open mouth. Andi had probably drawn this for them over and over. They made a face out of the branches but then turned the open mouth into a smile. "Oh, I see, now it's not a monster tree!"

"Well, as her grandmother told her; a tree doesn't have legs, so it can't run after you," recited Grant, "or it doesn't have arms to grab you."

"Can't you just see those branches gobbling up little girls and boys who get too close?" Gary started clawing and growling at Grant….

Susan laughed, "What a special story. So what do you do when you see or hear something scary?"

"Gary cries, but I'm getting too big to cry. I'm eight now." Grant went on, "We learned a verse at church; *'The Lord is for me so I will not be afraid.'*" (Psalms 118:6a)

"Do you know any stories? Can you read from the Bible Storybook?"

Garrett put his cell phone away, "Oh, no you two don't! You guys are stalling. Susan and I have business, and where are you supposed to be?" Garrett pointed to the stairs, "one at a time, remember?" Taking the steps two at a time tonight was not a problem as Grant and Gary slowly scooted off the sofa and inched their way towards the staircase. They both stopped, as if on cue, and ran over to Garrett, each one wrapped around a leg. "Hey, guys, tell Susan good night, and I'll take you up."

Gary and Grant ran over to Susan, hugged her and even kissed her on the cheek. "Will you be our new mama?" Gary begged.

Susan swallowed. "We'll plan on being friends for right now, okay?"

Gary grinned and skipped back over to a red faced Garrett.

"Be back in a minute," and he was up the stairs with the boys.

Susan's impulse had been to gather the boys in her arms, but she didn't know how wise it would be considering the ambiguous relationship she had with their father. What did her friendship with them or to Garrett mean?

Garrett came over and sat next to Susan.

She was going to love this. "Well Garrett, I must say Gary's proposal is the strangest I've ever received."

"Heartfelt I'm sure, but don't get too elated. I should have warned you. I think Gary is desperate."

"Thanks a lot!"

"Do you know how many un-proposals I've had to concoct? I might have to start taking off my shoes and socks, so I can use my toes to keep count!" He got down on one knee, as if to take something back, just as Andi walked into the room. Susan looked down at Garrett. He peered up at Susan, not realizing Andi was standing there. When he turned and saw Andi, he froze as if he had been *caught with his hand in the cookie jar.* He rose so fast he lost his balance. It couldn't get any better than this; how was he going to explain? Susan visualized waving a yellow caution flag, but for Andi's sake, she knew she would have to suppress a hardy belly laugh.

"I, er, Garrett, I'm sorry; I didn't know you were busy. I knocked and said 'hello,' but I guess you didn't hear. I wanted to talk to you about the puppy," Andi started toward the door, but Garrett gently put his hand on her shoulder.

"Come on in, Andi. You know Susan, the real estate agent for the wet lands property. My sister-in-law, Iris, wanted me to look over some papers Susan brought over. We haven't started yet," He led her back into the room.

Susan held up the folder, "Here ya go. I was wondering about the puppy, myself. The boys didn't say anything about the puppy. Where is he?"

"I didn't have a chance to tell Susan, Andi, what you told Gary and Grant and how you are handling it. Go ahead, but let's keep it down because the boys are supposed to be going to sleep."

"I told them Mama wasn't friendly to people, but she loved her puppies. I explained she would be very sad if she couldn't find her lost puppy, and if Mama wanted to have her puppy back, then we should give him back to her. I suggested maybe Garrett would buy a different puppy for Grant and Gary. They didn't like it, but they allowed me take the puppy home with me on Saturday. I still have it."

"So you still have the puppy, and you're going to take him back to Mama? Please tell Garrett and me when you are going. Not to change the subject, but maybe you'd care to know, I heard your Monster Tree story tonight. The boys both know it well, especially the picture of monster turned friend. I was very impressed!"

Andi's eyes sparkled. "They've heard it enough times. Grant and Gary are both getting pretty good at turning a devouring scowl into a welcoming grin; don't you think? As far as the puppy goes, my mother doesn't want me to keep it much longer, and she's probably right. The puppy was very weak, but he seems stronger. I'll go this week sometime. I don't know how Mama will react. We haven't ever touched any of her puppies, until now."

Susan couldn't believe the words were coming from her own mouth; "Let me know when, and I'll go with you."

Was she out of her mind? Go with her to the spiders, the bats and the vegetable house cellar with the growling black horse/dog and meekly say "here's your puppy Mama, no bad feelings. See we took good care of him. Don't eat us alive, please, Mama." The possibility Andi would accept Susan's offer was unlikely. Thank goodness! Andi would simply ask her three musketeers to be ready to parry. Well, she had offered and noble intentions count. Didn't they?

"Don't go by yourself, Andi. Don't count on Matt, Dan or Jesse either. I believe they're grounded on all activities, as well as off their computers until graduation. All three of them said you weren't in on the hacking, so you're in the clear." Garrett waited for her reaction.

"Oh!" was all Andi said.

Again Susan marveled at this lovely girl; she had a slim figure, naturally blond curly hair to the middle of her back, green eyes, rosy complexion and countable freckles sprinkled across the bridge of her picture-perfect nose. Her smile revealed magazine-cover teeth and deep dimples. Her clef chin and long smooth neck completed the picture. What could not be described was a reticence or sadness which permeated Andi's whole being. Was Andi aware of her beauty? Did she take it for granted? Perhaps she was bored? Andi was more than skin deep, and Susan knew it. Andi's shoulders slumped as she left to go home across the street.

Garrett watched until Andi was in her house and turned to Susan, "I don't know about you, but I could use something to drink. If I drink coffee this late, I'm awake for hours, but I can make you some. I can also offer, believe it or not, lemonade. I have ice, too. Offering anything is pretty good for me," Garrett paused.

"No coffee for me. Lemonade sounds good. Do you have a table where I could put out these reports?" Susan was almost desperate to get away from the sofa. She had to face her attraction to him, but all of his behavior could be explained away as something other than attraction to her. She also noted, when they were together, there was almost a childlike relationship between them. She had no explanation. The table would be safer.

Garrett turned the light on in the dining room and left to get the lemonade. Susan opened her file, but she suddenly had no desire to go over any of the contents. So, she decided, he could read the reports himself and then call her if he had any questions, or if he felt there were any problems with any of it. She was still debating whether or not to share what had happened to her at the lake. Maybe she never would…. She wasn't asking God for an intimate relationship, but if she were, she would certainly consider Garrett a fish, not a snake.

"I hid these two from the boys, so I could offer you something tonight. They don't know all my hiding places. Do you like chocolate?" Garrett had two glasses of lemonade and was balancing a small tray, probably not necessary for just the two small cakes and two napkins. Instead of seating himself across from her, he went over and pulled out a chair on the same side next to her.

"I love chocolate. I haven't had a Ding Dong in years! Thank you, Garrett." She hoped he hadn't noticed her involuntary rapid intake of breath when he sat down next to her.

"Iris called just after you arrived. She went over some of this and said she was interested in a report you have from yesterday. She thinks I should read it and give her my opinion. I guess she knew one of the developers had gone out with survey equipment and taken a look around. The report is in here?"

"Yes, it's really rough copy though—mostly just opinion. You're welcome to read it at your leisure…."

"My idea exactly. I'll read it later. Do you remember Friday night at the L & B when Clarissa stopped by? I owe you an apology."

"An apology for….?"

"I don't know about being what you called a *mansel in distress* though. I met Clarissa at a grief support group right after my wife, Carol, died. Clarissa's husband passed away a couple of years earlier. When a teaching vacancy became available at my school, she applied for and got the job. In order to be a part of the group, the move made sense for Clarissa, so she didn't have to drive from Columbia. Well, she didn't hide the fact that she wanted to get better acquainted with me."

"Aha, a candidate for a Gary proposal?"

Garrett groaned. "She hasn't had much contact with the boys, so to my knowledge, Gary has not *popped* the question to her. Gary is wearing me out!"

"Iris mentioned Clarissa at the meeting in my office. She seems to be influenced by her. Is there anything I should be concerned about?"

"I was under the impression Clarissa knew you, well knew the real estate agent who listed the property."

"No, the first time I met her was at the L & B restaurant."

"Oh, before I forget it, I want to bring you up to date on the Promethean-board scenario Clarissa referred to Friday night; Matt, Dan, and Jesse admitted to disrupting more than one class. Before they were identified, they also had hacked into the system and changed the date on the order for pizzas for the senior class: An unfortunate decision which backfired.

"The administration and staff always schedule a final outing for the seniors, and this year it was a pizza bash with the afternoon off. When the pizzas were delivered yesterday, instead of next week, the Principal sent a memo cancelling all extracurricular activities for the seniors.

"I'm going to be spending some time with each of the boys to discuss consequences. Andi's in the clear, but just the same, I'm just a little worried about her; nothing much really matters to her. She tells so many stories." Garrett frowned and pushed his hair back.

This must have been what Trevor was talking about. Susan munched on the Ding Dong. She ordinarily would have disregarded any idea of involvement unless it was business related. …. Now, Susan mentally began to list some persons who were quickly embedding themselves in her world; Andi and Andi's mother, Joycelyn (though she hadn't met her yet), and even *the three musketeers* were becoming important to her.... *How do I love you Lord? How do I love those you love, for you? If I truly receive God's love, then I'm better able to give love to others.*

Garrett waited until Susan finished her Ding Dong. "Would you like more lemonade?"

"No Garrett, thanks, I've had plenty. This Goldsmith property is the strangest place. It will sell, but I'm a little sad. I guess I'm just curious enough to want to know what makes it different. The place is remarkably quiet, almost as if time stops. I have a sense of other worldliness which reminds me of the mysterious, hidden world of Shangri-La.[4] Well, anyway, Floating Bone Lake is unique; I feel close to nature and close to God." Susan waited for Garrett's reaction but got none. This was not the time for her fish story either. "I'd better go."

"I don't want to keep you. I'll look the notes over yet tonight. I'll call you tomorrow, maybe by lunch time. You intrigue me, you know." He stopped her at the front door, "There's a bit of frosting on the corner of your mouth, here let me…." and before Susan could react, Garrett ever so gently licked the corner of her mouth in the beginning a gradual, slightly lingering kiss. "Hum, good!"

Susan stood shaken. He was teasing her again, but she asked herself if a kiss might mean something other than the caregiver hats he wore? Susan, skilled at composure, had come pretty close to her limit, but she had a comeback; "Boy, you better get more Ding Dongs!" He could take it anyway he wanted.

"Not a bad idea!" Garrett agreed as he escorted her to her Malibu. "Don't wave, but smile for the camera. Didn't I see you with an older couple at church Sunday? Ezekiel, huh? Call you tomorrow." He waited while she started the car and backed out of the drive.

"What about all those one liners? Camera? He must have been talking about Maggie." Susan smiled at the thought of Maggie seeing Garrett kiss her—not a chance, she guessed. "What about Ezekiel? I'm going to find out. So, he goes to Community Church." Aunt Em and Uncle Owen said they liked it. She finished her conversation with herself as she parked in her space

4   From 'Lost Horizon' by James Hilton, 1933.

at her cotton mill condominium apartment. One further thought lingered; Clarissa moved from Columbia? Clarissa knows Iris. Iris knows Mr. Keller. Does Clarissa know Mr. Keller or Jackson?

Susan, after staying up late reading and studying about the prophet, emerged next morning confident of finally getting the last word on Ezekiel! She was now an expert. Who, why, when, where, what? Bring on Ezekiel.

She was also anxious to hear from Garrett about what he thought, and what Iris was thinking. At first, all she could focus on was selling the property, and now she felt she was on a runaway stagecoach; she was unable to stop or control what was happening. Was her long sought goal no longer important? How could she forget the SPOTY?

Just about lunch time, Garrett called, "Susan, this is Garrett. I'm still at school. I was planning to take you to lunch and discuss the file, but it's been a busy, busy morning. It won't be possible. I need to go over a couple of details with you, but it's the same situation as last night. Could you possibly come over about the same time as last night? If not, I can check with Maggie. Forgive me, I'm sorry. I don't usually try to conduct business over my dining room table."

"You coming Garrett?"

Was that Clarissa calling Garrett?

"I gotta go, Susan. Call me if you can make it. If you get an offer on the property yet this afternoon, could you bring it with you? Iris mentioned the possibility. Talk to you later."

Susan left the office during her lunch hour, so she could go sit in her Malibu and meditate and pray. Garrett had said nothing about taking her to lunch when they spoke last night, so why was she disappointed and even angry? She was doing a lot of praying lately. Certainly she could go to Garrett's in the evening. She had no other plans other than planting her earth boxes, *again*. Gary and Grant were clearly in need of female attention. Should she encourage closeness or stay detached from them? Garrett was spinning like a yo-yo, up and down. He was playing a game of hide-and-go-seek, or maybe tag; you're it, come and get me. "Lord, I don't know if I want to be close to the boys or even Garrett. If I did want to be close, would it be for the best? How do I love you Lord?"

"Come follow me, Susan. I am the Way, the Truth, and the Life. One step at a time…. Don't be afraid to love in my name….."

Susan closed her eyes and leaned back in the seat, her head against her car window. She almost fell out when Garrett opened the door. "For a minute there I thought you were asleep. Didn't you hear me? I was knocking on the window. One nice thing about our little town is one place is not far from another place. Right? Scoot over, let me in."

She did her best to move over as Garrett squeezed in next to her. "I didn't get to explain; I've been trying to spend more time with the boys and not be gone so much in the evenings. After about the third or fourth 'will you be my mommy,' I got the idea I needed to spend more time with them. Some of the situations were a bit embarrassing. You can imagine. I hate taking off my shoes and socks. Remember, I explained to keep track of all his proposals to unsuspecting ladies; I would have to use toes to count. Ha, ha. You can come can't you? I'll call you later." He scooted out, pulled her back to her place behind the wheel, and left.

Susan, who hadn't said a word, sat quietly while the tears came unbidden. She dried her eyes and went back into the office.

No sooner had she gotten back to her desk, when Jerry from J.M. Ryan Brothers Construction, called. "Miss Walen, are you available this afternoon?"

The Ryan Brothers were busy discussing the lake as they walked into Susan's office.

"Miss Walen, I'm Jerry Ryan. This is my brother Michael. We were just going over some final thoughts about the property, especially the lake. We figure the lake isn't big enough to be recreational, and without the trees and wilderness, it loses its ascetic value anyway."

Michael stepped forward and shook Susan's extended hand. "After looking over the town, Jerry and I have to say there's just not very much *flat* land around here."

"It's good finally to meet you after talking to you so much on the phone. I'm told it's not good business to appear too interested in a listing, but we're throwing caution to the winds. Do you have any coffee? You know some kid out on his bicycle said we'd need a boat if we were going to work out there. Funny little guy! You got our notes, Miss Walen?"

"Susan will do just fine. I gave a copy of the draft of your assessment, notes on the appraisal report and your observations to the seller. Is that what you mean? I'm meeting with their advisor this evening. This coffee is from this morning, I can make fresh, Jerry."

"No, I'll take it. We did a walk around, comparing the lay of the land to the surveyor reports and our maps. We did a fly over, too. It is difficult to ascertain the size of the lake because of the irregular shape, the canopy of the trees and the amount of the underbrush, but it could be filled in nicely. Hills on the property could be used for fill dirt."

"Jerry, you're giving her selling points!"

"What did you do, put your poor brother on a caffeine-free diet? He's inhaled his coffee!"

Jerry did not seem to be listening, "Because of the lay of the land and the current subdivision, platting into lots will take some extra planning. We met with some of the city and county officials. We might have to negotiate for some easements. They seem very cooperative."

Michael went to look out the window, "With two, possibly three, brand new factories and a major mall planned less than fifteen minutes away; this area is expanding at a phenomenal rate. Housing is at a premium."

"Michael, she's got us pegged. Look at her."

Susan listened as the brothers marketed the property to themselves.

"The bottom line Miss Walen, Susan, is we're willing to deal, but time is of the essence as you said, or as we said, anyway it's evident; housing is at a premium. By the time, these businesses are here, up and running, we have to have beautiful homes to show."

"We're from Florida, but our main office is out of Atlanta. We're both ready to make Plaincreek Crossroads our stompin' grounds for our next little bit of lifetime."

After Susan had poured Jerry another cup of coffee, she poured one for Michael too.

He was gesturing so wildly, he nearly knocked the cup out of Susan's hand. "Oh, sorry. No, no coffee for me, just Jerry. Because we are ready to move on this, to save time, we have what we think is a substantial, final offer. 'On such a full sea, we are now afloat, and we must go with the tide or lose our ventures'; Shakespearian wisdom I believe."

"Michael, my brother, how right you are. Susan, what you pointed out to us is true; with the existing subdivision on the backside of the acreage, access to city utilities is do-able and reasonable. When this is platted into lots we will be able to build a subdivision equal to and larger than Bone Brook."

"Yes, Jerry, and Susan we will be able to provide at least two difference areas, and thus, a variety of price ranges. Our subcontractors are anxious to begin work. Business has been at a standstill. Now you know all our secrets!"

Susan began to look over the offer. "Neither of you has referred to a couple of conditions: the stream and a line of trees separating the subdivisions?"

"Look at what we are proposing. We have our financing in place and would be prepared to begin construction as soon as possible. Since you are the exclusive listing agent, you would know if anyone else would come close to this. I think the sellers will be pleased."

There it was. This might be the fastest transaction ever. She was almost disappointed; she wouldn't have to explain about the noises and the wild dogs or the floating bones, after all. The vegetable house, historic or not, didn't matter. She finished the afternoon with an offer beyond being refused. She should have been elated. Why wasn't she happy about her success?

Chapter 8

When she arrived it was much the same as the night before only this time Gary was taking his bath, and Grant who came to the door was in his pajamas. She waved as she entered, but Garrett was on his cell phone. She went in with her brief case and a large shopping bag which she set just inside the front door. Next, she went to the sofa to sit with Grant. Gary evidently had heard the door bell and was down the stairs just as soon as she was comfortable. With a child on either side, Susan was prepared for most anything.

"Will you be our mother?" Gary voiced his same plea.

Garrett who had overheard sat down, with the cell phone at his ear, and began to pry his left shoe off with his right foot. It looked as if he were going to try to remove his sock. Susan couldn't suppress her laughter.

"Gary, honey, I thought we were going to work at being friends before you put your order in for a mommy."

Gary was dejected but only for a moment. "Will you tell us a story before we have to go to bed?"

The only story Susan had familiarized herself enough with to tell was Ezekiel in the Old Testament, but she wasn't sure a 5 year old and an 8 year old would be interested. "Well, I can try if you are willing to sit still and listen. I can always read a story to you, if you wish."

"No, just tell us one. We've read all our books. Tell us something new." Both boys nodded.

"Didn't you say all good stories begin with *Once upon a time*? Would you say *once upon a time* for true stories, too?"

"We have some Uncle Elmer books, and he always says *Once upon a time*. Andi says *Once upon a time*, too. Yes, begin it like Uncle Elmer and Andi stories." Grant had decided.

"Once upon a time there was a man named Ezekiel who lived a long time ago. He listened to and obeyed God, but the people of his time were very wicked. They had turned away from God; their country was in ruins. Do you know what ruins are?"

"You mean like old and run down and not good to live in? Were there children, too? Did they have to go to school? Did they have bicycles? I'll bet my uncle Melton was a boy back then?" Grant nodded to Gary, and Gary nodded back.

"I think you got the right idea about the ruins. No, I don't think they had bicycles back then. So, you think your Uncle Melton would have been a little boy in Bible times? You can ask him sometime." Susan wanted to be there when they asked Uncle Melton.

"Usually children played and laughed, but everyone was sad. Now Ezekiel tried to encourage them. He knew if they obeyed God, they would be happy again."

"Has either of you ever done anything wrong?"

"Grant does!"

"Did either of you ever get punished because you were disobedient, naughty, lied or broke something?"

"You're not going to tell Dad are you?"

"Oh what are you hiding? No, it's your job to tell your Dad, not mine. Do you remember how you felt when you had to go to your room; sit in the corner; go apologize to the neighbor; miss playing outside; whatever you had to do? In bad times, you don't believe anyone loves you, right. Well, the people didn't listen to Ezekiel."

"God said 'If you are my people, I will be your God', but people just didn't understand. So, God gave Ezekiel a vision which is like a dream only in the daytime. In this vision, God showed Ezekiel a valley full of dry bones. Not deer bones, rabbit bones or …" Susan waited.

"Or fish bones or squirrel bones or chicken bones." The boys were seriously getting into it.

"They were leg bones, foot bones and arm bones."

"Andi said there's a valley of dry bones at the lake. She saw them. She says she thinks it's a vault." Grant jumped up from the sofa.

"You mean a fault, like a crack or yes, a little valley. Is there a place full of bones out by the lake? I haven't seen any yet. Just wait till you hear what happened to Ezekiel's dry bones." She would have to check that out later.

"I hope those bones by the lake don't belong to people." Gary was worried.

"I'm sure not. In Ezekiel's vision, it was people bones. Now, what's connected to the foot bone?" Susan pointed to Gary's feet.

"Leg bone." Gary answered.

"No silly, the ankle bone is before the leg bone. There are at least two leg bones." Grant was older and wiser than Gary.

"Don't forget the knee and then?" Susan patted her knee.

"Our hip."

"Then?"

"Our backbone." They answered in unison.

"Yeah, here we go, then the shoulder bone, the arm bones, the hand and finger bones, then back up to the backbone, the neck bones and, finally, the head bone."

"Bonehead!" Gary laughed.

"Why don't you show me how it might have looked?" These boys were a delight. Both of them stood up and began to twist their feet, then their legs. They swayed at their hips, flexed their shoulders, and flapped their arms. "Let's sing while we're being put together." So, Susan, more like a chant than a chorus, began "the foot bone's connected to the ankle bone; the ankle bone's connected to the leg bone…." On she went to the tag, "now hear the Word of the Lord."

Gary and Grant were sprawled out on the floor laughing.

Susan motioned for them to come up beside her. "After those bones came together, they were still just bones. God wasn't through with the vision. He began to cover those bones with muscles and skin."

"And freckles. Andi has some freckles on her nose. They're pretty on her." Grant was emphatic.

"Freckles, and maybe a missing tooth here and there." Susan pointed to Gary.

Gary put his hand over his mouth.

"Then God created eyes, ears and noses on the bones. Then he breathed life into them!"

"Yeah!"

"God is life. Only God gives hope. If God can do it with a bunch of dried up ole' bones, He can certainly give hope to those who, even though times are rough, are willing to obey Him. I know you boys, even as young as you are, think some days are not as good as other days. What do you do when you feel sad?"

Gary was quick with an answer, "I go find Daddy. He holds me close and makes me feel better."

"My church school teacher says we can always pray," Grant was serious.

"Say, you're both on the right track. Maybe you understand more than the ones who lived in Ezekiel's time. You see, God is our Heavenly Father, and we can go to him just as you go to your daddy when you're not feeling good. If we sin and don't obey God, we are dead inside, but God can make us alive again."

"If we had a mother we could go to her too, couldn't we?"

A subdued Garrett stepped up. "Are you guys ready for bed? Why don't you tell Miss Susan good night and thank her for telling you a story?"

Each of them hugged her and kissed her on the cheek. Gary started to say something, but then he smiled when Susan gave him a high five.

Garrett looked at Susan, and down to his stocking feet, grinning as he did so.

"Oh, I almost forgot. I hope you don't mind, Garrett. I got the boys a storyboard. It's in the shopping bag by the front door. I didn't say anything earlier because I didn't think there was enough time before bed tonight to read the instructions and set it up.

The boys made a beeline for the bag and with one boy on each side, brought it back to the sofa. She could tell they were curious, but they waited for permission to open the bag.

"You can look at it now, but you can't play with it until tomorrow after you get home from school." Garrett negotiated. The boys dove into the bag.

"Oh, look! Stories of Jesus. Hey, there are some toys in here, too."

In addition to the story board, Susan had included a cement mixer and a dump truck which had been prizes from conference dinners and contractors. She had saved them, thinking someday she would be able to give them to some little boy.

"Where's mine?" Garrett mimicked a pout.

"Here Daddy, you can have this." Gary handed him a white plastic horse he found on the bottom.

"Yeah, perfect, Gary! Ah, I'll have to keep it with me at all times, just in case." He winked at Susan.

Garrett came down after having put the boys to bed and went to the table where Susan was opening her briefcase. "Well, we'll see what survives, the truck or the child, after Gary sleeps on it all night. Maybe I'd better take it away after he falls asleep." Garrett entered Susan's space. "I couldn't help overhearing, but I didn't get the entire story. Can you tell me what's connected to the jaw bone, the lip?" Garrett pursed his lips and landed a loud smack on her mouth. "Ezekiel?"

Again, he was teasing her. "Sorry, those trucks are pretty sturdy, so you'd better rescue him. You have your steed." Without giving him a chance to retort, she handed him the offer she had received only hours earlier.

Garrett opened the folder, "No wonder Iris was in a good mood!"

"She should be, don't you think? There was another construction company interested, but they have not made any serious attempt to investigate or contact the city, county or state regarding development. They thought they might have trouble with financing. What it does mean is, for all practical purposes, the property is sold. Just a couple of weeks ago, I would have been ecstatic, but today, though I don't have reservations about the company or the sale, I worry about how it's going to impact a lot of people, negatively."

Susan closed her briefcase. "Changing the subject, did you hear what Grant was saying about a fault and dry bones? Do you know what he's talking about?"

Garret looked up, "That's something Andi has told them. Undoubtedly it's just a ravine or a crevasse with typical animal bones. There are fault lines in this area, the Brevard Fault or more likely the Pax Mountain Fault line, but I can't imagine it could actually be seen on the property. Andi would have learned about the fault lines in geography years ago, and evidently put two and two together to equal the possibility of the earth splitting apart in our own back yard, exposing more floating bones, haunted caves and you fill in the blank." Garrett continued to look through the sale terms. "I can assure you, it's nothing with which to be concerned."

"Good! I began to wonder and envisioned a whole new *valley of dry bones*." Actually, Susan could not envision what God had shown Ezekiel. The truth it represented was what she was trying to absorb; A Loving God can make a dried out life become new and exciting.

"Garrett, I've been with Andi, Matt, Jesse and Dan when they've been out exploring Floating Bone Lake and surrounding attractions. How are they going to handle this? If the property owners in Bone Brook ask me about their property values, I honestly don't have an answer. How passionate are the homeowners in the Association about staying or not staying when the property is developed? You know this area and this people. What do you think?"

Both Susan and Garrett turned when the front door opened, and a tear-streak-faced Andi stumbled inside.

"He's dead, the puppy is dead!" Andi was trembling.

Andi laid her head on Garrett's shoulder. Susan watched as Garrett tried to comfort Andi. Susan stayed close, willing to help. "Andi, you mean Gary's little brown puppy?"

"No, no, another one!"

"What puppy, Andi?"

"Mama and Brownie had four or five puppies. It was another one, not the one Gary found." Andi's words were punctuated with sniffs.

Both Susan and Garrett sat her down between them on the sofa. "How do you know one of the other puppies is dead, Andi?" It was Garrett speaking so gently to her.

"Run o-o-over by a car. Found him on the road." Andi was crying openly now.

"Andi, I'm sorry. We can bury him tomorrow. Maybe we shouldn't tell Grant and Gary." Andi nodded in agreement with Garrett. "How's the puppy Gary found? Have you taken it back?" Andi shook her head.

Susan went to the kitchen and found a clean cloth which she held under the cold water faucet. Then she looked into the refrigerator and poured some lemonade for Andi.

It took the better part of half an hour to soothe Andi, and even then, Garrett took her by the arm to escort her home across the street. Andi's cavalier attitude did, indeed, cover a multitude of strong emotions.

"I'll go with you when you take the puppy back to the vegetable house, remember." Susan reminded her. "Garrett, I'll stay till you get back."

A minute later, Garrett came back shaking his head. "I have never seen her so upset."

Susan folded her shopping bag, picked up her briefcase, and stepped out on the front step to leave.

As Clarissa drove up, it was Susan's turn to be surprised. On the other hand, Garrett did not look surprised. He walked out to her car.

The only way Susan could interpret Clarissa's unexpected arrival was as a statement of sorts. Clarissa insisted upon getting out of her vehicle, took Garrett by the arm and systematically tried to wrap herself around him.

"Why, hello, Susan! Does it look as if I'm proficient at interrupting? I just stopped by to remind Garrett about the formal-dress senior awards banquet. You know how men are at forgetting key dates and events. Garrett and I are going together, and we'll be presenting awards. It's such an enjoyable event. He needed to know the color of my dress, and I just decided on a pale peach outfit. It always helps to know the color when ordering a corsage. Speaking of awards, aren't you being nominated for the SPOTY? You'll have to tell us what all you do *above and beyond* the call of duty to make a sale. I hear the competition is fierce. Don't you have to sell the lake out there to win? Of course, you only need one buyer, huh."

Susan could hear the *meow* in Clarissa's tone, but she acknowledged her remarks with a nod and feigned calmness. If Garrett tells Clarissa about the offer, Susan could only imagine what Clarissa would say. As far as the SPOTY was concerned, she had not been notified, so how did Clarissa know? Clarissa made Susan's possible nomination for the award sound like an indictment or the latest item on the gossip circuit.

"Remember to check on the cement mixer," Susan reminded Garrett. She wasn't sure if Clarissa's account could make her gestures to the boys become just sales gimmicks or not. Clarissa's words had cut her to the quick. As far as Floating Bone Lake, the entire Goldsmith Property and Garrett, Susan had done nothing of which she was ashamed or embarrassed. She was honest. She was ethical. True, she had been relentless and even tenacious in securing listings and closing sales. Just what was objectionable? And what was so undesirable about being nominated for the SPOTY award? Clarissa had made it sound so cheap and underhanded. Just peachy!

Was this the change she had hoped for? Whatever else, she felt alive. Alive is better than—yes—yes, dry bones! She had a flash of insight about Andi too. Andi was beginning to feel something—led by a puppy of all things.

Chapter 9

Today J.M. Ryan Brothers would be placing earnest monies for the Goldsmith land.

Susan did bargain to keep a line of trees on the east side of the lake and to leave the brook untouched, except for the springs from the lake feeding into it. The speed with which she had worked this transaction was commendable. She expected she would be notified of her nomination for Salesperson of the Year award soon, but the victory would be bittersweet. It was the tone Clarissa used when she said, "You'll have to tell us what all you do above and beyond the call of duty to make a sale," which bothered Susan. Was Clarissa inferring Susan used Garrett for Susan's advancement?

As Susan reached for a book of meditations given her years before, a slip of paper floated to the floor. Susan immediately recognized the handwriting. Yep, Aunt Em. Susan was red faced to realize she had never even opened the pages of the book, and so she had never read the poem. What did Aunt Em think when Susan made no mention of it? She would have to thank her for the poem.

Morning was greeting her with sunshine, and she needed the morning to giggle.

Prelude
Giggle, oh, Morning,
Call to the sun, "Here am I",
Tickle the clouds to laugh with you,
So all the tears will dry.

Float on the very horizon,
Fly on whispered wing,
Sprinkle the mist of Joy dust,
On every living thing.

Breeze through the trees,
Direct the birds to dance,
Swing wide your dawning gates;
Singing of second chance.

Paint till you cover the hill,
Brush beyond to the mountain,
Beauty like blossoming grace;
Fresh as the Living Fountain.

You know your Creator, God;
Present at gathering storm,
Escorts away the darkness,
For your brightening form.

Oh, Morning, you are a Prelude,
Always an opening chart,
"Arise, oh, sleepyheads,"
A new day with a brand new start.

On this same positive note, Susan read about the Apostle Paul and joy:

> *"Always be full of joy in the Lord, I say it again—rejoice! Let everyone see that you are considerate in all you do . . . . Tell God what you need, and thank him for all he has done. If you do this, you will experience God's peace, which is far more wonderful than the human mind can understand. His peace will guard your hearts and minds as you live in Christ Jesus."*
> (Phil. 4:4-7)

After lunch, Maggie called. "Susan, okay, now I know it wasn't you."

"What?" Susan blurted.

"If not worth mentioning, then it isn't me. If it is wonderful, I might want to claim it. Just kidding. What's up?"

"Please don't laugh. About ten minutes ago, I thought I saw you go into the woods. I waited just to see if you were coming out, but whoever went in is still there. Must be Andi. If I had seen her when she first started to cross the meadow, I would have recognized her."

Oh, no! Susan was going to have to put her faith into action. Put her faith where her mouth is. She had to grin, because she offered to go with her when Andi returned the puppy. Forget the snakes, spiders, the wild dogs and bats; she was going after Andi. She had to. Andi must have decided to take the puppy back and skipped a couple of afternoon classes to do so.

"Maggie, I told Andi I would go with her, so I'm going to leave work, go by my apartment and change into jeans and sneakers. I'll call you when I'm ready to leave from my apartment, in about ten minutes. You can tell me then if she has come out."

At her apartment, she whispered a prayer, changed into a jogging outfit and called Maggie. "Any activity? Has Andi returned home?"

"No, nothing. Are you going in there too? I don't know what she would do by herself this time of day. According to Trevor, Matt, Dan, and Jesse are not allowed out of their homes after school, so they can't go."

"Maggie, to save time, I'm not going to stop by your place. I'll park up the street by Garrett's instead of on the cul-de-sac. I'll try to stop by later. Thanks for the information. By the way, can you see Garrett's front door with those binoculars?"

"Oh, yes, I can. Want a report when Clarissa stops by? Sorry, trying to be funny. Let me know if you need anything."

Andi was probably taking the puppy back, and she was going to the vegetable house behind the lake. By the time Susan caught up with her, she would have already returned the puppy. She wasn't terribly worried, but she did want to be a friend, if needed. Her plan was to cross through the meadow until she could see the back of the lake and then cut over into the woods toward the vegetable house.

Again, she marveled at the isolated moodiness of the place. Could the now crumbling vegetable house once have been a part of the Underground Railroad? The cellar was deep and large enough to hide twenty or more slaves on their way to the mountain trails to the north; it was an unverifiable, intriguing thought. Susan shook her head. She inched her way around to the back. Surely Andi would not be inside the cellar. She peered into the eerie darkness dreading to see a moving object or hear a growl.

"Andi? Andi, are you here?" She whispered.

Susan waited and listened. After a moment, she heard a faint whimper. She stepped inside and gagged at the smell of rotting flesh. She flinched at the buzz of flying insects.

"Andi, come out!" Andi was sitting just inside the broken wall hugging a squirming puppy. Susan, only one step inside, took Andi by the arm and helped her to her feet. She tugged on her until finally she came outside with Susan.

"Mama's gone! She's not here. The puppies are not here. Brownie is dead! I called and called, but Mama hasn't come. She always comes when I call her. She would want to have her puppy back, but she's not here. She's not here."

Andi's face was tear-streaked, and she continued murmuring, "She's not here. Mama's not here."

Susan's foremost concern was to get her home. Now outside the cellar, she took a gulp of fresh air. "Come on Andi, we can make sure this puppy has a home. Grant and Gary will love him. It looks like Mama just moved on after Brownie died. Animals can sense what we humans often do not and cannot know."

Andi took a slow breath, but led her over to an area of the lake Susan had not seen and climbed to the flat top of a huge rock outcropping. "I sometimes come here just to think." The puppy had fallen asleep in Andi's arms.

"This is serene. Andi, a lot of people would appreciate a solitary place like this to work out problems, think out solutions and get away from trouble or troublesome people."

"Do you see that ravine? It's deeper than it looks. I think it's a fault line. Garrett doesn't think so, but I do."

Ezekiel's valley of dry bones thought Susan. "Do you come out here by yourself very often, Andi?"

"Garrett keeps an eye on me. I think Maggie does, too. She has those binoculars. She said I was out here, didn't she? You know Maggie is taking some courses, so she can get her investigator license. She always seems to know what's going on, even if she does have to cook, clean, do laundry, other house stuff and then get to her own lessons. She baby-sits for Gary and Grant a lot, too. I can't always watch them. Most of the time they're good."

Susan leaned back and stretched out. "This rock is warm, and it's pleasant."

"Don't lean too far, and it won't hurt to make sure we're alone on this rock. I always check and watch too. The snakes slither up here to this warm rock in the sunshine."

"That's what I get for relaxing." Great! This inviting rock is a favorite space to one on her un-create list. *Since I'm on a more personal and frequent talking basis with You Lord, and You know I hate snakes, maybe You could….* Susan decided that prayer would not get any higher than the tree tops.

Andi must have read her mind: "Lots of people are afraid of snakes. Most of the time they don't need to be afraid. I saw a huge indigo snake out here a couple of weeks ago. In the light, it's a beautiful, almost iridescent blue. It's non-poisonous. We have rattlers, copperheads and cottonmouths, too, but I don't think I've ever seen any of those out here."

"I guess after the episode with the spider webs you probably figure I'm scared of everything. By the way, where did you learn that spider-web-flame throwing trick? I've never seen the likes of it."

"There's more than one way *to cook out*, ha!"

"Ha, funny, we think alike…" Susan recalled her *spider cook out* thoughts. "You talk about a snake like you would talk about a pet. Yeah some might be beautiful, but in my opinion, all snakes are poisonous. If I didn't freeze when one came near, I would probably take a good shot at outrunning them."

"You'd run one direction, and the snake would probably run the other."

"Now a snake crawling off in the opposite direction is a good thought. Andi, I need to tell you, if you don't hear it from me, you would most likely hear it from Garrett, this property is as good as sold. I thought I would feel overjoyed about moving it off the market, but I have become aware of how much you kids love this place. I also know the homeowners in the subdivision are not going to welcome their little part of the country taken away from them. It won't be the same with other streets and houses instead of the lake and woods. I said before, sometimes animals can sense what's happening before we humans do. Who knows, maybe Mama instinctively knew a change was coming and just moved on after Brownie died. Do you suppose?"

Andi stroked the puppy gently behind the ears. Something within her broke, and the tears came slipping unnoticed down her cheek and onto her shirt. Suddenly she groaned, and the tears came in streams. She slumped forward and began to weep. "Why does everything change? Why does everything I love have to go away or die?"

Susan sat just within reach.

Andi's shoulders shook. She slumped over swiping her face with her sleeve. All this over a dog? Perhaps not.

"Tell me about your father, Andi."

Andi sat so still Susan didn't know if she had heard.

"My dad died in an accident. We had an early ice storm, and the roads were slick. I don't know why my dad and Carol were somewhere near Spartanburg. We had some packages to wrap at home. It was getting close to Christmas. Dad was a contractor and helped build some of the houses at Bone Brook. He did a lot of work on Garrett's, you know. Garrett lets me come and go in the house anytime. He knows I feel as if a part of my father is still there. Carol, Garrett's wife, had special trim and details added to that house. My dad said if it weren't for his skills and Carols' demands, the house would be nothing exceptional. Did you see the breakfast nook? It is natural wood and hand carved. The window on one wall is curved glass with a stained glass frame in the center."

"No, I'll have to look next time. Now I know why you and the boys don't like Christmas trees."

"I used to love Christmas, but now I hate it. Mom and I never did wrap the packages the year Dad died. It was awful. Carol's Grandmother, Clara, became bedfast after the accident. Garrett and Carol had moved into their house even though Dad was still working on some of the projects. After Carol died, Garrett just sent the workers home and didn't do anything else. Two of rooms upstairs aren't even painted yet.

At first, the boys were little brats; it seemed they were always crying, fighting and wetting the bed. Gary started biting. He was four when it all happened. They always wanted me to tell them stories. I read them stories, and I made up stories about when I was a little girl. Have they told you about the heliotropes yet?" Andi smiled through the tears.

"Heliotropes? Should I know what they are?"

"If you're surprised, they will love it. So don't go look it up."

"Okay. Andi, how did your mother handle all this? I'm not sure I've even met her."

"Mom is Mom. Often during the night, I could hear her cry. Maybe she thought I didn't love Dad because I didn't cry, but she wouldn't talk to me. Sometimes, she was sad; sometimes, she was angry. For awhile I was sure it was my fault. Maybe Dad was just going too fast to get home; he knew I was waiting. Some driver turned onto the highway and hit them broadside. The other driver said he didn't see their car and couldn't stop because of the icy road. He hit them on the driver's side. The impact sent their car over the side of the ridge but stopped his car from going over. My dad was driving. They were on a hilly, curvy part of the highway not far from Spartanburg and when they went over, the car caught fire. It took a long time to get to them and to identify them. The police did say both of them probably died instantly."

Andi held the warm, soft puppy up to her cheek. "Gary will have to name him. Do you think the puppy is sad, because he doesn't have a papa or a mama?"

"I'm so sorry about your father, and even about Mama, Brownie, and the puppies. You know, don't you, it's not unusual for a child to feel responsible when a parent dies for whatever reason? I did the same thing for years after my own dad died."

Andi nodded without looking up. "Your father died when you were young, too?"

"He drowned after saving me when we were fishing. I was ten. I didn't know it, but looking back, I was angry with the whole world, plus the One who made the world. I was mad at myself, feeling if I hadn't gone fishing with him, he'd still be alive. I felt it was my fault. My mother had left us without a word the year before this happened. So, there I was, with no parents."

"Where did you grow up?"

"My Aunt Em and Uncle Owen took me in and raised me. Uncle Owen was my dad's older brother. They didn't have any children. I must have made it extremely difficult for them; I was so busy hating everyone. I need to make it up to them somehow.

"Believe it or not, it's because of this little lake I began to see what I had been. I didn't care for what I saw. Do you recall the day I was covered with mud when the kids hosed me off? I was supposed to meet Angus. It was the same day Gary went into the field and came back with the puppy. Well, I had fallen into the lake. The slope of the bank was wet, and I slid into the water and couldn't get out for awhile. I had time to think and talk to God. I was an awful mess! I wouldn't want to get stuck in the lake again, but I'm thankful for the experience. I think I am beginning to be a better person because of it."

"I'm sorry."

"Sorry about me beginning to be a better person?"

"No-o-o-...."

"There's nothing for you to be sorry for...."

"Yes, you may as well know. Don't you tell Garrett; I asked Matt to send you an email to meet Angus at the lake."

"Angus didn't email me? Okay so he didn't know anything about meeting me at lake. Who received my return message? Hum."

"While I'm confessing, there's more."

"More?"

"I went out and splashed water from the lake onto the path leading to the lake where we took you fishing and where I knew you would go."

"You what? Why?"

"Don't be angry. I just wanted to scare you, so you wouldn't want to come anymore. We don't want adults in here. If something bad had happened, I would have felt horrible. I saw Garrett go back into the woods. Maggie lets him know when I come back here, so maybe she thought it was me."

Susan could not believe what she had just heard. Did she actually hear Andi say she was responsible for Susan's dunk in the lake? Susan had been willing to grab any floating bone to pry herself out of the muck.

Well, if the kids leaving her at the vegetable house rated an apology and one pizza, then a fake email plus a dunk in the lake would warrant an apology and two monster pizzas. Garrett was probably too preoccupied with Clarissa to be concerned about how Susan was being treated by the kids. She wasn't at all sure of what she could share with Garrett anymore.

"You know, I could have been paralyzed by the hiss of a slithering snake? I could have been just plain scared to death by shadows. What if my skin became invisible like the weird fish I caught? You might have had to call the fire department to get me down out of those pine trees if I heard haunting howls coming from the vegetable house. I could have been eaten by wild dogs. Why, who knows what I could have gotten into? Can you imagine being stuck in our pitch black lake with floating bones rattling in your ears all night?"

"Susan, I'm sorry. I didn't plan for you to end up *in* the lake. I just wanted you to come close. I would have made sure we found you. I was mean. Do you hate me?" Andi was half crying and half laughing at Susan's exaggerations.

"I can't hate you Andi. It turned out very well despite what you planned. Do you know about Joseph in the book of Genesis, in the Old Testament? That would be a good story to tell Gary and Grant. You'd have to watch

Gary when it comes to the part where Joseph's brothers throw him in a pit or the part when some of them pull Joseph out and sell him to a slave caravan. Wouldn't Gary have fun? I guess I could feel a little as Joseph did, when, to his brothers, he said, 'you meant to hurt me, but God meant your actions for my good and His glory.' May I emphasize? Don't do it again."

They started back towards the subdivision.

"Since we're talking Andi, your lack of reaction to the fish I caught has been bugging me. Wasn't the fish just a *little* different? Why didn't you say something or at least acknowledge it was weird?"

"It reminded me of my father, I guess. I didn't want to think about it."

Andi's father? Susan didn't understand, but maybe another time they could talk about it. "Are you ready to take this puppy to Gary? If this little fellow grows as big as his mama, then we have a progeny of the legendary wolf/dog big-as-a-horse creature guarding Floating Bone Lake. You know, when I was growing up, I never let Mom and Dad keep a dog. Before I went to live with them, when my real mother and father had…. Well, I had a puppy, but it got sick and died. Heartworms they said. I didn't want one again. My dad, Uncle Owen, would love to have a puppy. I wouldn't even know where to start picking one out for him."

"Have you ever seen a bichon frise? They're like little snow balls and smart. Look it up. You'll fall in love; you know I know about dogs!"

Yes, Andi did know about dogs. Susan couldn't argue. "Well, I have one request, if you are willing, without pressing the point, keep me informed, let me in on what you and the three musketeers are up to – I'll be all ears. Let's go."

"The Three Musketeers? Oh, you mean Matt, Dan and Jesse? Oh, what a fantastic analogy, the Three Musketeers and their sidekick, d'Artagnan, me. We had some times I'll never forget, but it's over, isn't it? Do you know I'll be eighteen a couple of weeks after graduation? I'm not sure I like growing up. Everything changes."

"Andi, after my father had died, I chose to be angry, bitter and to be unforgiving for *twenty years*. I hope you handle it better than I did. It's such a tragic price to pay; hanging on to bitterness will *not* bring your father back, but it will drive everyone who loves you away from you."

Andi sat listening.

"What are you going to do after graduation, Andi? Are you going to college? What's your mother going to do when you leave home? Sorry, I ask too many questions, but you can pick and choose which one to answer this way."

Susan took the puppy and felt its ribs under the silky-long brown hair. The little fellow began to lick Susan's fingers. "I've never had your problem, but I can just imagine how hard it is to be so pretty. You'd never know if someone really likes you for who you are or is just drawn to your appearance. Adding insult to injury, you are a natural blond, and again, I can just imagine how you have had to live down the dumb blonde jokes. After awhile, you could just give up thinking that people are going to treat you a certain way, no matter what you say or do. Am I right?"

Andi rolled her eyes.

Susan shrugged at Andi's sideways glance. Had Susan grown a second nose?

"What? Susan? Is *your* mirror cracked? Oh, here comes Garrett."

"Hail, the driver of the whamperjob-parked Malibu and a class-skipper. How are you two? Oh, you've got the puppy. Where is its mother? Gary woke up this morning crying about his missing cement mixer and his puppy again. I had to make some promises; this little fellow will help me keep one."

"Mama is gone, Garrett, and Brownie is dead! So I guess there's no reason why Grant and Gary can't have the puppy. What do you think?" Andi wiped at her nose with her sleeve.

"Well, the boys were counting on getting him back." Garrett took the puppy from Susan. "You'll never guess the name Gary gave him. Guess." Garrett gave a lopsided grin. "I could prolong the agony, but I told Maggie I'd only be a few minutes depending on whether I would need my steed or rope. The puppy's name is Zeke. Do you know where he got that name? Come on you two, guess. Okay, okay, I'll tell you. Zeke is easier to say than Ezekiel." Garrett turned his attention to Andi and the puppy.

Susan slipped away unnoticed.

Chapter 10

"Maybe all my efforts are futile. Everything is pointless." Susan muttered as she shuffled across the slate floor to her coffee maker, along the way bumping against the refrigerator knocking off a couple of magnets. On the floor, along with pieces of a porcelain banana magnet was one of her memory scriptures:

> *"For God has not given us a spirit of fear and timidity but of power, love and self discipline."* (II Timothy 1:7)

"You need to know, Lord, I feel like finding some chocolate and crawling back under the covers." Chocolate! She remembered the Ding Dong and involuntarily touched her lips. Yesterday, with Andi and the puppy, Garrett made no move to joke or feign intimacy with her and paid no attention when she left. What had changed with Garrett? His focus was elsewhere. Her only answer was Clarissa.

She wanted to give up, but Susan was not a quitter.

Her devotions from Hebrews chapters 11 and 12 were about the *great race*. She pictured Aunt Em and Uncle Owen cheering her along the course. "Thank you, Lord, for Aunt Em and her prayers. Thank you, Lord, for Andi and her misguided attempt to derail me at the lake. Thank you for all friends I am coming to know. All right, even Clarissa. If it's in Your plan for me to receive the SPOTY, it will be because it would glorify Your name. I sense You are bringing me to a place where You want me to be. Yeah!"

Thinking about the coming week, Susan knew the schedule was going to be full of meetings. She didn't anticipate any problems, but the sale of the property was so rapid she hadn't even gotten some legal documents, such as the clear title report from the abstract company.

Foremost on her mind was the senior banquet and Clarissa's *peachy keen* dress. "Stop it, Susan!" She lightly smacked her own mouth.

It was also graduation. For Andi and her three musketeers--Matt, Jesse and Dan, she had decided on a card and some cash, but she wanted something else unique for Andi. An idea began to emerge; Andi was devastated at losing Floating Bone Lake and the camaraderie of her friends on the adventure to the vegetable house. Why not a memory book?

Susan didn't have much time. Gary and Grant could help; they could draw pictures of the puppy. She'd have to get some snapshots. She would need to go into the meadow, the lake and the vegetable house. What could happen? She'd already taken a splash in the lake. Those spiders? She planned to stay away from them. It wasn't as if the place crawled with them. Mama was gone, and Brownie was dead; she didn't know of any other man eating mammals out there. She might see the snake, but wouldn't Andi be ecstatic over a photo of an indigo? Andi did say they were nonpoisonous.

Susan would have to make the trip by herself. She couldn't ask Garrett. The musketeers were still grounded, but maybe they would write some little shorts about their many excursions back into the wet-lands. Angus hadn't come back yet. Maggie had Gabi.

"Susan, God did not give you a spirit of fear."

As the day progressed, Susan did get excited. She formed a plan; change into jeans and old tennis shoes; gather up her camera, her cell phone, and a rope, though she didn't know why she would need a rope; eat a snack bar; tell Maggie to keep an eye on the meadow. She felt guilty; what had she left for God to do? What a silly thought, leaving God out. Nonsense. Prayer would cover Susan's propensity to calamity. Well, after her trip to Floating Bone Lake and its hindermost parts, she needed to see Garrett to ask if the boys could help her during the weekend or even early the following week. She loved it when she formed a plan. She loved it when it came together just right.

Approaching the rusty, twisted barbed-wire fence, she spoke directly to it. "Am I getting good at this, or what?" She was on schedule and her determination firm as she stepped over the fence and walked towards her nemesis. She looked critically at the truly lovely panorama before her, unaware she had been tiptoeing toward the tree line. She was a part of the silence of the woods as she chose her first angle and shot. The wild flowers were a rioting contrast to the placid pines, scattered maples, oaks, birches and sweet gum. The lake gave not a twitch. She enjoyed framing her shot with an eye on the lighting and design. She crouched to get an eye level shot across the lake. "Come on, come on." Waiting to see if the bones would come to the surface at her command was ludicrous, of course. So, she turned to go back out in the meadow, around the lake to the rock outcropping, and to the vegetable house. Out of the corner of her eye she saw a movement, another deer, she snapped. It evaporated; she blinked, and it was gone. "Oh, Lord, thank You"; there out in the middle of the lake were the familiar ripples. She wondered if the transparent fish did flips and pirouettes like salmon, dolphins and whales. "Keep busy Susan, don't stop and feel!"

"I'm not going to ask for a snake, Lord, but if there just happens to be one sunning itself on that rock, please help it sleep through the take. I want this to be special." If she got the shadows just right the vegetable house would be a classic, spooky, rival to any haunted house. On it went through the afternoon, and Susan's five or six turned into twenty. She couldn't wait to print them and show Garrett.

She was almost to the Bone Brook Subdivision when Trevor came barreling toward her on his bicycle. He nearly did a doughnut to avoid hitting her when he put on his brakes. "Guess what I got. Come on, guess. You're going to be very, very excited. Come on, guess."

"Trevor! Let's see, you signed me up for a side show and sold out of the tickets! I'm right, huh!"

"Nah, come on be serious. Come on, guess...."

"Your mother gave Gabi away for a week."

Trevor laughed. "It tops even that possibility. Follow me, and I'll show you."

"Not unless you tell me your mother is out of popsicles." Knowing Trevor, she knew this was something truly exciting, but she didn't trust him at all. She had to skip to keep up until they reached his back yard.... "Trevor, does your mother know?"

"I'll show her, too. Come on. Mo-o-m! Come see what I got. You won't believe it!"

"Gabi is taking a late nap. Hi, Susan. See you made it okay. I didn't have to dial 911 or anything. What's going on, Trevor? What are you doing with the earthbox? We need to put the plants in it this weekend."

Oh, Susan hadn't planted her earthbox yet either. She hoped her tomato plants were still alive. She had taken everything outside on her patio.

Maggie reached to remove the black plastic cover off the earthbox. Trevor yelled, "Mo-o-m, stop!"

Maggie stepped back and froze. "Trevor?"

"Yeah, isn't it wonderful? Miss Susan you want to see? Careful, just a peek."

Susan felt her heart take a flip. She caught her breath, took a quick gulp, glanced down and stepped back. She only caught a glimpse of the answer to one of her less than logical prayers. "Trevor, is…?"

"Beautiful, huh."

"I need to take a picture. Where and how did you catch the snake? You are going to turn it loose aren't you?"

"I didn't catch it. It was here in the box when I came home from school. It probably was eating all those bugs in the bottom."

"Trevor, what bugs!" Maggie stood back from the earthbox.

"Me and Grant got worms and bugs to go fishing."

"Ugh, what kind of snake is it?"

"Maggie, unless I'm mistaken it's a long indigo snake. According to Andi, it is non-poisonous. She said she saw one last week. I'm told when the light is right, it is a beautiful blue. We need to be still and very quiet, so we do not scare it away. I will focus and take a picture. Trevor, the picture will be your surprise. Deal?"

"What do I get for it? May I take the picture?"

"Trevor!" Maggie warned.

"Sure you take a couple, along with mine. The snake won't stay around long."

It was almost dark by the time she had taken pictures of all the kids who showed up to see the snake. After the snake had slithered off, the kids begged, posed and generally had a carnival-good time. The photos would be like no others and might be unclaimed by their parents. What fun! Her heart felt as light as a helium balloon.

"Maggie, will you allow Trevor to come over Saturday morning? I was going to stop to tell Garrett what I was doing with the memory book and ask if he would allow the boys to help, but maybe I'd better not. He's been distant lately, and I think he may be serious about Clarissa. I'll just go home and call him."

"I'm guessing Trevor wouldn't miss a Saturday morning with you, Grant and Gary. Susan, please do not play a will-of-the-wisp. For what it's worth, I think Garrett is nervous about being involved, because he's not sure if he can trust again. The scuttlebutt, as I told you, was Andi's father, Russ, and Garrett's wife, Carol, had an affair. No one could figure out why they were in Clara's vehicle on the road near Spartanburg and the mountains. Wouldn't you have doubts? Know what I mean? According to David, David and Garrett, you know, are close friends; Garrett has had a real problem understanding his role and fault in all of this. It won't help if you stand back and let Clarissa get her claws into him. Anyway I've told you what I think. Now, at least get over there and talk to him in person."

And so, at the risk of feeling a little foolish and vulnerable, but on a mission, Susan stopped by Garrett's. "Hi, Garrett, got a minute? I need to borrow Gary and Grant for a couple of hours on Saturday, if possible. I have this idea about making a Floating Bone Lake memory book for a graduation gift for Andi. I thought the boys might like to help. To keep our project a secret from Andi, I believe my apartment is the best place to work. What do you think?" Susan came close to putting it all in one breath and did not enter the door Garrett was holding open.

"Whoa, wait a minute, I might have to get my steed, you're about to hyperventilate!" Garrett laughed. "Sounds good. Can I help?"

"Oh, you know what, stand still," Susan moved to the side for better lighting. The flash went off as she snapped the picture. "It can't be complete without a photo of you with your hair like that." Susan said no more.

Garrett brushed his hair back. "Well, let's see, how about Saturday morning? Do I bring Grant and Gary, or do you want to pick them up? If I bring them and leave them while I run my errands, you will be at my mercy as to when I pick them up."

"I'll take a chance. Oh, could you pick up Trevor also? I have several things to do, though nothing time sensitive. Just call me, so I can be ready. I'll fix lunch, so you don't have to bring them at the break of Saturday dawn." Susan turned to go.

Garrett lifted his arm and opened his mouth to speak, but then he just turned and went into the house.

Susan hoped Maggie had her binoculars out and saw she was talking to Garrett, in person, instead of calling. Susan mentally planned her menu as she backed out of the driveway. Do kids like vegetable soup? She could leave out the lima beans and go light on the carrots. Early on Susan discovered soup was a quick leftover. She would make sandwiches. Hopefully Trevor would come. She would get some Ding Dongs. Garrett said the boys loved them and so did Garrett.

Aunt Em used to let Susan invite kids from the youth group after church on Sunday night… many yesterdays ago. Those were good times, but Susan didn't realize, until right now, just how good.

"Why was I always resistant to what Aunt Em and Uncle Owen tried to do for me?"

Saturday morning was warm and rainy, so the kids weren't giving up outdoor play time to come to her apartment. Susan was thinking especially of Trevor who was always on his bicycle. At 9:30 am sharp, Garrett, Trevor, Gary and Grant, all under one huge umbrella, stood on her doorstep. Well, Garrett was under the umbrella; the boys were playing catch-the-rain-drops running off the umbrella, a game to get as wet as possible around the umbrella.

"Come on in. I guess we'd better start off with something hot. Do any of you guys drink hot chocolate?"

"You got those tiny marshmallows to put in it?" Gary made his wishes known.

"Yes, I do think I have some instant chocolate mix with miniature marshmallows. Will that do?"

"Where they at?" Gary was ready to get things going.

"Gary, please go to the cabinet in the hall and bring three small towels, one for each of you, while I get the cups and chocolate." Susan was glad the kitchen was pleasant and warm with the aroma of slowly simmering vegetable soup. Garrett stood to the side. "Garrett, how about some chocolate, or I still have coffee?"

"Thanks but I'd better get at my errands, so I can be back in time. I have my cell phone, but I don't think I've ever given you the number."

"Well then here's my cell phone. Would you be so kind as to go ahead and enter your number with my contacts? Before you leave, I want to show you what we're doing." After Susan had stationed the boys, with their cups and towels, at the kitchen counter, she took Garrett by the hand to the dining room where she had all her scrap booking supplies. She had worked unusually late to get all the photos printed and laid out. She had corner cutters to crop some of the snapshots. She had backgrounds of a variety of colors, designs, and textures.

Garrett was silent. She didn't know whether he disapproved or just wasn't interested. "I'll keep my cell on, in case you need me for anything or need me to come sooner. Guys you remember what I said…." He hugged all three of them and left.

Susan watched him leave and then showed the boys the pages which didn't have to be in any certain order. As soon as any of the three boys finished a page, it could be put in the book, and a page cover put over it. She showed them how to do it.

"Can we each make a page of our own, both sides?" All the boys seemed to want to do it.

"Anything you want to do is okay, but you remember, this is so Andi will have happy thoughts about you and good memories of Floating Bone Lake."

The Indigo snake photos were impressive; Trevor got his thumb in one of the pictures, but it was still a jolly good shot of the snake. Susan suspected he did it on purpose; just to prove he took the picture. She helped him write a couple of sentences about Andi; she wasn't afraid of snakes and bugs. As Susan anticipated, Gary and Grant colored pictures of some of the things they did with Andi. They both drew and colored a picture of Zeke, the puppy. Grant included a picture of a large black dog with *Mama* written at the top. They had fun with the decorative strips and stickers. Susan was delighted; it certainly was the boys' work, and it looked like it. Trevor took the photos Susan had snapped of the neighborhood children, trimmed them, arranged them in every odd imaginable way, and put some of them in photo corners and others with the two sided adhesive blocks. On one page with a picture of just the meadow, he drew his bicycle and his mother, father, and Gabi; you could see their house (although one would need a magnifying glass) in the corner.

"Boys, here's a photo of the vegetable house. What does it look like to you?"

"Ooo, it's a haunted house. Is that where Andi and her friends go all the time?" Trevor had never been back behind the lake, Susan guessed.

"Let's use these ghosts and black bats."

Susan agreed about adding the bats to the photos of the vegetable house.

"Is a pumpkin a vegetable? We can put them there too. You said it was the vegetable house…" Grant was busy looking for more vegetables.

"I'm going to put a ghost on their vegetable house 'cause it looks scary," Gary moaned and groaned as he slapped on the stickers.

Susan neatly mounted all the angles of the lake and the rock outcropping with Floating Bone Lake lettering in the middle. She thought she had some pretty impressive pictures. After all, she had to do some pages too.

"Oh, you know who we forgot."

"Who?"

"Zeke." Your father has a digital camera, doesn't he, Grant. "I'll phone him." She grabbed her cell phone. Oh, she couldn't believe him! So she would be calling *Me*?

"It's me."

"I know. Well I'm glad I got the right number. I didn't want to ask if this is the correct number for *Me*.

"Do I need my steed or rope?"

"No, Garrett, no disasters, and none of the boys are homesick yet. Say, is there any way you can take a picture of Zeke and either send it in an email for me to print, or if you can do it, print one?"

"So, I can be of assistance. Yes, I can take an award-winning photo. Do you want to see him while he is chewing on my shoe or my pants leg? Are you about finished with the lads? Oh, I was supposed to tell you to leave three blank pages. Matt, Dan, and Jesse all agreed to send a picture, who knows in what pose, and a written something. I'll bet their parents threatened to ground them for another week if they didn't do it. You talked to them didn't you? How did you get their numbers, names, whatever?"

"I've got my sources… Thanks Garrett. We'll finish what we're doing within the next hour, so I can feed the boys. Plan accordingly."

"This has Maggie's name on it. Did she *investigate* for you? I'll see you in about an hour and fifteen minutes."

Susan turned her attention to the boys, "Gary, what you got there?" He had been drawing a picture, but he wouldn't let Susan see it. "Come on, now, I'm dying here." Susan slumped in the chair, enough to set Gary to giggling.

"What are you making?" Trevor was his usual gracious self. Not.

"Oh, I know." Of course, Grant did.

"Don't tell. I want Miss Susan to guess."

"You didn't give me a chance to see it. Do I have to guess? Why don't you just tell me?"

"The picture is about a story Andi tells. She'd want stories in a memory book wouldn't she?"

"Absolutely! Why won't you show me the drawing?" Susan had no idea.

"Cause you would guess about the story."

"Well, you need to tell us the story. Then we can all look at your page, put it in the book, and then eat lunch. Anyone hungry?"

Gary started; "Once upon a time, remember, all stories begin with once upon a time. Once upon a time there was a beautiful little girl named Andrea. I'm saying she was beautiful. She went to see her grandmother each summer, and a couple of times a week the growin' man in a clunky old truck came with fruit and vegetables. He always brought a surprise for Andrea, too. This time, he handed her five tiny striped bugs, but they weren't alive like the jumping beans. They were not marbles or shiny. She was disappointed, because she didn't know what to do with them. The farmer man said they were *heliotropes*. Miss Susan, do you know what a heliotrope is?"

So, here it was. She had forgotten to look it up, so she could answer him honestly. "No, is it some sort of rope used on a helicopter?"

"No!" Sputtering laughter, "Guess again!"

"It's a bug which, when it bites you, causes your head, your eyes, your teeth and your ears to light up, so you can see all the way down through your nose to your stomach. Am I, right? I think my guesses are pretty imaginative."

Gary had such a marvelous sense of humor. "No. No. No. You have to hear the rest of the story to find out."

Trevor was annoyed, "My stomach is growling, Gary. Tell it quick!"

Grant took over, "Andrea took the heliotropes to her grandmother who said they were seeds. After Andrea had planted them, she watched them every day, but nothing happened. She got tired of going to look."

"Then one day about a week or a month later, she saw some green leaves coming up out of the ground. She watched and waited. Some days she watered them. They grew and grew." Gary contributed.

"How tall?" Susan asked.

"Even taller than the fence and even taller than you." Gary stretched his arm over his head.

"Even taller than anybody standing on two books," per Grant. Susan could tell they had fun with this story.

"So heliotropes are very, very, tall green plants."

"Not just tall and green!" Gary stomped his foot. "Pretty soon Andrea saw a bud. A bud is a baby flower; it starts out little but gets bigger. She watched it. She went in the morning and saw it was getting very big. It was round and yellow. She waited until the afternoon the next day, but it was turned the wrong way. When Andrea and her grandma looked up heliotrope in a book it said the sunflower turns toward the sun. Andrea did not believe it at first. Miss Susan, have you ever seen a sunflower turn towards the sun?"

"Indeed I have, but I didn't know sunflowers were heliotropes. Such a big word for you, young man. I've learned something I didn't know before today. It is a great story. Yes, I guess we can say the sunflower is a flower facing the sun."

"Well, I have more of the story to tell you. The growin' man had a surprise for Andrea. But now you know what a heliotrope is, I'll show you the picture. If you're good, I'll tell you the rest of the story sometime, but now we're hungry. My stomach is gurgling."

Susan covered her mouth to keep from bursting into laughter. She could imagine Andi going through the motions telling the story.

Gary was showing real leadership qualities. She better snap to, or she would be fired. "Gary, your picture is super. Do you think you could grow heliotropes? You boys put Gary's picture in the memory book."

From the kitchen nook, dry and cozy, they could hear the rain splattering against the windows. She still wasn't sure her choice of vegetable soup was right, but she hoped they would give it a try. She gave each of them half a bowl of soup and a plate for a sandwich, crackers, and cheese. She had arranged all the extras on a deli tray. It did look appetizing.

"Did you make all the soup in the big pan on the stove?" Trevor wanted to know.

"Wow, you opened a whole lot of cans!" Gary was serious.

"Stupid, she made the soup. It's not out of cans, duh!" Maggie would be proud of Trevor.

"I only gave you half a bowl to see if you like it. If you do, there is a lot more, and you can have more. You can put the crackers in your soup or just eat them with the soup, either is okay with me. The sandwiches are peanut butter and strawberry jelly. Just enjoy yourselves and eat." Susan was so happy; she wanted them to have fun. Grant reminded them to pray first.

They were on their second bowl of soup when Garrett arrived. He handed Susan a picture of the puppy. Zeke was trying to lick the lens. Funny! "Would you like soup, Garrett?"

He shook his head.

"While the boys lick their bowls clean, let's go to the dining room, so you can see what we've done so far." She left him to look at the completed pages. "Look at the last three," she called from the kitchen. She had saved them for Matt, Dan and Jesse, as requested. Across the top of each, she had stenciled, *One of the Three Musketeers*. "I'm going to give her some blank pages to add whatever she wanted. Well what do you think?" Susan came back into the dining room to stand next to Garrett. She was sure Andi would recognize the love in each page and picture. She wondered if Garrett could see it, too. Susan was baffled; she wasn't sure, but Garrett seemed disturbed, sad. She was not going to allow him to be a basement person, to drag her down and cause her to feel sad today.

The three boys came into the dining room.

"We're done for today, so I'll give you the dessert to take with you. Do you like Ding Dongs?" Susan asked.

Garrett's head came up.

"Yeah, you mean we get both of them?" Susan had gotten them in packages of two and had handed each boy one package. "Thank you!" the three said in unison.

Susan couldn't resist, if only Maggie could see her now. "Here Garrett, you can have one." She handed him one chocolate cake and licked the corner of her mouth unconsciously. She turned red when she realized what she had done. "Garrett, I made lots of soup. I'm sending some home with you."

Trevor went to the door. "Is it still raining? You're not going to try to go fishin' again, are you?"

"No Trevor, not today." *Today's trouble is enough for today.* (Matt 6:34b) What was bothering Garrett?

Chapter 11

Why do alarms sound impatient? Susan could have set her clock radio as the alarm, but she had to be sure she would get up and not drift off back to sleep. She considered herself, a fairly early riser, up by six thirty or seven but not five thirty! She rolled over trying to remember why she set her alarm so early. What day was it? Sunday. Oh, Sunday. She rubbed her eyes and sat up. Today was Mother's Day. *Her* Mother's Day. She had to drive for about an hour and a half, run an errand, and take care of some last-minute details, before she could surprise Aunt Em, her mom, by slipping in for the ten thirty church service.

She hoped Uncle Owen had kept her secret and not told Aunt Em she was coming. Susan prayed she would not regret filling him in on her plans for the day. Was it not the smart thing to do? Not many people ever *got one over* on Aunt Em. Susan remembered a butterscotch pie incident which was a source of several years of guilt. Aunt Em had baked two pies, and then she went to town. The buttery, caramel smell made Susan's mouth water. So-o-o good. While Uncle Owen took a nap, eleven year old Susan, hiding between the rows of corn in the garden where she would not be discovered, ate a whole pie. Despite having a stomach ache, Susan denied any knowledge of what might have *happened* to the pie. Years later, as Susan was creating a story project in school, Aunt Em, just as an aside, suggested the vest for her Pinocchio puppet should be a *butterscotch* color!

She couldn't dwell on whether or not Uncle Owen would keep his promise not to tell. She could only allow plenty of time to get everything in order without making hasty moves or clumsy mistakes. After all, Garrett could not arrive to rescue her from any mishaps. Susan dismissed Garrett from her mind and was on her way. Susan had sent flowers earlier in the week to sidetrack Aunt Em. Thinking Susan would not be coming, Aunt Em would be surprised. Gifts of a new Bible, embroidered Bible cover, and a gold-leather purse were in the back seat. She also had note paper and pen.

Mother's Day was traditional; Uncle Owen always ordered a cake and bought a card. Most years, the church passed out carnations, or the Sunday school children gave their mothers a little pot of petunias planted from seeds weeks before. Today was going to be hugely different.

Oh good! It had quit raining, and the sun was shining in a partly cloudy sky.

On schedule, her first stop was to pick up the carrot cake from Belinda, a long-time neighbor and a caterer. They both knew her aunt and uncle would be at church early, catching up on news and visiting with the Headliners Class of more mature shakers and movers, for coffee and doughnuts. The class actually started at nine. Then the church service was from ten thirty until about noon.

"Belinda, how can I thank you for going out of your way, so I can do this for Aunt Em? I wasn't up for the hassle of trying to bring a cake with me." Susan followed her into the back office. "Oh, my! Look what you've done! I love it! Aunt Em will go nuts." The cake had white frosting trimmed with yellow and pink roses with green leaves. In the center, a reclining *Maxine* was clothed in a shimmering metallic dress, a gold hat with curly gold feathers, sequined shoes and matching purse. It was exquisite. In green, the cake read *Go for it Mom*. Any other cake would be pale in comparison. It was so what she wanted.

"Here you go. I must say this is my masterpiece. I almost hate to let it go. I think it's absolutely adorable. With only a week to create it, don't you think it's great?" Belinda was undeniably proud of what she had accomplished.

"Belinda you are the best! You know what, don't be surprised when Aunt Em shows this to her friends and members of the club, and they come a courtin'. Where did you get such a figure with those clothes?"

"I can tell you just a tiny bit of one of my trade secrets. Of course, this carrot cake recipe is a blue ribbon state fair winner. I have all kinds of figures for cake decorations, and this is one of them. I did have to make the clothes, but then I am an artist. I'll just give you one little hint in the form of a question. Have you ever gone to a baby shower and had diaper nut cups made out of stiffened fabric? Oh, Aunt Em will like this; the figurine can be taken off to save. I've put it on a clear plastic base which keeps it from getting in the frosting. If it had been for someone other than Aunt Em, to be honest, I probably wouldn't have put so much into it."

"Belinda, thank you. Happy Mother's Day to you, too! I only told Uncle Owen I would have a cake. I didn't want to tell him too much, because he could have given it away. You can tell how much I trust him with a surprise."

Susan still had a key to Uncle Owen and Aunt Em's house, so she let herself in, carefully placed the cake, still in its box, on the table and surrounded it with the gifts she had chosen. She let the gift bags do the wrapping for her and was pleased with the festive look of the table. She had one more thing to do, and it was the most difficult. She only had an hour ....

Dear Aunt Em,

Can you believe it's been nearly twenty years since you carried me, a kicking, screaming ten year old, into your safe and loving home? You opened your door and your heart to me. It's taken all this time for me to recognize your gift.

I must have changed your world but, much of the time, not for the good. How patient you were to stand back, giving me space to grieve and express my anger against myself, God, and everyone in general. You and Uncle Owen, I fear, got the brunt of my hurt and frustration. I lashed out because I didn't have what I wanted most, my parents. You had sympathy for me in spite of my bratty behavior. It is most traumatic for me, now, to admit the same behavior in an adult is nothing less than immaturity and self-centeredness.

Throughout the years, you provided me with more than just life's necessities. What was your source of gentleness every morning? You greeted me with a smile, a song or poem and a scripture. Clearly I remember your apron was never without a trace of flour; you smelled like breakfast. I came to know I could depend on you each morning. It was stability in a life which, for me, had fallen apart. Chores and responsibilities were a part of living in your household, and it was a waste of time trying to get out of them. Thank you for discipline (an admission a long time coming, huh).

This note is a little like a prayer. When we pray there's nothing we can tell God He doesn't already know, but He wants us to tell Him, not for His good, but for our good. I've not said a thing you didn't already know. You could set me down and remind me of those years, but by writing this now, you know I, too, recognize your sacrifices.

Words won't do it, but they cut the path. Thank you for a home full of love. Thank you, from the bottom of my heart, for providing an education and for leading me to develop skills for achievement. Thank you for encouragement and inspiration to be my best. Thank you for modeling honesty, integrity and the highest moral character.

I'm running out of time today, so I just have just one more observation: Aunt Em, I have come to understand, you not only gave up your time, resources and energy to parent me, you also gave up your interests, tabling your own personality a bit. You've probably already admitted to having some freedom because I'm down the road an hour and a half, living away from you. I can't believe you would dance on the table, but I will be excited to see what you do and what replaces your apron. If it glitters and sparkles, it will be a hoot.

You are in every way my mother, and I honor you this day. Mom, it is going to be such fun to have you, not only as my mother but also as my real best friend.

All my love,

Your daughter, Susan

P.S. One day soon remind me to tell you about *my lake experience*. It is a *brand new day* and a *new start*; I believe you will be pleased.

Susan had just enough time to get to the church and slip in next to Uncle Owen. "Happy Mother's Day," she whispered as she scooted in. The look on Aunt Em's face said it all. "Uncle Owen, you *done good!*" She patted his hand.

The choir began; "Who will teach the children? ... Whoever does not love, does not know God...Let the morning bring word of Your love...." The flute obbligato rang out, "Jesus Loves Me...."[5]

Susan leaned forward to look around Uncle Owen and nod to *her* mother, Aunt Em. How different her life would have been without her.

Susan's father had done his best to be both father and mother to Susan after his wife simply had said, "I'm done," and had moved to parts unknown. How does a youth minister face a congregation or his adolescent daughter? How does he explain what happened? Her father then quietly resigned, moved closer to family, his brother Owen and sister-in-law Em, and took time with his little girl.

Certain her mother's disappearance had been her fault, Susan was, at first, inconsolable. Her father became her whole world, and then he, too, was taken from her. She had nothing left. Then Aunt Em and Uncle Owen stepped up.

My Dear Loving Father, thank you for your default plan on my behalf. Aunt Em taught me about you. She showed me your love. She led me to you each morning and tucked me in with you each night. Thank you. Oh how, I need to learn unselfish, boundless love. Thank you, oh, thank you for my mother and for this day. Susan wanted to be ready, as her Aunt Em had been, to go where love might lead her.

---

5   Who Will Teach the Children? By Anna Laura Page/John Parker

Chapter 12

"Hey, it's Monday evening. I'm inviting myself over if you don't have other plans. Trevor told me all about Saturday morning. According to my son you are the best cook ever, and you are a lot of fun. I want to see the masterpiece for Andi first hand! I'm on my way."

"Consider yourself invited and come on over, Maggie. I'd love some company. Do you like vegetable soup? If you don't help me eat it, I will either have to freeze it or have it for lunch all week. Maggie, Trevor is the Masterpiece. Grant and Gary are too. It was such fun. Yeah, I think you'll be surprised at what they've done."

Susan was prepared for Maggie's reaction when she led her into the entry way of her apartment. As Maggie stood looking into the family/living room and dining room with its stone fireplace and cathedral ceiling, she gasped. "I'm in love with this apartment!"

"Compliments of the old cotton mill. The antique furniture is from my father's estate. I'm proud of what decorating I've done, but I have other ideas for when I have time."

While they were snacking on the vegetable soup, Maggie read each entry, nodding as she turned the pages, "It's more than I expected. Susan, you are a talented photographer. Oh, look! Didn't Trevor take this picture? He did everything but kiss the snake! These crazy kids. I'm sure Trevor didn't say he's planning to give Andi a rose. If I say anything, he says I'm *yucky*, but he thinks the sun rises and sets on Andi."

"A rose? I was thinking about flowers, too. A good idea." Susan added.

"Oh, these last three pages from Dan, Matt, and Jesse are still blank? You'll have to have those to finish the book. Their parents said they would make sure Garrett got something from them to give you. When and where are you going to give it to Andi?"

"I haven't heard from Garrett, but it should be soon. He'll see the three musketeers at school." But Susan had been wondering about the best time to present the book to Andi. Susan was pretty much still an outsider, and though she had begun to get acquainted, she had not been invited to any graduation or reception. Maggie's question was relevant. "I'm not sure when to give it to her." This was the only answer she had.

"You don't know, do you?"

"I guess not. What am I missing, Maggie?"

"This is a small town. True, it's growing rapidly. In fact, the last I heard it was the fastest growing area in the state. However, we have not outgrown our traditions; everyone who wants to attend is welcome to the high-school graduation and the reception immediately following. The graduation is a football field event scheduled on a Saturday afternoon. The reception is in the gymnasium where, by the way, Clarissa and Garrett will be at the Senior Banquet Friday night. The same decorations are used for the reception. Two birds with one stone."

"What if it rains?"

"Only a stranger suggests it might rain. One year, during the March of the Meistersingers, it began to sprinkle. Everyone enjoyed it. I suppose if severe weather is forecast, it could be delayed or postponed until Sunday afternoon. It's never been a problem."

"They enjoyed what, the music or the rain?"

"Both!"

"You mean the whole town is invited to the reception too? The event could become quite an undertaking."

"Right Susan, the Parent Association plans all year. Girl, the women in this town stumble all over themselves to bake those cookies. Can't you hear it now? 'Oh Mable, how ever do you do it? Each time I have one of your cookies, I think I have gone to heaven! Did you try one of you-know-who's plate over there at the end? She's using this same recipe for the fair.'" Maggie strutted around the room, pantomiming sampling cookie after cookie, laughing as she went. "Some men in this town bake for the reception, too. They claim the greatest bakers in the world are men. The greatest compliment of the afternoon is a wet finger pressed upon any remaining crumb, so it will not be lost, leaving a licked-clean plate. Some check to see the name on the bottom of the plate as soon as it is emptied."

"My mom loved to bake, and she had several delicious cookie recipes, but she had this one I think is like no other. I'll have to whip up a batch to share with everyone. Maybe next year I'll tell the association to include me."

"I told the committee I'd bake at least twenty dozen. I mostly bake *traditional* cookies with one special batch, but I haven't chosen a spectacular recipe for it, yet. Garrett wanted me to watch the boys Friday night during the banquet, but I had to turn him down. I know full well I'll still be stirring cookies. It's unlikely he would take the boys with him. Andi and Joycelyn will be tied up. Had you thought about taking care of them?"

"Garrett didn't say anything to me. You know, I could watch them. Grant and Gary are great kids; I don't think I would have any problem. Did I tell you Gary asked me if I would be his mother?" Susan missed the knowing look Maggie gave her.

"Are you going to offer to watch Gary and Grant for him, then? I understand it's a sticky problem because, if you are too eager to *help him*, he could get the wrong idea, whatever. Then, too, what would *Clarissa* think? Back to the reception, the seniors can have pictures taken with a couple of different backdrops. It is, of course, probably not the equal of prom night, but it is the last hoorah for them. The seniors can have their own individual reception, especially if they have out of town family. Even then, they usually come to the school reception as a family, then go out to eat, or do their own celebrating afterwards. I, personally, will vote to keep the tradition as long as possible. You wouldn't believe the strong sense of friendship and the community it creates."

"We could bring the memory book and give it to Andi at the gym? What do you think?"

"It would help if we talked to Joycelyn. We can tell her about our surprise and find out what plans she has made. How does that sound? I'm ashamed to say I don't already know. I'll call her tomorrow when Andi is out of the house."

"Thanks. I'm changing the subject, but where do you and your family attend church? I think I will be trying Community again. When my mother and dad were here, they seemed to like it. I'm going Sunday to the nine o'clock service, but I don't like sitting by myself. I thought, if you were going, we could sit together?"

"Uh, no it just always seems there's some reason we don't make it, even if we plan. We've been to Community twice since we've lived here. We went mainly because it was close."

"I hate to admit it, but I've lived here in Plaincreek Crossroads for six months and have attended only once."

"Hey, I'll just plan on going. If I can get my family up, then we'll all meet you. If I can't get them up, then I'll come by myself. The Hospitality Room is just inside the main door area. We can meet there. Oh, one more piece of information about the graduation, since it is on the football field, you probably won't want to wear high heels. I have to tell you, this is a gala event, and we all dress in our best—it's tradition. Why don't you plan on sitting with David, Gabi and me, during the program?"

"Oh, thanks, great! Oh, I need your number to put in my cell contacts. Look how Garrett put in his." Susan showed her Garrett's *me* entry. Again, Susan missed the knowing look Maggie gave her.

"Why did you ask about Garrett being in the range of my binoculars? Hmm?" Maggie was still snickering as she went out the door….

Susan was embarrassed, but she did see the humor. It felt right to laugh. At least she wasn't talking to a piece of rusty barbed wire this time around. She closed the door, walked to the kitchen, fixed another bowl of soup, and picked up the gift memory book. Something was missing. As she glanced through the pages, it slowly dawned on her. *The fish* was nowhere in the book. "I will have to draw it. It has to be included. It is my part of the story of Floating Bone Lake."

The fish was hush, hush. According to the kids' own account, they often would say they were going fishing as a means to be allowed to go into the property. Her guess was no one ever caught a fish. She was sure Garrett didn't believe her fish story. The boys might not have gotten a real close look. Susan still didn't understand Andi's reaction and what it had to do with Andi's father, but the fish was still a part of the mysterious saga of Floating Bone Lake. It must be included. Floating Bone Lake would go out with a bang or at least with a mystery, not just a whimper.

Susan knew she was an extremely good photographer which helped her as a realtor, but, as an artist, she was, as the Biblical saying goes, "weighed in the balance and found wanting." She hadn't thought about it for awhile, but she remembered a vacation Bible school lesson about God being a potter. For a project, the teacher passed out clay, so the children could be potters and make anything they wanted. After the artwork had dried overnight, they painted their creation. When it was her turn to share, Susan had no idea of what to call her blob. The other children laughed and quickly ran out of guesses. She was on the verge of tears and ready to bolt, when she got an idea; "It's a dinosaur egg!"

What a stroke of genius on her part, or was it? The other children agreed it was a truly unusual dinosaur egg. Susan named it a *veriosauras* egg. She had no idea where she came up with her own special dinosaur name either. Susan voiced her sudden insight. "Would God have given me the idea of a very unusual, striking dinosaur egg? What a loving thing for Him to do."

Well she couldn't get away with drawing a *veriosauras* fish. As an adult, she didn't think she would be given much allowance or guessing room. She remembered the fish wasn't broad but rather elongated. It reflected a rainbow of colors like oil in a puddle of water. All internal parts could be seen. How could she adequately draw such a strange, beautiful fish on a piece of paper? When she was searching the library book about fish, she did find a tiny tropical minnow zebra fish where the insides were visible for four weeks of its life. Maybe she could use the minnow as a pattern, come to think of it, if the fish were larger? She wondered. "I haven't returned the library books yet. I can envision another Rembrandt."

As she worked on her *fish* page she, too, wondered about the water in the lake. Did Andi think Susan was serious when she, jokingly questioned if her skin would become transparent by standing in the lake? Surely the water couldn't have some chemical to make the fish transparent! What *was* the truth about Floating Bone Lake? What *was* she missing? Was any opportunity to unravel the mystery drawing to a close? Susan was heartbroken; she visualized herself with a torch at an ancient book burning; only instead of a book, it was Floating Bone Lake with all its history and secrets. The torch was a bill of sale to a construction company.

The fish was still on her mind when she awoke the next morning. During meditation time, her sense of anticipation intensified. Did the fish fit into the category of the dramatic, or was she trying too hard to go beyond the mundane? I have to know more. She would call Maggie for help.

"Maggie, I hope I'm not calling at an inopportune time. You can call me back if...." Susan stumbled over the words.

"Susan, good Tuesday morning. Oh, for heaven's sake, I've been up for over an hour. Gabi is now talking to her Cheerios before she eats each one. I have to start at first rooster crow for Trevor. He wakes up in stages, and stage four, fast arriving, has a penalty of extra chores after school. He was banging around just now. David is just leaving for work. What's up?"

"Maggie, I'll just take a minute. I have to finish getting ready for work, myself, but I have a request. If you don't want to or don't have time, don't feel obligated, please."

"Okay I got it; I'm not obligated. I'm curious. What's up? Let me guess, you want me to spy on *you know who*. I won't say the name(s) just in case *for quality assurance your call may be monitored or recorded....*" Maggie gave a convincing impression of a call center answer.

"Maggie, I want to give your investigative skills a workout. I don't think I told you about the fish I caught in the Lake. It was very unusual. I need to have information. ... "

◠◡

At the office, by midmorning Susan realized, though she had been extremely busy with additional listings, her mind was elsewhere. In spite of her best effort, she could not focus. Garrett's phone call was an additional distraction.

"Susan, hi, it's Garrett. I just received the last of the three boys' contributions for the memory book. I've got a meeting this afternoon, but if you're going to be home, and you don't mind, Grant, Gary, and I will stop by a little later."

"Oh sure, no problem. I'll be home this evening. In fact, how about planning to stay for dinner? I'm going to make a casserole, and I need someone to eat it. Do you think you could take the time? I miss the boys."

"Uh, ah."

"Oh, you too." Susan couldn't believe him.

◠◡

Susan had set the dining room table with salads and had just cleaned up the cooking mess when, as a duet, the oven timer, and the door bell sounded. The timing was perfect. *Lord, if this is a door or a window, I'll take it, if not, Your will, not mine.*

Like two welcoming puppies yipping and yapping with tails wagging, Grant and Gary greeted Susan as if they had not seen her in three years instead of just three days. Grant grabbed her hand, and Gary attached himself so closely she almost tripped over him. Garrett was still standing on the doorstep. "Oh, come on in. Are you boys hungry? You're just in time. I'm right now taking the casserole out of the oven."

"Well, I could have brought my trusty steed, but he's been ignored and not needed lately." Garrett grinned from ear to ear. "It sure does smell yummy. Most of the flour is on your jeans." Garrett anticipated Susan's playful swing and ducked.

Susan didn't quite understand this childlike behavior, but the thought was quickly replaced with the realization they were *friends*.

After praying Gary asked, "Do you have any jelly?"

"What kind do you like? I've got strawberry, orange marmalade, and honey. Which would be good on those biscuits? I'll just bring them all out for you."

"Can I put my stuff on my biscuit?" Grant wanted no part of the jelly.

"You mean the hamburger, green beans and tomato sauce with mashed potatoes? Grant, anyway you want is okay with me."

"Will God be mad if I don't thank Him for the green beans?" Gary was already sorting the green beans from the ground beef.

"Boys, what have I told you about eating what is on your plate? We thanked God for this delicious food; you won't make God mad if you don't like it; He might be disappointed, though, if you don't try it before you say you don't like it. If your stomach doesn't feel good after you eat some, you don't have to eat the rest. Of course, you won't be able to eat dessert, either."

Susan nodded in agreement. She turned to Garrett, "Have you looked over what Jesse, Dan and Matt sent?"

"Oh, no, I forgot. I left them in the car. I'll be right back."

Garrett immediately came back in and handed the envelope to Susan. "Go ahead and read now if you want. I've got to clean my plate. I don't think I've ever had this dish before, but I like it."

Susan whispered, "Shepherd pie. I didn't tell them there's onion in it, too. Look, they ate the green beans. I'll take a peek at these now. When you're ready for dessert, I'm ready." Susan opened the manila envelope and picked out the letter and picture from Matt.

> Brat,
>
> We won't be going out to Floating Bone Lake much anymore, I guess. They're gonna put in a street and build houses. They'll probably tear down our vegetable house. It's too bad, but you didn't keep it neat and clean. Such a housekeeper! Ha, ha.
>
> Matt
>
> P.S. Whatever you do, you'll be good. I know.

"I imagine his mother or father one made him add a post script," laughed Susan. "Garrett, look at this picture." It looked like the ones taken in a photo booth at the mall. Well, it was authentic!

Susan opened the one from Jesse.

Andi,

I'm supposed to say something for your memory book about the good times we have had. I think it is too bad Floating Bone and the vegetable house won't be there. Even if none of us will be there, it's weird to think it will all be gone. Thanks for your friendship and the memories.

Whatever you want—go for it!

Jesse

Susan opened the last one from Dan.

Andrea,

Thanks for making school a little less of a bore. I never could figure out why Mama liked you better than the rest of us. We never did anything to her.

Maybe you should learn to work with animals. I will always think of you.

Remember how to *burn* the enemy and life for you will be good!

Dan

"My how sentimental. The Musketeers, all three, are brilliant, aren't they? My, what a way with words." Susan tried not to seem too critical, "Years from now Andi will read these notes, look at these pictures, and her memory will come alive. These boys certainly are who they are. I'll put these in the book later. Are you ready for dessert? Why are you laughing?"

"You told the parents to have them write special thoughts and memories they wanted Andi to remember. Right? You hold in your hand, Susan, evidence of how tender and sentimental high-school males will be."

"How do you know?"

"I work with them, remember? Besides, don't you think I was ever one myself?"

"Oh, Garrett, I just thought the way they followed her around and did her bidding meant there was some tenderness there."

"Don't worry. Andi knows them and would not expect anything else. She will enjoy the pictures. When are you going to give the book to her?"

"When are *we* going to give it to her? We should all, not just me, be there. After the graduation, I think, otherwise it would be hard to get everyone together. Maggie was going to check with Joycelyn, but I haven't heard yet. Boys, I have some scrumptious cake and ice cream. My mother insisted I bring some of her Mother's Day cake home with me. It's a blue ribbon carrot cake and out-of-this-world delicious. What you don't eat for dessert, I'm sending home with you. I've had plenty myself."

"Your mother? I thought I heard you say your aunt and uncle raised you," Garrett wrinkled his eyebrows.

"Yep, Aunt Em. She's more than earned her right to be called *Mother*. I went to Columbia last Sunday for Mother's Day."

"Oh," Garrett just stared. "I wasn't sure whether you'd be at church or not."

༄

After they had gone, Susan left the dishes and went up to her closet. Graduation was in four days, and Maggie had insisted Susan choose a very special dress to wear for it. Susan's only glamorous outfit was the one she was saving to wear when she accepted the SPOTY. The two-piece ensemble was simple, soft and flowing. The bodice was burgundy with white and black accents, sewn with hundreds of tiny crystal beads. The scooped neck was encircled with a braid of crystal beads also. The sleeves were elbow length with a fluted hem and the solid, rich burgundy skirt hung below the knees to the middle of the calf, also with a fluted hem. She had felt elegantly feminine and classy when she first tried the outfit on and planned, even then, to style her hair in a twist with a couple of loose curly strands. Maybe this would be a *saleswoman of the year* event anyway. She had to admit she wanted to be smashing, and this designer dress should do it—just in case Garrett was interested.

Garrett hadn't said anything about watching the boys on Friday night. She would have to volunteer.

Chapter 13

Susan had just arrived at the office when Garrett called. She sat down and took a slow breath, not wanting him to know how much the sound of his voice affected her.

"Susan?"

"Good morning Garrett; isn't it a great May morning?"

"Yes, well, I just wanted to say thank you for the carrot cake and for dinner, as well. The boys were getting tired of hot dogs; not really, they would eat hot dogs for the rest of their childhood if I would allow them. They did say the casserole tasted pretty good, even the green beans. So, thank you. The cake was wonderful, and I confess I had another piece. I didn't have any Ding Dongs left over; you see *I* was only given one."

"Oh, you poor thing. I'll keep a couple in reserves for you next time. Garrett, seriously, have you found anyone to watch Grant and Gary on Friday night during the banquet? I understand Maggie, Andi and Joycelyn are unavailable. I didn't know if you had someone from the church on standby. Anyway I haven't made any other plans, and I am offering my services, if needed."

"Oh," Garrett paused, "how thoughtful of you. I did think of you, but then I decided it was too much to ask."

"I guess I'm not the babysitting type, huh. Your boys are delightful, and it would be a privilege to spend some time with them."

110

"Oh Susan, I can't thank you enough. You are gracious. If you're sure, I do have a list in front of me of possible ladies from the church to call this morning. None of them really knows the boys, so I was putting it off a bit. I have no other reason. Do I understand you don't mind babysitting my boys while I'm at the school with Clarissa?"

Susan laughed gently, "Oh, Garrett, you're at the school with Clarissa every day, but I know what you mean. Do you think it will be okay with Clarissa to have me at your house while you two are at the banquet? Maybe that's the question."

"If I say I have to bring the boys, clearly my next choice, she might not care."

"Well then, what time is the banquet, and what time should I come to your house?"

As Susan hung up she was a little disturbed by their conversation, but she had to leave Garrett in God's hands. Garrett obviously cared for Clarissa. Susan's motive in watching the boys had to be a genuine caring for the children and being a friend to Garrett. *With Your help, I'm up to it Lord.*

Her next call was from Maggie. "Hey, Susan, you said something about a special cookie recipe the other day. I want to try something different. Is there any chance you would share your recipe with me for the reception?"

"I'd love to! I'll look it up and bring it to you on my lunch hour. I should have time. The cookie is two cookies in one and a filling which will remind you of s'mores, because it has, any or all; graham cracker crumbs; caramel; pecans; chocolate; and marshmallow creme."

"Whoa, sounds rich. From your description of the cookie, I could improvise if I wanted to. I'll bet your mom used different fillings too."

"You guessed right. Did I say I'm going to watch Grant and Gary? Wish me well."

"Good for you. I have a couple of tips; Grant, as you probably have already figured out, is the quiet one, and Gary is the extrovert, into everything. Gary is candid, and you have to be careful what you say around him because you'll hear it back later, only in his own version of it. Tell you what, I'll stop by Garrett's while you're babysitting and bring a couple of your special recipe cookies as a sample, so you can see how I did. After graduation activities, we'll have to talk about the *fish project*. I have a hunch this whole fish thing involves something none of us could even imagine. Don't worry, we'll talk. Oh, remember I told you the town dresses for graduation? Did you take me seriously? I hope so, talk to you later."

❦

Friday evening when she rang the doorbell, Susan could not have more closely resembled the stereotype of a babysitter; she had her hair pulled back in a pony tail, and was wearing jeans and sandals. Garrett said he would have to leave by 5:30, so she arrived five minutes early for any last-minute instructions. After waiting a minute or two, she feared no one was home until Garrett finally came to the door. He was handsome in, probably, a new suit, and she loved his cologne, a little on the musky side. She swallowed, and ignoring her intimate thoughts, simply said, "Hi, I'm here, is my timing okay?"

"Come on in," Garrett stood back as she entered. "The boys had their baths earlier, so they'll just have to get into their pajamas at about 8:30. Since this is Friday night, they are allowed to stay up until 9:00 pm. They are in the kitchen finishing up their hot dogs, potato salad and baked beans. Does it sound like a picnic? Actually Maggie often grills, and since she will be helping out with the graduation and is trying to get her cookies baked, she fixed the beans and salad earlier. She grilled the hot dogs for her family for tonight and brought some for the boys, too. She and David are caring friends and excellent neighbors, believe me."

Susan had never seen Garrett as nervous. He had talked nonstop since she walked in the door. "Any special instructions and tidbits I should know about? Will they try to pull anything over on me?"

Garrett hesitated, "No, but I'll keep my cell phone on, in case you need to call me."

"Oh, yes *me*, how could I forget?"

He chuckled.

"Dad, we're done!" Gary, with Grant behind, burst into the hallway and stopped when they saw Susan. "Are you our surprise?"

"Surprise? I don't know. Dad, am I their surprise?"

"I figured they would be too excited if I told them who their babysitter was. I know them pretty well, and they would have made *special plans*." Garrett whispered to Susan "I was trying to save both of us."

Susan had never thought of herself as special, exciting, or as a surprise, but generally considered herself as ordinary. She had not been around young children since she was a teenager, so she was praying she was not in over her head. As she closed the door behind Garrett, she had the strangest sense of a mother sending her child off for the first day of kindergarten, though she didn't think he would come back crying.

"Listen, I have a favor." Both boys came to her side and nodded. "How about a tour? I've only been here in the hall and dining area. Since it's sprinkling, you can't go outside this evening, anyway. I hope it doesn't rain for tomorrow."

"Oh, it never rains on graduation," Grant assured her.

"So I've heard. I hope you're right. I'm wearing my new dress to the graduation."

"Dad has his new suit on tonight. He even bought some really smelly stuff. Did you smell it when you came in?" Yeah, Gary had something to say.

"So do you boys share a room, or have one room of your very own?"

"Gary won't sleep in his room, so his bed is in my room for awhile until he grows up like me."

"It gets dark, and I don't want to be alone. Miss Susan, come look at my trucks." Gary took her by the hand, led her up the stairs to the second floor.

"Oh, you have a bonus room over the garage. Is this your play room? Look at the trucks!" Gary remembered who and for what occasion he received each one. He must have had fifteen to twenty of them. As Susan quickly scanned it, Grant's room with Gary's bed in it also, had sports posters, autographed baseballs, and several baseball bats.

"Here's Dad's room. You can look 'cause he made his bed and it looks nice." Gary opened the door.

Susan didn't go into Garrett's room, but as Gary had said, she could see the room was extremely neat. She noted the computer and a small file with books and papers. "Your dad must do his work in here?" The room across the hall was shut.

"That other room is my mother's work room. We don't go there anymore. Dad says he can't handle it." Grant had just said a mouthful.

Gary stood in front of the closed door. "I had told Dad I want to be a big brother just as Grant is my big brother, but Dad said we would have to wait for another mother. When dad can go into my mother's room and can keep his shoes and socks on, I can ask you again to be my mommy."

Susan was speechless. She was overwhelmed, and she'd only been there less than half an hour. She figured it would be wise to change the subject. "Oh, by the way, where's the puppy? His name is Zeke, right?" Both boys started jumping. "Let's go downstairs, and you can show me the rest of the house. Then we'll see Zeke. You'll have to tell me your father's rules because

I don't know what they are. Don't try to fool me because, if you do, then next time I come you'll be in trouble with me."

They were young and innocent. When they went downstairs to the kitchen area, she took note of the nook which had hand-carved trim and a stained glass inset in the bay window. The floor was slate. The upper cherry cabinets had beveled glass doors. The counter top looked like marble, and all the brass hardware added a polished elegance. The master bedroom was on the main floor, postcard perfect, like it had never been used.

The boys wasted no time pulling Susan towards the back room just off the garage. She could hear Zeke sniffing around. Grant took a baby gate out of the closet and put it up between the kitchen and the dining room. A second gate was already in place between the kitchen and the hall and only needed to be expanded and hooked. Gary opened the door to get the puppy.

The three of them sat on the kitchen floor with Zeke, petting him, holding him, giving him just one treat, and teasing him with his rawhide dog bone. Watching the boys play, Susan began thinking over the times she spent with Garrett and the boys; she would never forget how the boys became so involved in the Ezekiel story of the dry bones, or Garrett throwing his rope to her …. A rush of warmth overwhelmed her.

The doorbell rang, but neither boy moved. "Stay here with Zeke." She unnecessarily instructed.

"Maggie, come in. The boys gobbled down the hot dogs and food you sent."

"I'm running just a little late. This light rain, you wait and see, will disappear before graduation tomorrow. I only grabbed a couple of cookies. They're pretty decent sized. The boys can share. I'll finish baking later tonight, but I wanted you to taste one. I think they're wonderful. I thought, if you wanted, you could share yours with *me*. Including your cookie recipe, I have baked four different kinds of cookies. I'm doing my part. Do you have a fantastic dress? Looking sharp is your part."

Susan frowned, "What about my dress?

But Maggie was out the door. "Have to go y'all; call me later."

"Miss Susan, Grant put Zeke back in the mud room."

"He was getting you all wet. His papers are in his room." Grant said.

"Let's take the gates down. Why don't both of you go wash your hands after playing with Zeke? Maggie baked cookies for us to try. She brought two cookies, one which you boys can split because it's pretty big, and the other is for your father and me. She wants us to tell her if we like it."

Both boys hurried back in after washing their hands, "Sure is a hu-mon-gous cookie, isn't it, Miss Susan?" Gary gave Grant half and then wolfed down his own without pausing even to smack his lips. "I'm going to get another one at graduation."

"I'm putting a piece for your father on this little plate and putting it in the cabinet. Remember it's for him." Susan took a bite of hers. "I believe we have a winner. Yes, Gary and you too, Grant, there will be more after the graduation tomorrow."

"Cut the kitchen light, Gary. Let's tell stories! Miss Susan, can you tell us a story?" Grant asked.

"I meant to ask about the storyboard. Have you been able to put it together and play with it?"

"No, not yet. I'll go get it. You can show us how to tell a story." Grant ran in to the living room.

As a child, Susan spent hours making up stories based on events from Sunday church school lessons; she added her own characters and made up her own endings. She was pretty sure she'd have to reread the Bible stories to be able to tell them correctly. This storyboard was a modern version of New Testament stories of Jesus written on the elementary level, so the children could read it for themselves. Her childhood storyboard was called a flannel graph, and the figures had a flannel backing. This new board was plastic, and the brightly colored figures were pressed on and peeled off easily.

"I got it." Grant handed it to Susan.

The storyboard had been opened but not taken apart. "Let's start with when Jesus was born."

"It's not Christmas!" Gary protested.

"Since Jesus birth was the beginning of Jesus being on earth, we'll just start there and go on." Susan handed the first story to Grant and the corresponding figures to Gary.

Grant read about Mary and Joseph who looked for a place to stay.

Gary knocked on the floor, hard. "Let us stay here!" He shouted.

Grant read about the birth of baby Jesus. He told Gary to put up the star, the stable, angels and then the shepherds who were gathered around the baby.

"Do these animals eat that hay?" Gary had placed a cow, a sheep and a donkey at the manger.

"Yes, the stable was like a barn where the animals stayed, and the manger was where the animals would get their feed. The baby Jesus didn't have a bed, so he slept in the manger with the animals all around." Susan answered.

"Then some of the hay would fall on the ground, right?" Gary ran upstairs and came back with construction paper, markers and scissors. "I'm going to make some hay for the floor."

Grant just rolled his eyes.

Susan wasn't at all sure the *hay* would stick, but Gary was determined. He didn't care if it stuck or not, although he licked it to make it stick.

The phone rang. Garrett wanted to know how Grant and Gary were behaving. "I said they could have a treat if they were good. I'll let you use your judgment, and if they would like a crème oatmeal cookie, they are in the cabinet next to the refrigerator behind the boxes of cereal."

"Thanks. Maggie stopped by with a couple of cookies, so they may not want one. We're just finishing with the Christmas story on the storyboard. Gary is making extra hay. Everything is fine."

Garrett became unusually quiet, but just when Susan thought he had already hung up, "Well, great, Susan. See you after a bit. Remember, you can call anytime you need me. Bye for now."

Gary came to Susan wanting her to help him get his shirt off. "Gary, what do you have on your shirt? It looks like caramel."

"From the cookie. I can put my pajama top on, but I don't have to go to bed do I?"

"No, you don't have to go to bed; you get to stay up a little while longer on Friday night. Instructions from your father." Gary left to go upstairs.

Grant was sitting quietly at the storyboard. "Miss Susan, why did my mother die?"

How do I respond, Lord? What brought this on? Oh, no. The accident in which their mother died was in December, around Christmas time. So now she knew why Garrett became so quiet on the phone. She should have remembered the time of the accident before starting with the Bethlehem story. Susan could just kick herself. Grant was fighting tears.

"Come on, Grant, let's go sit on the sofa." Grant came and hugged Susan, as they sat down together. "Grant, I don't know. I'm not going to pretend I do. Bad things happen in this world, and they are very tough to go through. I know you miss your mother."

Grant mumbled a "yes."

"Do you want to tell me about her?"

When Gary came back, not just in his pajama top, but both top and bottom, he sat down on the other side of Susan and joined in as he and Grant began talking about their mother.

"Every night Mommy read a story to us. She was so funny; she made faces and sounded like an airplane or a bird. She warned us about the mean ole' farmer with his wicked hoe." Both boys began to laugh. "We had to watch out for his meany hoe!"

"She hugged us and said she wouldn't let anything get us. When Daddy came home, he would read with us too, but he wasn't as much fun as Mom was." Grant had to wipe at a tear.

As she listened to Grant and Gary share about their mother, Susan was nearly in tears herself. It had been a year and a half, going on two years. Perhaps they didn't get to talk about her much. Grant, Susan surmised, remembered much more than Gary and was the serious one of the two. They were still real young to hurt this much.

Gary was getting restless, "I want to cut out some more hay."

"Tell you what Gary, we'll tell one more story before your dad comes home. How about a story about fish? Grant and I can practice reading the story while you make fish."

"I'm good at making fish. I can make hundreds."

"Oh, you can? Well this story is about 153 fish. How far can you count?" Susan asked.

"I can count to one million ninety nine!"

Grant rolled his eyes.

"Well, just a few fish will do. The storyboard only has a picture of two or three, but we can add as many as you can make." While Gary got busy drawing and cutting the fish, Grant, who was an excellent reader, went over the story with Susan.

The disciples saw Jesus die. "So what do we do now?" They didn't know what to do, so, they went back to what they knew how to do. They went fishing. They fished all night and didn't catch a single fish, not one.

At dawn, someone had a fire going on the shore and yelled to them, "Catch anything?"

"No, not one."

"Put your nets over on the other side of the boat."

What did they have to lose? So, they put their nets on the other side. Suddenly the net was filled with 153 large fish.

"It's Jesus!" Peter who was in the boat jumped out and into the water. He hurried to Him.

From then on, Jesus taught them to be fishers of men. He taught them to tell everyone about the stories Jesus told and how much God loved them.

When they got to the point in the story about the 153 large fish, Gary began to bring on his fish to add to the storyboard. He had cut them out of a piece of marbled, multicolored construction paper. Susan caught her breath. Gary had drawn each fairly good-sized fish as if they were transparent, with bones and inner organs visible. As if perfectly normal, Gary plopped them down, one by one, all identical. "I don't have enough, but I can make more."

Susan had been so absorbed with Gary's fish she had not heard Garrett come in. He was standing with his mouth open.

"Daddy!"

Garrett knelt down in front of Gary, "Gary I love your fish, but why did you draw them the way you did?"

Garrett did not believe Susan's story about catching a fish. How would he accept a transparent one? Now what?

Grant was nonplused about the fish. "Andi told us about catching a fish, and she drew a picture like Gary's. 'Member I said she caught one."

"Andi caught a fish like this?" Susan and Garrett asked in unison.

Grant shrugged his shoulders. "Yeah, she gave it to her dad, and he told her not to say anything about catching it. I told you Dad, remember, but you didn't believe me. You said it was just one of Andi's stories. I forgot until just now."

"You can ask Andi. They always go fishing, but they don't bring any fish back…" Gary pouted a little. "Daddy, we have a piece of a cookie for you. It's in the cabinet." Gary led the way to the kitchen and pointed to the cabinet.

Garrett looked a little confused but opened the cabinet. "Oh, I see. Tell me why you are in your pajamas, Gary, and why are you not, Grant?"

"Gary got some sticky caramel on him and changed. I didn't."

"One Ding Dong and now half a cookie? Tell me again why I have half a cookie?" Garrett pursed his lips.

Susan had to grin. "Maggie came by on her way to the high school and left a sample for all of us. She baked them for the reception and wanted us to try them. You only get a half. I made sure both halves were identical." She waited for him to respond. "Gary and I can straighten up the living room and put the storyboard away. Oh, Gary, may I have a couple of your fish for Andi's memory book?"

"You can have them all. I can make more fish than I made before for the fish story."

She would add Gary's fish to her fish page. She was wondering how Andi would explain her fish. Andi didn't react when Susan caught her fish, but Andi had not only seen one before, had she caught one herself? Why didn't she say something? What did Andi mean when she said Susan's fish reminded her of her father? What was it Grant said, Andi gave her fish to her father and, he told her not to say anything? Then, too, Maggie said she wanted to talk about the fish after graduation. Maybe she found something.

Susan had just gotten everything put back and was ready to go tell Garrett she was leaving, when the doorbell rang. She could hear the surprise in Garrett's voice, as he answered the door.

"Clarissa! Ah, er, come in. Don't just stand there. It's still trying to rain." Garrett brought her into the living room. "You've met Susan, our realtor and, tonight, our babysitter. You know the boys, Grant and Gary."

Clarissa was lovely, and her peach outfit was indeed *peachy keen*. She had a Gardenia corsage with peach, salmon and dark pink ribbons which coordinated with the color in her suit beautifully. Clarissa's smirk, which clearly marked Garrett as her territory, for Susan's benefit, was not as attractive or beautiful as the rest of her.

Susan knew she looked the epitome of a teenager with her jeans, sandals and pony tail. She knew it and wanted to cry, but she had to leave it with her Lord. "Clarissa, it is good to see you again. You are beautiful! I was just leaving. My job here is done for this evening. See you tomorrow, boys, Garrett, Clarissa." The boys grabbed hold of Susan for a hug. She turned to leave.

She didn't want them to see her tears.

Chapter 14

The next morning, wispy, white clouds decorated a bright blue sky. The breeze was warm. Why did she doubt? It *never rains* on graduation day at Plaincreek Crossroads.

Her plans were to sit with and Maggie, David and Gabi, out in the field where chairs had been set up for family and towns people. Trevor would be with students in the bleachers. The high school, middle school, and elementary school, physically in the same area, made a large, convenient complex.

Susan had put the finishing touches on the memory book, which included the fish page with Gary's handful of fish. She put it in a gift bag ready to give to Andi and couldn't wait to see how Andi would react when she saw the page with the fish. Why hadn't she told Susan she had caught a similar fish? She had said the fish was connected with her father somehow. Why would he have told her to be hush-hush? Susan wanted to talk to Andi, but she had not been included in anyone's plans so, she was prepared to leave after giving the book to her at the reception.

Examining herself in the mirror, Susan had doubts. "Now I think of it. I should have checked with Maggie about this dress." Susan preened and turned to view all angles. "Too late now. I sure don't want to be overdressed, but then I want to be at my best. I'm going to give the Lord a hand."

For whatever reason, wearing her lovely SPOTY dress for the graduation seemed right to Susan. She wasn't worried about her nomination for the award. It was perplexing, though, why she had not been contacted if she were one of the nominees. Did getting the award really matter so much anymore?

"What's happening to me?"

( )

The lawn care experts apparently had rolled the area, because it was solid when she stepped out on the field walking toward the rows of chairs. The school age children, on the bleachers, were laughing and yelling, pointing out parents and family. Maggie was waving wildly as she stood three rows from the front on the right side. As she walked over to Maggie, Susan glanced over the graduation program. The commencement speaker was no less than the President of the University of South Carolina. Susan also noted Andi was not only beautiful but also smart, as indicated by the asterisk for the National Honor Society next to her name on the program.

"Hey, Maggie, I didn't know...." Maggie was standing with her hands on her hips and her head back.

"Uh, huh, girl! You have done it! I almost didn't recognize you. You look so much more sophisticated, classy *and pricey*. I really love your hair, and your outfit is beyond gorgeous; it's a long way from mud-decorated feet or clay-encrusted overalls."

"Do I clean up good? Oh, Maggie, am I overdressed? I took you seriously when you said the town went all out."

Maggie laughed—"Oh, heavens, no. You're perfect. Just wait until Garrett sees you. I got a mean streak in me, and this is gonna be fun."

( )

In an hour and a half, from start to finish, under partly cloudy skies, with a fair breeze and no rain, Andi, her three musketeers, and classmates switched their tassels and bowed to applause of family and friends. With the sea of burgundy gowns and white mortarboards for girls and black for boys, the living river surged toward the gymnasium.

Gabi could walk, but she also loved to run; so Maggie and David had her in a stroller. The toddler didn't object being pushed and enjoyed the ride as everyone left the field and swarmed into the festive gymnasium. Balloons were everywhere. The floor was covered with a tarp and tables lined the perimeter where finger sandwiches, cookies, and punch were being served. It smelled like a bakery.

121

Leaving David to watch Gabi, Maggie hurried over to her station. Trevor and his classmates were already going from table to table, and parents congregated in noisy, laughing groups. Susan stood alone in the back, next to the entrance. She had realized, as each student received his/her diploma, the class colors were burgundy, white and black. She fit right in. She was trying to decide what to do when she was bumped from behind by her two favorite elementary age boys. Gary started to grab her legs, as he always had, but stopped short when she turned around. Grant rolled his eyes. Both boys stood away from Susan.

"It's just me, a little dressed up." She hugged them both. Sad, if a single dress could make much difference, since she was still the same on the inside.

"Grant, look at her shoes!" Gary began to stoop to touch her low heels trimmed with black beads but straightened up quickly.

If her shoes had been red, she could have clicked her heels *to go back to Kansas*. Susan grinned at the image. She sure wasn't in Kansas anymore. This was a new territory, new people, and new purposes. She felt joy and a fresh sense of life as she looked into the adoring eyes of these little boys whom she loved very much.

"We didn't know it was you at first. Your hair is different, and you look different, but it's you." Good for Grant.

"Yeah, Grant, I hope you like my hair, dress and shoes. Where's your dad? Let's ask him if you can go with me to my car to get Andi's present. I found a parking place real close. Aha, there he is."

As Susan and the boys reached them, Garrett and Clarissa, still in their graduation robes, had their backs toward them and stood speaking with a student. Susan stood and waited--not wanting to interrupt or eavesdrop, either.

"Hey, Dad, can we go with Miss Susan?"

At the sound of Gary's voice and his son's insistent pulling on his sleeve, Garrett turned around. When he saw Susan, his eyebrows went up, and his mouth dropped open for just a moment. They stood looking at each other. Clarissa smirked when she saw what had Garrett's attention and frowned at the trio standing before them. Clarissa gave Garrett, what could only be interpreted as an I-told-you-so look. Again Susan was sad to get this reaction.

"Look at these two spiffy gentlemen who are my escorts." Susan nodded her head towards the boys, one on either side, holding her hand.

"Dad made us wear our suits. He says it won't hurt us for weddings, funerals, church, sometimes, and graduation day. Can I take my tie off now, Dad?"

"I guess so…," and with that permission from their dad, both Grant and Gary as if on cue, pulled off their ties and tried to hand them to Garrett. He refused, indicating they could put them in their pocket. Susan took them, folded them neatly and put them in one of the compartments in her purse.

"With your go-ahead Garrett, I'll take Grant and Gary out to the car with me to get Andi's gift. I'm parked very near the doors over there, and it will only take a minute. By the way, where is Andi?"

Garrett took an audible breath, "Sure, they can go only if they will promise, first to walk and not run, and then not to leave the building again unless it is with me. Did you hear me, boys? We, Clarissa, Mrs. Murray and I, are staying around for any pictures the graduates might want to take. Andi should be around somewhere; just look around for a group of four, hopefully not engaged in mischief."

"We'll check in with you when we get back, so you won't wonder or worry."

To the boys she said, "We'll find Andi and the three musketeers when we get back. In fact, if we can find him, we should get Trevor to come with us. I need to ask Maggie something. She's over there."

As Garrett's gaze followed her across the room, Clarissa took his arm, turning his attention back to a couple of students who wanted to have their pictures taken.

"Maggie, we're going out to get the memory book. When we get back and find Andi, could you and Trevor join us over next to one of the photo booths to give it to her?" Then Susan whispered, "Maggie, did Trevor bring a rose for Andi?"

Maggie whispered back, "He sure did. I've got it back here ready when he wants to give it to her, if he doesn't forget."

"Oh, good, I've got a couple of carnations for Grant and Gary to give her. Do you feel Trevor will mind if they have a flower for her, too? I left them in the car in a cooler; I hope they're not wilted. You weren't exaggerating when you said the whole town comes. There are hundreds of people here. Everyone is in a good mood. I like this."

"Told ya. Not a bad get-together huh? About the rose, I'm going to get gray hairs early if Trevor is jealous and fearful of losing Andi's attention. I can see he might want to be the first one to give it to her though. He took great care in picking it out and, personally, paying for the rose. Grant and Gary are his friends, so I think it will be fine. See you in a bit."

"Watch for us to come back in."

"Oh, Susan, I'll bet Garrett might have whiplash."

Whiplash? If only he did care, but a dress does not make a person.

Between them, the boys decided Grant could carry the gift bag with the memory book because it was heavier, and Gary would be extraordinarily careful with both of the roses. Susan walked between them with a hand lightly on their shoulders. As they re-entered the gym, two of Susan's fellow realtors smiled and waved. She acknowledged them and continued towards Garrett with the boys.

"There's Andi! Hey, Andi!" Gary shouted.

Andi, Jesse, Dan and Matt all waved and started towards Garrett. Maggie found Trevor and came over with a woman whom Susan had not met but instantly recognized.

"Susan, this is Joycelyn Stokes, Andi's mother." Maggie introduced her. This was where Andi got her looks; Joycelyn had short wavy blond hair, brown eyes, and a lovely figure.

How could her husband have cheated on her? There. Susan had done it. She had made a judgment about a situation of which she had no firsthand knowledge. Maybe Joycelyn was right in backing off, thinking people, friends, neighbors and even strangers were gossiping behind her back, judging her about her possible failings as a woman and a wife. She was unusually quiet, almost backward, and Susan sensed her pain even on this joyful day. Maybe it wasn't a joyous day actually. It marked a milestone in Andi's life; it also meant Andi might be leaving; Joycelyn could feel yet another loss.

Grant looked to Susan, asking, with his eyes, permission to give the bag to Andi. Susan nodded. Grant handed the gift to Andi and immediately took a carnation from Gary.

Trevor stepped forward and shyly handed Andi a velvet deep red rose. "This is from me; I picked it out for you. I just want to say congratulations and happy graduation stuff." Andi laughed and bent down and hugged Trevor. His face turned beet red as she kissed him on the cheek. If Maggie was right and Trevor secretly had a crush on Andi, odds were Trevor would not wash his face for awhile.

Grant and Gary, as they figured it was their turn, handed Andi their pink-with-red-fleck carnations and asparagus fern, hugged her, and kissed her on the cheek. "Miss Susan said we could give you these flowers, too. They'll look good with Trevor's, won't they?"

"They certainly will!"

Susan pulled cards out of her purse and handed them to Andi and the boys. The guys seemed pleased to be noticed for the first time. The size of the group was growing as Dan, Jesse, Matt, their parents and Garrett joined them.

"Make sure you take a look at Andi's book. Thanks to all of you. In years to come, I think Andi will treasure every page of it. I hope we have occasion to get better acquainted in the future." Susan acknowledged them all.

"Andi, Andi," Gary pulled on her robe. "When you look at your book, look at the heliotropes I drew." Susan and Andi exchanged grins.

"Oh, you did. Did you sign the picture?"

"Yep, but I didn't sign the fish—there were too many, and they are not big enough to sign, but I made them." Gary was thinking. "Maybe I can put my name on the big page." Nothing shy about Gary.

"Fish, what fish?" Andi pulled the memory book from the gift bag and began to rapidly leaf through it. The *fish* page was the last page before the blank pages. She just stared. "Oh, Gary, you drew a picture of the fish I caught over a year ago. You did a neat job there buddy!"

Garrett didn't say anything, but looked from Susan to Andi and then down at Grant.

"We didn't tell anybody, except Dad, until now," Grant was nervous and looked about ready to cry.

"That's fine, Grantlee," Andi used her pet nickname for him. Andi looked over at Susan. "Miss Susan caught one, too, see her picture here, they're just alike. I'll look at this book later. It has some wonderful pictures." She nodded to the musketeers, "When I check over what you guys said, I'll be surprised if the words don't jump out and growl at me."

"Be sure to look at the snake pictures." Trevor added.

"You're kidding! I went through too quickly, didn't I? I will make sure to look thoroughly at it when I've got more time. Did you really see the indigo? Incredible! Oh, Trevor, thank you!" Trevor turned red again. He might not survive this day.

"Dad, there's Aunt Iris and Uncle Melton." Sure enough, Grant was right. Susan's boss, Franklin Wallston, was with them.

"Garrett, Clarissa!" Iris spoke as Clarissa again joined Garrett. Her boss seemed also to know Clarissa. It was as if everyone knew everyone. The graduates and their parents had wandered off. Maggie and Joycelyn had returned to their refreshment tables, and, as suddenly as Susan had felt she belonged, the group dissolved, and she stood alone, at a loss at what to do. Although she was the listing agent and had made the sale, these five people were discussing the Goldsmith property as if she weren't there. How did Iris always make Susan feel she was intruding on Iris' territory? Susan was deciding it was time for her to leave when Andi tapped her on the shoulder.

"Susan, I need to explain to you about the fish, maybe next week?"

"Right, Andi, good idea. I'm a little more than curious about your fish, and why you didn't mention it before. How about Monday? I'm free during the evening, so, call and let me know for sure. In fact, how about I treat you and your mother to dinner at the L & B?"

"You know, I think Mom would like to come, and she can hear what I have to tell you, too. I'll let you know."

Before the party was pretty much over, Susan toured the tables, sampled cookies and had some punch. She was lighthearted as she was again ready to leave. She turned, almost bumping in to her Uncle Owen. "Mom, Dad! Jackson?"

"Jackson called and, just on the spur of the moment, we all decided to take a chance you'd be home, so we could take you to dinner." Her mom was all smiles.

"How did you know where to find me?"

"Jackson said this town was probably so small we still could most likely find you if you weren't home. I guess he was right. We saw your Malibu right next to the main entrance."

As she recovered, Susan hugged her mom and dad as if she hadn't seen them in a month of Sundays. She had not seen or heard from Jackson in over six months, and so she stood back, not quite sure of his reason for bringing her parents, or what her reaction should be. She stepped towards him and gave him what might have to be described as a half hug. "What brings you to Plaincreek Crossroads, Jackson?"

"Oh, to see you, naturally. You look your usual magnificent self. Love that dress, Susan. I'd have to say the style in this little burg is cutting edge. From all the people and the crowded parking lots, I guess this is a major community activity. Jackson looked all round the gym the whole time he was speaking with Susan.

Susan was used to this. He was always fond of being around lots of people. It had never seemed as if he were content to be with, or speak to, just one person at a time. His nickname in the office was Ken, the male counterpart of Barbie. He did fit the image; blond wavy hair; blue eyes; broad shoulders; an ever present smile. Susan was surprised at her own thought: what a stir it would make if Andi and Jackson walked into a room together. When Susan, herself, was with Jackson, the snag was always his self assurance and his absorption with himself. He had to be the center of attention and made Susan less important. This blast of insight hit Susan square in her gut. She certainly could not judge Jackson without judging herself.

Garrett with his graduation robe over his arm and the boys each with a handful of cookies walked up behind her.

Mom motioned to Susan to look behind her. The boys weren't paying attention to anything but their cookies. Garrett stood waiting.

Her heart was literally in her mouth as she turned to include Garrett in the circle, "Mom, Dad, Jackson, this is Garrett Taylor, a counselor here at the high school, and these are his two sons Grant and Gary. Garrett, this is my Mom and Dad. You've heard me refer to them as Aunt Em and Uncle Owen. They live in Columbia and surprised me with a visit this afternoon. Jackson Weatherly is a former co-worker. I still don't know how they found me."

"Susan, this was easy. We kept track of you through your teenage years didn't we?" Her dad grinned from ear to ear.

"I can only imagine. If you'd only seen the times I've had to rescue her," Garrett smiled at Susan's discomfort. "We'll have to get together to discuss this sometime."

Susan didn't blame her mother for looking puzzled.

"We're taking Susan to dinner. We'd love to have you join us." Dad invited.

"Yes, do, and tell us how Susan is getting along in Plaincreek Crossroads." Jackson extended the welcome.

"Sorry, we can't this evening." Garrett looked from Susan to Jackson. "We have graduation plans, and we'd better get going. See you later. Grant, Gary, tell Miss Susan, Jackson and her parents, bye."

Gary came alive. "I only got one of those cookies you cut in half last night," he complained.

Grant seemed on top of things, "I got two. Dad said to get him one, so he could eat a whole one. When are you coming over, Miss Susan?"

"Well, I'll have to get more stories ready. You never know…. Bye now," Susan kissed them both on the cheek. They dragged their feet as Garrett took them off.

Jackson and Garrett were opposite. Jackson was animated, talkative, and always glancing around when someone was speaking to him. Garrett was quiet, reserved and direct when speaking with someone, as if he or she were the only person for miles around. While she was considering the men, Susan didn't see the questioning looks between Aunt Em and Uncle Owen.

After Garrett had walked away, Aunt Em turned to Susan, "Isn't this the outfit you bought and were saving when you received the SPOTY?" She treated it as a rhetorical question and went on, "I'd say I'm glad you chose to wear it today. It looks as if you fit in and more. That's all I'll say. You're not in Kansas anymore."

Jackson opened his mouth to speak....

"Hey, Miss Susan!" Gary pulled away from his Dad. "'Member, you gotta hear the rest of the heliotropes me and Grant have to tell you."

"Grant and I," corrected Garrett, as he retrieved his youngest son, nodding to them.

"Okay Gary, I'll remember!" With those words from Susan, Gary actually smiled as he was being pulled away.

"I want you to meet Maggie." Susan saw David and both children were standing at the nearly empty table, too.

Maggie came to the front of the table, "Let me guess, this is Aunt Em and Uncle Owen and...."

"Mom, Dad, and Jackson, this is Maggie Riley, her husband David, and Trevor and Gabi. You have to watch Trevor; he'll hawk anything loose and make a profit out of it."

"Awe, she's still mad 'cause we hosed her off."

"You what?" Aunt Em wasn't sure she heard right.

Susan patted Trevor on the arm as if to say, enough.

"Jackson and I worked together in a real estate agency, in Columbia. He drove Mom and Dad down for the day and found me here. Maggie, you'd appreciate how they were able to find me. Maggie is working toward an investigator's certification, and she keeps close watch over Floating Bone Lake. She's a good friend. Maggie, if you are available on Monday can you meet with Andi, Joycelyn and me at about 4:30 pm at the L & B?"

"I love the L & B. If it's okay with you, David, for my *night out*?" David shrugged. Then Maggie addressed Susan's parents, "Susan has nothing but compliments regarding you two. I don't mean to be in a hurry, but I've invited some of Trevor's classmates and their parents for a cookout. Say, where are my manners? I'll have plenty. Come on over in about an hour. You can meet some of our Plaincreek Crossroads folks."

Jackson stepped up. "Thank you, Maggie. Nice to meet you, but we'll need to be starting back as soon as we finish dinner."

"Next time, then. Gotta go. Jackson, you'll have to fill me in on Susan. She doesn't talk too much about her *former life* in Columbia. Oh and Susan, remember to be at the hospitality room in the morning."

"So, you've got plans for in the morning?" Jackson probed.

"We're going to church," Susan took her mother's arm.

"Church?" Jackson shook his head and looked down at the floor for a moment.

As they left the gym, Susan thought she saw Angus at the far end of the room. She had been wondering about him. He had been away for only two weeks, and so much had happened.

"The L & B is a favorite. How about we go there?" Susan asked. "The letters are for Light and Bread. I'll drive my car, too. Just follow me. It's not far and hopefully not too busy."

As they entered the restaurant side, Jackson glanced at the postcard he was handed. He quickly stuck it in his suit jacket pocket.

It hit Susan. Why was Jackson so formally dressed? Didn't he say it was a spur-of-the-moment decision to find her home on a Saturday afternoon?

Susan chatted about Garrett, Grant, Gary and Maggie's family because Jackson and her parents had just met them. She only mentioned the Goldsmith property in passing. Jackson certainly could not have understood her feelings about the land and her ambivalence towards selling it.

She felt closer than ever to her mom and dad, but because Jackson was there, Susan still did not share her spiritual experience in Floating Bone Lake.

"Susan, Jackson is anxious to get back, and you know us. We prefer our own bed and our own church. We're just getting more and more set in our ways; we treasure being at home. We're only a little over an hour away, so we can visit anytime. In fact, we should do this regularly."

"Sure enough, you know we could visit more often," Jackson agreed.

Susan was not convinced Jackson meant what he had just said. Her focus was, though, on how to get her mother alone before they had to leave. "Mom, could I talk to you for a minute?"

While Jackson and her dad went to bring the car to the front entrance, Susan took the opportunity to talk to her mom. "Mom, would Dad be open to receiving a puppy as a gift from me on Father's Day? I've picked out a darling little white fluff ball for him. If you think it would be acceptable, I will get the puppy and surprise him."

Like a deer caught in the headlights, her mom stood and stared at Susan. After all, Susan's aversion to dogs had been vocal and definite down through the years. Susan hated the incessant barking of little dogs trying to be fierce and terrible. Susan feared larger dogs, so asking if she could get a puppy for her dad was one hundred eighty degrees out of character.

Susan had never shared the loss of her own puppy, Mars, back before her mother had deserted her and her father. She only had her puppy for a couple of weeks before the puppy died. Susan had named him Mars, after the *red planet* because he had a beautiful deep reddish-brown colored coat. After he had died, she refused to have anything to do with another puppy. Someday she would tell Mom and Dad. Today she was asking for permission to love these God-given parents in this special way.

Susan, chuckling and still preoccupied with her mother's reaction, almost forgot about Jackson.

Jackson seemed ill at ease as he came around to open the door for Aunt Em. When he closed the rear passenger door, Jackson took Susan's hands in his. "Susan, I see it's you, and you're the same, but I'm not really sure. Something is different. I've had a pleasant afternoon and evening, though. Thanks Susan. Why didn't you call or try to contact me? And, Susan, you do look smashing!"

Why didn't you call or try to contact me? What? Had he expected her to get in touch with *him?* Why didn't he make any effort before six months to talk to her or see *her?* She had no answers, but her thoughts were on her mom and dad. Would her dad notice her mom was a bit *shell shocked* on the ride home?

Andi had suggested a bichon frise when Susan asked her what kind of puppy she should get. Her search ended when she fell in love with Danae, a six week old, fluffy, soft, pure-white puppy ready to be adopted. According to the sellers this particular puppy was proving to be very smart, even tempered, playful and loving. She knew her mom would approve because Danae didn't shed, was known to travel well, and by Father's Day, would be somewhat trained.

In the past, Susan never put much thought into a gift selection. Now, she had the same sense of joy and freedom choosing the puppy as when she had worked on Mom's Mother Day gifts, the storyboard for the boys and the memory book for Andi. Since she now had her mother's consent, her mom did nod without a word, Susan would sign for Danae on Monday. She couldn't wait until Father's Day.

Sunday morning before church, Susan read the story of Jesus raising a little girl from the dead:

A distraught father had fallen before Jesus, begging and pleading for Him to help. "Come, please! I know you are able to help my daughter. My house is not far. Please, make way for Jesus. Please come!" From down the street, mourners wailed.

Jesus, a mist in his own eyes, answered, "I'll come." As Jesus followed, the crowd grabbed at Him as though their reaching fingers would draw power from Him. Jesus was pushed and jostled from all sides. "Who touched me?" Jesus demanded. Upon hearing weeping, He turned to a woman just within arm's reach. "Woman your faith has made you well."

The father pulled at Jesus' robe, urging Him to move on.

When they arrived, Jesus simply said, "She's not dead, only asleep."

Foolishness! Of course the little girl was dead. After all, they had seen her lifeless body lying stiff and still on the mat.

A deep hush fell over the house. Outside, mourners ceased their groaning.

Inside, Jesus handed a breathing child to her parents. No more funeral dirges. Joy was wrapped in sobs as the little girl hugged her mother and insistent father. (from Matthew 9:18-26)

Susan imagined what the people in the crowd would be saying as they followed Jesus from the house. Person to person whisperings: His healing strengthened limp limbs, gave sightless eyes a vision of life, and cleansed souls with forgiving love. His power stole life from death giving hope to all who believed.

Susan wondered whether this particular story was in the storyboard, but she did know one story was the parable of the farmer. Oh, what fun Gary would be. She could see Grant rolling his eyes. Would Gary want to cut out seeds? She could see him putting plants under a hot sun and watching them wither or be choked by weeds. Grant would have to make sure Gary didn't think Grant was a withering seedling.

As she thought about the lesson of the farmer, Susan began to think of songs to accompany the story. She envisioned a play or some object lesson. Like a light turned on in the darkness, she realized this was something she would love to do. She could help out with Sunday school classes. What fun it would be to have children come to her apartment for snacks and games.

She glanced down at her watch surprised at the late hour. "I'd better get dressed, or I'll be late to join Maggie at the Welcome Center, or did she say Hospitality Room?"

Susan parked in the first open parking spot which turned out to be the equivalent of a daily exercise run.

As she entered, Trevor was muttering, "Mom said the minister would be speaking in vain if we didn't take Gabi to the preschool. But Mom's making me sit with you guys."

Maggie gave Trevor a good-humored little smack on the head. "David's still sleeping. Maybe next time he'll come."

"Maybe next time, I can go to a kid's class," Trevor fired back.

He was pacified when they took their seats next to a family with a boy close to his age. By the end of the service, Trevor had learned the boy's name was Nathan, and he was moving to Plaincreek Crossroads in the fall.

"If you're looking for a house, she's an agent," he said about Susan.

After the service, Susan walked with Maggie to her car before going on to her Malibu.

Trevor who had run ahead called out, "Did you see Mr. Taylor? He saw us, but there were too many people between us. He was with someone. I don't know who."

Clarissa?

Chapter 15

For six years, Susan had lived and breathed to seek out new listings; show properties; match sellers and buyers; make deals; organize all the details that came with dealing real estate. She had devoted the entire year proving to be the best among her co-workers, but today none of this mattered. Today she couldn't wait to get home go to the L & B with Maggie, Joycelyn and Andi to talk about the *fish*. She watched the minute hand finally make the hour hand click. She rushed to change into casual clothes. Was her career now less relevant? Maybe, just maybe, her real life was beginning to have more meaning.

When Susan arrived at the L & B, Maggie, Joycelyn and Andi were in a festive mood.

"I think we should order first. It's my treat; you all can order to your heart's content." Susan dismissed her earlier boredom, "Do you come here often?"

"Often enough to recognize Tyler. So, he's going to be our waiter. He's a classmate of Andi's. How about that, Andi?" Maggie teased.

"Just so he doesn't pour water all over me!" Andi over-emphasized a pout.

Maggie and Joycelyn snickered.

Tyler approached. "Andi, I'll be your server today. What would you like to drink?"

"Just water with lemon for everyone right now." Maggie offered.

Tyler looked over at Andi, "Yes, and I'm sure you want a full glass."

That did it! Joycelyn and Maggie burst into laughter.

"Yes, right, a full one—with no ice please." Andi looked directly at Tyler.

Even he couldn't keep from grinning.

Maggie laughed until she had to wipe a tear.

"If I have too, I'll have Kat bring your water, Andi." After more laughter from Joycelyn and Maggie, Tyler shook his head and walked away.

"A little hidden agenda here, I think." Susan had no idea of the reason for the humor.

"Susan," Maggie dramatized, "you had to be there when it happened. Last time, Tyler tripped all over himself when he saw Andi and dumped an entire glass of ice water down her neck. She jumped up and almost knocked him over. I tell you, he looked as if he wanted to find the nearest manhole and pull the cover in over him. What was so comical was Andi looking at him as if she were a mother with a naughty child. When he tried to dry her off with a napkin, she rolled her eyes and resigned to his ministrations. She rolls her eyes better than Grant does. Have you ever seen Grant roll his eyes? In fact, now that I think about it, maybe Grant gets it from Andi."

So Susan had to shake her head and chuckle. "Poor Tyler, how embarrassing." As she looked around the table at the two blondes, Joycelyn and her daughter Andi, and then at Maggie who was friendly and bubbly, she was getting a different picture of them. In addition to the light and frivolous conversation, Susan couldn't ever remember enjoying herself as a friend among friends. She looked across the room to the booth where just a few weeks ago, she and Garrett sat so close and ate their dessert after Clarissa left. She felt warm and all fuzzy until Garrett walked up. He and Iris were together.

If he noticed her flushed cheeks, he didn't show it. He was, in fact, a little somber. "Well, what do we have here?"

Maggie answered, "There's room for two more. Join us."

"We just stopped in at the bookstore to find a couple of books for Gary. His birthday is coming up. Their Uncle Melton is staying with them for an hour. I dislike missing out on all this delightful company though." Garrett's gaze swept over all of them, resting on Susan for a moment.

"Oh, boy! Take some bandages back with you to repair Uncle Melton's ego. Susan knows what I mean. Do you suppose they'll ask him if he helped create the moon and stars? Do you know how many times they have asked me questions using Uncle Melton's age for comparison." Andi feigned a gesture of helplessness.

"Oh, yes, Grant and Gary asked if kids had bicycles when Uncle Melton was a boy. I suggested they ask him. I think they have a list of questions ready for him." Susan contributed.

Iris frowned.

"May I ask what the occasion is for you ladies to be having an evening out?" Garrett probed.

Andi pulled her memory book from under the table. "I wanted to talk to Susan about the fish in my book."

Iris scanned the table, eyes resting on Susan. "Fish! Who cares about a fish? Mother had said something about a fish before she died, but I didn't know what she was talking about. Carol had some crazy idea about some fish, but no one knew about it either, so it died with her. It doesn't matter anyway. The property is sold; unless someone screws it up?"

This evening was taking a turn for the worse. *How prophetic I am*, Susan chided herself as Clarissa walked up.

"What have we here? Hail, hail, the gang's all here or something. I hope I'm not interrupting. That seems to be my role in life lately, doesn't it? Garrett dear, I still have some odds and ends to tie up to complete averaging the grades, so I can turn them in to be sent out next week. Never mind, I'll talk to you about business later. Will you be in the office the rest of the week? I wasn't there today. I took the day to recuperate from the weekend. Are you going to be working at the school during the summer? I'll just call you later." Clarissa gave Susan a backward look.

"No, Clarissa. Come with me now. I'm heading home. We can talk there." Garrett nodded to the group, took Clarissa by the arm and led her out of the restaurant with Iris in tow.

So, Garrett was taking Clarissa home with him. "Anyone ready for dessert?" Susan shrugged.

"After that wet-blanket-trio, we all need some instant gratification," Maggie jumped in. "Here comes just the guy!" Tyler was the brunt of yet another remark. "We'll have to leave a hefty tip for him."

While they were quietly eating their dessert, Andi opened her book to the *fish* page. "Susan, I saw the fish you caught even though you dropped it, and it got off the hook. But, I'll bet you are wondering about the fish Gary cut out last week. The boys didn't see my fish, but I told them about it, and I drew them a picture, just like the ones Gary drew here in the book. I told them not to say anything which was probably easy since it wasn't real to them anyway. They could have easily thought it was just another one of my stories, but I did catch a fish, and it was identical to the one you drew, Susan. I should have told you, and I don't know why I didn't. I still don't know what to think. It's been over a year ago, just before my dad's accident. Mom?"

"I'm fine Andi, now go on."

"Dad was excited about the fish. When I caught it, I put it in my fish water bucket. Yes, Susan, ahem…my *water bucket?*"

Susan hadn't said a word, but when Andi emphasized her *water bucket*, she knew she was talking about wetting down the clay path to the fishing spot at the lake. She nodded that she understood.

"Dad took the fish. He said he would have a great surprise for us, and I was not supposed to say anything to anybody. The accident was the next day. I just wanted you to know, Susan, you weren't imagining what you saw when you caught that fish. The strange fish is one of the mysteries of Floating Bone Lake I'll always wonder about, even after there are houses in its place."

"You know what? I've noticed more customers have come in, and our table might be needed. How about coming to my apartment? Maggie has some more information; I hope. My apartment is just around the corner. I'll go find Tyler and take care of the bill. You can follow me, or Maggie knows the way."

Susan caught Tyler's attention. "Tyler, if you have the check, we're getting ready to leave, but I wanted to tell you your service was excellent. I think you were a good sport when we ladies teased you about the time you spilled water on Andi. We had a good time, and we loved the food. So, thanks. I hope we get you if you're on duty the next time we're here. It's the little things which add so much."

Tyler and her mother would get along, Susan surmised; he looked like a deer in the headlights too. He just stood there for a moment, then smiled and turned to bring the ticket.

When the four of them entered her apartment, Susan anticipated that Joycelyn's and Andi's reaction would be like Maggie's reaction on her first visit. "Look at those floor-to-ceiling windows! Check out the loft. Do you sleep up there? Wow, what a neat fireplace. I love this setup."

After they had all settled down in the living room by the fireplace, Maggie took charge of the discussion, "I am glad we're here where you all can hear me. The L & B would have been fine, but this is better. I have a *ghostly* story to tell. In the beginning, God created the heavens and the earth. We should ask Uncle Melton for verification, right." Even Maggie chuckled at her own humor. "Well, going on, I think it was on the fifth day God made fish, all the creatures of the sea, and the birds, too, but we're only interested in the fish right now. There's this minnow, about an inch and a half long, called a zebra fish. Most likely what you saw in your library book, Susan, was a zebra fish."

"You're not going to tell me my fish was a zebra fish. I don't think I would have won any prizes with the size of my catch, but it certainly wasn't a minnow! I don't….."

"Susan, just hang in there…. At the University of Oregon back in the 1970's, Dr. George Streisinger recognized that the zebra fish was genetically similar to humans on the tissue, cell and molecular levels. Researchers began to use this fish to study cancerous tumors, stroke, scoliosis and spinal cord injuries. What makes this fish useful is, when hatched, it is transparent. What is developing inside the fish is visible. Experimenting with the fish at this stage allows scientists to be able to track cancer growth and metastasis as it occurs inside the fish. Are you with me?"

Susan wanted to understand, but she still couldn't connect-the-dots. "It's so unbelievable; a fish could be used to study cancer. But, you're talking about just a little over two inches. A zebra fish is not very big…. But mine…."

Maggie interrupted. "Ahem, Susan, just hang in there. Continuing…. The transparent stage of the minnow was about four week's duration, and then it becomes opaque, not transparent anymore. By the beginning of 2008, there were published reports about a Dr. Richard White and other researchers at Boston Children's Hospital who had succeeded in producing a zebra fish which remained transparent its entire life. You'll never guess the name of the fish. The name of the fish is Casper! *Casper the ghost!* Now, Casper is being used to study diseases such as Alzheimer's, inflammatory bowel disease and even birth defects in human children."

Susan caught her breath, "Maggie, could our fish be Casper Fish? How would a Casper fish get into Floating Bone Lake? How could this transparent minnow zebra fish grow into a fairly good sized fish? Are there others? Is the fish Andi caught a year and a half ago, and the one I caught two weeks ago the same kind, or is it a different species? If our fish were Casper fish, do the researches know this is possible?

"Susan, I don't know. I wish I could tell you, but from my investigation, the zebra fish breeds prolifically, and scientists began requesting embryos of Casper fish for their studies. I also know there is a massive amount of research being done and a huge amount of grant money, in the millions, just for Casper fish research. What happens in a laboratory dish, it would seem, can have far reaching effects on a living specimen. That's what I've got so far." Maggie had been pacing while she was reading her notes. Now she sat down.

"How long do the fish live?" Andi wanted to know.

Maggie jumped on it. "Oh, I've got more information somewhere." She shuffled through her papers. "Yes, they can live from two to five years under ideal conditions. The fish are native to the Ganges' fast moving water, but they are hardy and have been known to survive under far less than ideal conditions. They prefer water temperatures of 64 to 77 degrees Fahrenheit, but can withstand other temperatures."

"Well, if they live in Floating Bone Lake, they sure did get cold. Unless.... Do you suppose when those bones float to the surface they're actually brought up by, maybe, some warm springs? I think the whole area is over a fault...." Andi spoke as if speaking to herself and began to nod her head.

Joycelyn spoke up, "I had no idea they were using fish to study birth defects. None of you could know, and I doubt if Andi remembers. She was just a toddler. Russ and I lost twin boys at five months into my pregnancy. The doctors said there was no way they would have lived. We were heartbroken, but we did have Andi. I had a hysterectomy. If researchers knew more about the causes of birth defects, then I, personally, think doctors could do more to prevent them."

"Mom, I must have been really little. I just knew you were sick and had to go to the hospital. So, now I know why I don't have any brothers or sisters."

"Maggie, I wonder what Iris meant when she said her mother and, possibly, Carol, said something about a *fish*? I'm sorry, Joycelyn, I don't want to upset you." Susan was afraid she had just inserted foot in mouth by talking about Carol.

"No, don't worry about it. I've had so many questions, and I haven't been able to withstand any of them up to now, but now is an opportune time. The first houses in our subdivision were built about five years ago when Russ and I met Carol and Garrett. Russ had business dealings, of course, with Clara Goldsmith who owned the property where the subdivision was built. Carol was more a daughter than a granddaughter to Clara. We often wondered how Iris and Melton felt about Carol getting all the attention and benefits. Anyway, our house was one of the first. It worked out so well to be living here and Russ working in the same area. The company began building Garrett and Carol's house about a year after ours. We were so glad they moved in as soon as they did, even though the house wasn't nearly done. Gary was just a baby and Grant a toddler. I think Andi watched them at least once a week, didn't you?"

"Mom, I think I raised them!" All of them laughed.

"I loved Carol. We became best friends. I told her early on about the twins, and she shared with me about her father dying of cancer before she and Garrett married. I still don't understand what happened at the time of the accident. I thought everything was going well between Russ and me, but I can't help but second guess myself on everything. Looking back, I didn't see any *red flags*. I'm afraid to know what happened, but I need to know so I can put it behind me and go on."

Susan responded, "Anyone would want to know, Joycelyn. Andi, Grant said you gave your fish to your dad. I wonder what he did with the fish. Have you ever felt as if you were on the edge of a big discovery but not quite there? Do you think, as I do, that something is missing? By the way, Maggie, or Joycelyn and Andi, do you know Angus, whatever his last name is? I thought I saw him out of the corner of my eye Saturday at the graduation. He seems to know Garrett. Did he know Carol? Did he know Clara Goldsmith?"

"Susan, with your ability to ask questions, you and I should go into business. Actually, those are very good questions."

"Sorry Maggie, I was just had a couple of thoughts. Andi, when Grant told his father about the transparent fish, Garrett didn't take it seriously. He thought it was just another one of your stories. Garrett dismissed it and, in fact, didn't believe me when I said I caught a fish. He just laughed it off. You know, Garrett has never said word one about Carol. I guess she hadn't said anything to him about any fish. Gary and Grant said they never go in to *her room* upstairs. I wonder if Angus would talk to him; maybe he knows about the fish. I guess I don't want to make a mystery where there is none or stick my nose into another's painful experience." Susan was floundering to express the depth of her questions.

Maggie rubbed her forehead, "Well, I know one thing. A good mystery stirs my molecules. I wonder if Garrett would be willing to look in Carol's room for any *fish* clues. It will still be just like she left it, if what Grant and Gary say is true. David does say I can see a question when there's nothing to ask. Speaking of David, it's getting later than he is able to keep the children under control."

"Oh, it is getting late, isn't it—not for me, but for you. There are definitely some things to think about. Floating Bone Lake is about to be sold. I'm uncomfortable about it. Isn't that crazy, since I'm the realtor making the sale?"

Chapter 16

Next morning Susan awoke with questions on her mind. Was she making something out of nothing? A fish is, after all, just a fish. What could Casper fish possibly have to do with Floating Bone Lake? Maggie said she would talk to Garrett about the Casper Fish if he called and asked her. But, would he call? Susan didn't think so. She felt she needed to call him.

About midmorning, Susan went out to her Malibu to call Garrett on her cell. He answered on the first ring.

"Garrett, this is Susan."

"Good morning Susan, how can I help you?"

Susan was taken back a bit, but she understood he was at work, as was she. "Garrett, you asked us last night at the L & B what we girls were doing."

"Yes, I did, didn't I." Garrett sounded a little friendlier.

"I'd like to bring you up to speed, but not over the phone."

"No, of course, not. If you don't mind coming again, I guess if you want to talk, you can come after the boys are asleep. Would you want to come over this evening, maybe just a little later than usual?"

"Wha-t-t…? Sure, Garrett, see you tonight. Thanks for talking to me." Was it her imagination, or did Garrett just say she shouldn't come until after the boys were asleep? Didn't he want her to see Grant and Gary? By the tone of his voice, he wasn't just trying to be alone with her.

Her next call was to Maggie. "Maggie, Susan here. Could you come with me tonight to talk to Garrett? You have the information and details on the Casper fish."

"I can't! David's got a meeting, but I'll get out my binoculars."

"Oh, that's gonna help! Do you know if Andi or Joycelyn is busy? On the other hand, I'm sure they don't want to talk about Carol. Okay, I guess I'm it." Susan wanted to say, *keep me in your prayers*, but Maggie wasn't the one to ask for that, yet.

When Susan went back into the office, she noticed a few in the office checked their watches. Her imagination was bordering on paranoia. Were they clocking her movements?

C ?

Later in the evening, on her way to Garrett's, Susan wondered if the doorbell might awaken or alert the boys if they weren't asleep, but as it turned out she didn't have to worry. Garrett was waiting for her. He led her to the living room and motioned for her to sit on the sofa while he sat in a chair across from her.

Susan began, "Remember when I told you about the fish I caught but got away. I didn't tell you, but the fish was so transparent I could see everything inside of it. You know about the memory book for Andi and the fish I drew, and the fish Gary drew and cut out, and the fish Grant also recognized. You know, too, Andi said she caught one just like the drawings, and she gave it to her dad who told her to keep it a secret." Susan saw Garrett wince. It was now or never, even if it hurt. She continued. "Maggie did some research."

Garrett interrupted, "of course, you and Maggie, camera and all."

Susan didn't understand his response. Garrett and Maggie were close friends.

"Daddy, can we see Miss Susan?" Both boys were at the bottom of the stairs.

Gary, with Grant behind, ran over to Garrett. "Daddy, please, can we see her? I didn't get to tell her the rest of the story. It's real short. I gotta tell her. Plea-s-s-s-se!"

Susan didn't have a clue. What story? Then she remembered the heliotropes. "Oh, the rope from the helicopter!"

Gary ran over to Susan, "No, silly!"

"Gary!" Garrett warned.

"I'm sorry Miss Susan," he bowed his head a little.

Grant shrugged.

"I know I was silly. I was trying to be funny." Susan looked at Garrett.

"Wait a minute!" Gary ran in the direction of the kitchen. He returned with his hand balled into a fist. "Look Miss Susan," Gary opened his fist, "some bugs that didn't jump like jumping beans," he quoted from the story.

"Oh, the heliotropes," Susan said, pretending she had just remembered.

"There were only five of them. Where did you get more?"

"They're sunflower seeds. Dad says they're for us to eat. You break open the shell, and there's a kernel inside. Dad, can we tell her the rest?"

"I don't suppose you guys will be able to go to sleep until you do, will you?" Both shook their heads in a *no*. "Can I listen, too?"

With the *yes* and with Gary on one side of Susan and Grant on the other, Gary began.

"Once upon a time."

"Short, boys," their father interrupted.

Grant took over, "You remember about the growin' man telling Andrea he had a surprise for her?" Susan nodded. "He brought her a big box wrapped with a ribbon and bow even. She couldn't guess, so, he let her open it."

Gary jumped in. He was getting animated, but one look from Garrett, and he calmed down. "Miss Susan, Miss Susan," he pulled on her sleeve. "First, guess how many seeds Andrea had. Not just five. She had hundreds. Seeds from the sunflowers she planted."

"Wow, what was she going to do with all those sunflower seeds?"

"Grant, tell her what was in the package." Gary was holding Susan's arm.

"It was a bird feeder. The growin' man had made it for her."

"Why a bird feeder?" Susan asked.

Gary was laughing, "Because the birds can eat the sunflower seeds."

Susan had resisted elongating the story by not asking questions and egging the boys on, and now she summarized the story for them; "Oh I see, what a great story; Andrea was God's helper by planting the seeds, watering the plants, and then feeding the birds with the seeds from the flowers. I love it. Thank you!" She kissed them both lightly on the forehead.

"Story time is over, off you go again. Go on up, and I'll follow to tuck you in again in a minute." To Susan he said, "Be back in a minute."

"Oh," Gary ran back, "Here you can have these. They're roasted, and they're for people." He gave her his fist full of sunflower seeds, turned around, almost started to say something, but ran up the stairs instead.

When Garrett returned, Susan tried to explain. "I'm sorry if I have upset you. It certainly wasn't my intention. I just wanted to let you know what we were thinking."

"Go on Susan, tell me why you came."

"All right then, I asked Maggie to do some research on the kind of fish I caught in the lake. She uncovered data on a minnow-size fish called a zebra fish. Scientists have been able to alter it genetically to make it transparent all of its life instead of just the first four weeks. The transparent fish is called Casper, and because their systems are similar to humans, they are used for studies for cancer and many other diseases. So assuming my fish was a Casper, how did it end up in Floating Bone Lake? The laboratory Caspers are only an inch or so long, so how did the Casper fish grow as big as the one I caught or the one Andi caught? When Andi caught hers and showed her father, why did he tell her to keep it a secret? What happened to it? Iris mentioned Carol and Mrs. Goldsmith, both, talked about fish. Did Carol talk about the fish in Floating Bone Lake? Is this the same fish? Do you know what Iris was talking about? Do you think Angus, since he knows a lot about South Carolina, would know anything about this fish? Maggie has more information on Casper if you'd want more details…" Susan finished.

"Susan, I've listened, and to be candid, I'm not interested in any fish. I remember Andi's fish story, and I know you said you caught one, as it turns out, similar to hers, but I don't see what a fish has to do with anything. Have you thought you've tried to make a mystery where there is none?" Garrett concluded.

"I'd better go then, it's not my purpose to meddle in other's affairs, but it appears you think I am. I just had an idea…. Well, never mind. Good night, Garrett." She had been sitting on the sofa but now stood up to leave.

Garrett hesitated, but then asked, "Susan, are you a candidate for some salesperson of the year award in real estate? Why did you wear such an expensive dress for the graduation?"

"What? The SPOTY? I don't know. I haven't heard. Come to think of it, the banquet is later this fall, but the answer is I don't know. The dress? What about my dress, for heaven's sake? Maggie said to dress up. She said the graduation was an annual community event. I probably picked the prettiest dress, short of an evening gown, in my closet. What was wrong with it? Oh,

I almost forgot, I need to give these to you." Susan reached into her purse for the ties the boys had taken off at the graduation reception.

Garrett looked down. "You'd better check on whatever award you think you're going to receive."

"I will." Susan walked out. The last time she felt pain like this was right after she had plunged into deep darkness gasping for air and not finding her father. Now she felt a similar sense of loss and aloneness. Had Garrett come to mean so much to her? Had she come to mean so little to him?

As soon as she arrived back at her apartment, the phone rang. It was Maggie. "Susan, the shark is circling!"

Susan didn't want her to know she was crying. Besides she felt a headache coming on, if she didn't stop sniffling. "What are you talking about?"

"Of course, I can see Garrett's house, but when she has to come right by my house to turn around in the cul-de-sac, I don't even need my binoculars."

"Maggie, make sense."

"The entire time you were at Garrett's, Clarissa was going by every couple of minutes. She didn't stop at his place when you left though. She apparently just wanted to make sure you weren't there. Susan, Susan! You just don't know, do you? We'll save that for another day. Were you able to tell Garrett I have information about the fish? Will he be calling me?"

"I did tell him, but don't expect him to call."

"Okay, I'd better turn my attention to Gabi for now. Guess who is telling a story to her curtains to keep from falling asleep? If you think Grant and Gary are unique, just wait till you get to know Gabi."

"Thanks Maggie, you always help me feel better. I'll let you get back to Gabi. Talk to you tomorrow."

Susan thought she understood Clarissa, but not Garrett; why had he warned her to check about what was going on with the SPOTY? Why was Garrett concerned about it? So focused on the fish, Susan had nearly forgotten about the award. She had not heard she was even nominated. Two months ago it had been the most crucial goal of her life, but now it just wasn't.

She was dumbfounded over the dress.

Susan had a sense of foreboding as she woke refreshed, but with Garrett on her mind. In her study time, she savored passages in chapter ten of Matthew.

> "Look, I am sending you out as sheep among wolves. Be
> as wary as snakes and harmless as doves…. You will have the

right words at the right times.... It will be the Spirit of your
Father speaking through you... But don't be afraid of those who
threaten you... Fear only God... not even a sparrow, worth
only half a penny, can fall to the ground without your Father
knowing it...."

These two-thousand-year-old words from Jesus were still timely.

Everything at the office appeared normal. She didn't know what she was expecting after talking with Garrett last night. She had to work for the Internet on a virtual tour of a couple of properties. This was a part of the job she considered fun. When she had a moment for a break, she went to her car, where she knew she would not be interrupted or overheard, to make a call to Jackson.

"Hello, Jackson, this is Susan. I don't mind saying I was surprised, after six months of silence, to see you on Saturday. I still can't get over how you knew I was at the graduation. We didn't talk business when you were here, so what's happening in Columbia?"

"Susan. Uh, hum. Yes, it was good to see you. I've been busy, as usual, but sales are slow. I imagine you're anxious about closing on the Goldsmith property. I'm sorry I didn't see your apartment, because your Aunt Em and Uncle Owen tried to describe it to me."

"Thanks for bringing Mom and Dad. How did you know where to find me?"

"Cla..... ah hum, Iris told me about the graduation."

"I didn't think. Of course, you would have met Iris. She and Mr. Keller are good friends. Do you know Clarissa? You would have just missed her at the reception. I called because I want to know whether you know anything about nominations for the SPOTY."

After a long pause, Susan asked, "Jackson, you still there?"

"Yeah, Susan, the banquet is in the fall, I'm not sure of date and time."

"I have a fri....acquaintance here who said I was nominated for the award. I don't know how she would know, but I haven't heard a whisper."Susan explained.

"Ah, hem, the scuttlebutt is your nomination was withdrawn, that's what I heard anyway. There was some sort of mix-up, I don't really know much." Was Jackson shuffling papers? Was he trying to end the call?

Susan had to know about a withdrawal of her nomination. "Why haven't I heard any of this, Jackson? Why didn't you say something when you were here? Is Mr. Keller in, Jackson? I guess I need to speak with him. I'm sorry if I sound frustrated, but I don't like not knowing what is going down. Do you know what I mean?"

"You're right, Susan. Mr. Keller is the one to talk to. He would know more than I do. I don't think he's in right now, but you can talk to Virgie? Just a minute... Oh, Susan. I'm sorry; I know you worked hard for the award. They don't announce the winner ahead of time, so I'm as much in the dark as anyone. Here's Virgie."

Virgie was Mr. Keller's administrative assistant and a very sweet girl. "Hi, Susan, how's Plaincreek Crossroads? Wow, it's a mouth full!"

"I will fill you in next time I come to see my mom and dad. Jackson says Mr. Keller is out of the office. Virgie, would you please have Mr. Keller call me as soon as it is convenient for him."

She hung up. "Withdrawn?" The word was a dagger with jagged edges poised to strike. Jackson sure did treat her call as a *hot potato*, and she envisioned the squeamish look on his face when she *almost* asked for an explanation. So, even though he didn't admit it, he did know Clarissa. She needed to speak to Ron Keller. He had to know what this was about. Susan wasn't sure she wanted to learn anything from Jackson, anyway. A mix-up? She didn't seriously think her nomination had been withdrawn just because she moved. Mr. Keller was always a fair man—he would tell her.

Susan left her cell phone on, with volume on high, but put it back in her purse as she went back to her desk. She looked around to note there were no clock watchers this time. She was just getting back to a virtual tour site when Iris Felton walked into Mr. Wallston's office. Her brother, Melton Goldsmith, was not with her.

A half hour later, Mr. Wallston called her into his office. "Susan, I've called you in, so you can hear for yourself, first hand, what Iris is concerned about regarding your handling of the Goldsmith property." He gave the floor to Iris.

Susan sat unmoving.

Iris began speaking slowly and distinctly, "Susan, I know you're new around here and don't know our ways, but just because Plaincreek Crossroads is a small town doesn't mean we don't recognize *city* ways! Poor Garrett doesn't know what has hit him." Iris shook her head.

"Garrett! What about Garrett?" Susan wanted to yell, but remained calm. She also wanted to walk out, but she needed to hear what Iris was saying and try to make some sense out of it.

"Don't think, dear, we can't see what you're doing. Playing up to him and his boys the way you do. A little more than beyond the call of duty! Clarissa had you pegged from the very beginning. I'm glad she warned, Garrett, at least." Iris had gone from friendly to being coy and sarcastic. "Back in the woods with him. One crisis after another. Oh, and going over to his house in the evening supposedly to *look over papers*. Garrett, himself, said you and he didn't look over papers while you were there. You were seen at the L & B with him, all cozy. Then there's graduation and the dress."

The dress again, Susan was going to get to the bottom of this. She interrupted Iris, "Yes, what about my dress?" She looked Iris in the eye with a steady challenging gaze.

"Well, my first thought, when I saw you, was *show off*. I could hear the cash register, Ka-chinggg when you walked in! And I understand your deluxe apartment over at the Woodside complex is pricey, too!"

Iris straightened her shoulders; "the real problem, however, is the possibility of vested interests or underhanded dealings in connection with the sale of my property. It has come to my attention a second party might have been interested, but because of your stipulations which reduced the amount of land to develop and affected a cost increase, they chose not to bid. I want to know just what agreements were made to control the sale price and who would purchase the property." Iris took a breath. "As I said, this is still a small town, and your city ways and city deals are not welcome here. Did you think Garrett was your key to a bigger cut? Did you think you could end up with his part of the deal, too?"

Susan took Iris' pause for an opportunity to speak. "Garrett? If I remember correctly, he is not one of the sellers."

Iris sputtered..."well, ah, er, you didn't think we'd let Carol's kids go with nothing, do you?"

"You know, I didn't ever think about it." Susan looked at her boss who seemed absorbed in his desk calendar. "I'm a little confused. Let me see if I understand. First you think I'm trying to get in good with Garrett, so I can somehow benefit more from the sale. Then you accuse me of trying to fix the price, so it could be sold for less than what someone else might possibly pay? Please, be my guest, speak to both developers, evidently you haven't, or you wouldn't be saying all this."

Susan continued in an even steady tone, "Iris, I'm a successful realtor. I've worked hard and ethically to honor requests and requirements of both sellers and buyers. This is a beautiful area. No wonder it's growing. The South Carolina climate is attractive in itself. Plaincreek Crossroads is a stone's throw, well, a little more, to the Smoky Mountains and even the Blue Ridge. I can look out of this office window and see them. I've made some wonderful friends here already, and yes, my apartment is great, though not as expensive as you imagine."

Susan thought she should lighten up a little, "I'm sorry I have in some way made you my enemy. Perhaps someday you'll explain. For now, just know I have been honest and straightforward. I learned about the property first hand. Quite an experience."

"That's another thing," Iris was not going to be deterred. "You sent some kid in when the developer was on the property looking it over, and he said they would have lots of trouble because it floods all the time."

"Iris, Iris, you've got a lake fed by springs and a creek on the property; any developer would know they would have a water issue with which to deal."

Mr. Wallston was silent.

"As I was saying, I think you'll find in spite of me being a city girl, I'm pretty normal. I go to church."

"Sure, out of all the churches in this town," Iris had refueled, "you even followed poor Garrett to his church." Iris smiled smugly.

"*His* church? If you mean Community Church, it is the closest to my apartment. I didn't know Garrett even attended church, let alone Community. How many are in the congregation? I believe I saw in the newsletter something about four or five thousand. All beside the point. Where are you getting your information?" Susan asked. "I don't think you're shadowing me…or are you? Have you've hired a detective to follow me around, or do you have spies who report to you?"

Iris actually laughed, "No, of course not! I heard no more."

"You heard I was going to Community Church?"

"Well Clarissa said; Garrett said."

Susan interrupted, "Clarissa? Oh, yes, you two came by the L & B on Monday night." Susan didn't say anything else.

Iris stood, "Clarissa warned Garrett. I hope he listened. I am going to be looking into these matters further, and I warn you, there could be consequences." She jerked the door open and left.

Susan sighed. "Mr. Wallston, have you heard anything about my nomination for the SPOTY?"

He set clasping and unclasping his hands. "Susan, there's no fool like an old one, right?"

"Mr. Wallston, I don't know any fools. What are you talking about?"

"When you came in January, you were so reserved with everyone in the office. You just didn't interact much. A focused, quiet employee *could* be the best kind of employee; sometimes I don't know. You were so task oriented, constantly developing ideas to find new clients or new ways to treat them. You set the bar quite high, you know. Not everyone wanted to attain such high standards. So, I guess I can see where Iris got some of her impressions. I will say you have always treated everyone with respect. This afternoon sitting here with my head down just listening to Iris, I realized by the tone of her voice, if for no other reason, what ludicrous accusations she was spouting. I should have known better. Iris had her mind made up about you before she even met you."

"Mr. Wallston, what did she mean about consequences?"

"Oh, Mr. Fenton is well known in the whole northwestern area of South Carolina. He has influence with the Mayor and the city council. He could stir up problems with permits, zonings, and numerous other services. If not Iris or her husband, then her friend, Clarissa, could cause problems. Clarissa's brother-in-law is the current Mayor. If they thought they had the goods, such as ethic violations on you, they could make a real stink."

"What about the SPOTY? Do you know anything?"

"Why do you think I referred to myself as an old fool? This is hard, Susan, I'd rather be kicked down the street than tell you this, but I did get a letter and a form. Since I was your current employer, the committee wanted a recommendation. They apologized for the tardiness of the request, but there had been difficulties with the nomination. Iris has been angry, suspicious, certain you had ulterior motives and convinced you were deceitful. I should have been more observant; I didn't question the whole scenario enough. Listening to her rant and rave today opened my eyes, but it's too late. I'm afraid my recommendation, if I had gotten it in, would have included reserve pending investigations. Do I understand you've not been informed? I'm so embarrassed."

Susan had to laugh. "Iris is right about one thing. She was very descriptive when she said she could hear the ka-chinggg when she saw my dress. I got it on sale, if that matters, but it was the most expensive item of clothing I ever purchased. I saved it to wear to the banquet in case I was awarded the SPOTY. I guess I should be pleased she took such notice of it. I have to believe at this point my nomination was withdrawn. Mr. Wallston, please don't think another thing about it. I do understand. Thank you for being so candid and honest."

"Susan, just so you know, Mrs. Wallston and I attend Community Church, too."

As if she were a child returning from the Principal's office, Susan slumped to her desk. How could she fix what was broken when it wasn't broken? Everyone only thought it was broken. Hadn't she done everything correctly and by the book? For the first time in many years, Susan had become involved and just look what happened. Another minus. Another take-away. So she would not be nominated for the SPOTY. So Garrett, thanks to Clarissa, and Susan's own carelessness to become attached, did believe her to be a scheming ladder climbing agent whose only concern was getting the most money possible! How could he think of her in those terms?

As she sat shuffling through papers which an hour ago had meaning, she was cognizant of the office staff watching her. It was so quiet she imagined them straining to hear what was being said when her phone rang. She sensed whispers behind her back. No one came to her and asked what was happening. She guessed they all thought they knew. Who could understand?

Susan's head was literally spinning about Garrett, the Sales Person of the Year award, Iris, Jackson, and the entire office. Why would Garrett be inclined to assume the worst about Susan? After all her diligent work, the SPOTY had evaporated. From day one Iris treated Susan in an abrupt and brusque manner. Jackson was hiding something, and Susan did not want to get to the bottom of it. The office was a mystery. What had happened there? What else could go south? Her attempt to be at her best was reaping negative results. Where was the peace and happiness for which she had so longed?

She didn't even know herself anymore. Instead of taking it on the chin alone, she realized a deep desire to talk with someone. This insight impacted her as if she had been physically smacked. Where was the person she had been? She had been one who thought she could take care of herself without any help from anyone else. Was this weakness or strength?

Joycelyn could not face anyone for nearly two years but did survive the innuendos, suppositions and buzz around her spouse's behavior. Perhaps she could understand Susan's pain of being misunderstood and misjudged, also. It was comforting to know she was not alone—the Lord was leading her to others. She was sure.

Then there was Angus. Susan had this desire to talk to him. She wasn't sure why.

Chapter 17

As she sat in her apartment after work, Susan wasn't worried about Iris and her accusations in the long run, but she momentarily had the sap knocked out of her. Surely Iris would change her mind after talking to the developers, if they were upfront.

Clarissa was a problem. Any further contact with her could be disastrous, because Susan was sure Clarissa had been feeding venom to Iris and Mr. Wallston. Maybe Clarissa had cost her the SPOTY. She also suspected Jackson was responsible for some intervention before Clarissa took her stab. She felt a little guilty thinking Jackson had anything to do with the withdrawal of her nomination for the SPOTY. Why, though, had he come to Plaincreek Crossroads? Who did he hope to see?

Strange, Susan dressed up fit-to-kill at graduation, to be pretty and attractive, only Clarissa, Iris and maybe even Garrett judged her as a show off. She was guilty of wanting to look her best, but it would have never crossed her mind to try to outdo anyone else. Susan always thought Satan hacked at a person's weak spot, but this was her strength. She respected all peoples and believed in the value of the individual. She did not knowingly elevate herself above anyone, or so she believed. A snob? She couldn't have imagined it. Then again, how did the saying go: "what a gift God would give us, if we could see ourselves as others see us?"

She couldn't do anything about her co-workers. Apparently no one in the office was even curious enough to talk to Susan or to ask her any questions.

Is this how it was with Joycelyn and Garrett; everyone just sitting back and judging without even making an effort to affirm or clarify anything? Is it a virtue not to be nosey or a virtue to be involved and concerned? A fine line Susan concluded.

As Susan reviewed events, her biggest hurt was Garrett. She could only conclude he questioned Susan's behavior because he believed Clarissa and Iris. She had to admit her *fish* quest probably just made her appear *fishier*. Susan chuckled at the analogy, but it wasn't really funny. Susan just could not give up until she had some answers.

> *"Then Jesus said, 'Come to me, all of you who are weary and carry heavy burdens, and I will give you rest. Take my yoke upon you. Let me teach you, because I am humble and gentle, and you will find rest for your souls. For my yoke fits perfectly and the burden I give you is light.'"* (Matthew 11:38)

Susan read the passage slowly and then began to pray.

"Here I am Lord; it's time to end my pity party. I leave my hurt and disappointment with You. I've been thinking about Joycelyn. Is there some way I can be a real friend to her? I'm not going to ask about Garrett—I'll just leave him with you. All I seem to do is make matters worse. Now, about Clarissa, Lord, You know I'm not a saint, and I'm angry about losing the SPOTY. 7 X 70 is not an easy score. So, I'll just thank you, Lord, because I know your Spirit is working with me, even as I pose questions and search for resolutions."

Her mind kept wandering back to Angus. Perhaps he was the missing link. She had to go the library to find him, like watching for a moon flower to open, a rarity, but possible at the right time. "I'm planning to go see Angus, Lord. Am I taking on too much of a burden where it's not necessary? Please help me hear your voice."

Now to find Angus. Susan had no idea of the timing for his storytelling whether week nights or weekends. So, she first hurried to the second floor and peered into an empty South Carolina room. Then she asked at the information desk and learned nothing. They were still looking for a schedule when she walked off. She finally sat down in the lobby area and picked a book on the new release shelf to read while she waited for him. As hard as she tried, she could not concentrate.

When Angus walked in Susan uttered, "There are no coincidences where God is concerned. Thank you, Lord." She was at his side before he could greet her. On their way up to the South Carolina room, Susan promised not to take more than a couple of minutes, if he would talk to her after his story.

Susan learned that ancestors of Mrs. Clara Goldsmith were responsible for the establishment of a stage coach way station at Plaincreek Crossroads back at the beginning of the1800's, and the stage coach line was, in fact, how the town got its name. If Susan remembered correctly, Andi and her three musketeers found pieces of leather, parts of saddles, bridles, harnesses and jars of leather soap when they first starting exploring the vegetable house. What if the vegetable house had been part of a horse ranch or even part of a station for the stage coach line? It is such a shame it is in such a deteriorating condition. Since the vegetable house was on the Goldsmith property, there was a definite connection. A moot point now.

As they were leaving, Angus took Susan's arm and ushered her out of the library. "Let's sit in your car to talk. Do you mind? If we stay in the library, we won't have much of a chance to talk in private."

"No problem."

"Good, I'm curious why you've taken so much effort to talk to me, Susan."

"Angus, I'm in a quandary. I don't want to nose where I have no business. On the other hand, I have this strong sense I should pursue some of these questions until some answers surface. I have questions about a species of fish called Casper Fish used for cancer research. Andi and I both caught a fish similar to a Casper in Floating Bone Lake. When Andi caught hers and showed it to her father, Russ, he took it and told her not to mention it to anyone. Iris Fenton stated both Clara and Carol talked about a fish. If the fish Andi and I caught was a Casper fish, how did the Casper Fish get into Floating Bone Lake? Their normal size is one to two inches. How did they get to be at least 8 to 10 inches long? What happened to Andi's fish? Why the secret? Were Clara and Carol talking about the Casper fish? I ran this by Garrett, but he dismissed it as so much nonsense, just so you know."

"Garrett may be right," Angus rubbed his forehead. "I have not seen or know anythin' about the fish. Why is it so special and used for studies?"

"Oh, I'm sorry, I forgot to explain. The Casper Fish is transparent! You can see the entrails, bones and all. When they use the fish, scientists can see how the cancer is progressing. If you know Maggie Riley, she has a good bit of information about them."

"You mean you caught one of the fish in the lake behind the subdivision?"

"I sure did! I raised it up to see it and was so startled I dropped the line, and it got off the hook and swam away. I was so upset."

"Are you sure it was really transparent?"

"Yes! I held it up long enough for Andi, and maybe Jesse, Dan and Matt to see, too. Garrett doesn't believe I even caught a fish."

"Interestin'. I'll tell you what I can do. I have friends in the history department at the University of South Carolina Upstate at Spartanburg. I can ask them to check around to see if any of the research departments are familiar with this Casper fish."

"I can't think of anything better... Thank you, Angus. How well do you know Garrett? Did you know about Garrett's wife, Carol? Garrett won't even entertain the thought that Carol and Clara Goldsmith knew something about the fish."

"Knowin' Garrett as I do, I'm not surprised a *fish story* would not make any headway with him. We, Garrett and I, met through the church, after his wife died. We have since become accountability partners—not a perfect match, but it works none the less."

"I was wondering how you knew each other. So it was through the church, hum. Then you didn't know Carol at all."

"No, I never met Carol. To tell you the truth, I know little to nothing about Garrett's family. I'm on one of the hospital visitation teams from Community Church, and I'm a member of Promise Keepers. Garrett and I became acquainted through the men's group and, as I said, became accountability partners. My wife died a few years ago, and my only daughter, Laura, is a student at South Carolina University. I'm currently on sabbatical from SCU and am in the process of compilin' an up-to-date history of South Carolina, if you're wonderin' what I do."

"So, your storytelling is probably not just a hobby. You're not much older than Garrett, even though Trevor thinks so. I'm not asking for you to betray any confidences, but Garrett seems pretty closed when it comes to talking about Carol."

"You're right, though Garrett and I have both lost spouses, he has not been open, to discuss Carol or their relationship, even with me. If anyone questions him, he might close up and become terribly distant. Let's leave Garrett out o' this for now. Oh, and I have met Maggie Riley, so if you will give me her number, I'll give her a call. I will start on this in about an hour. Right now, I have a late dinner invitation which I'll just be on time for if I leave within five minutes."

He was on his way.

Next Susan decided to drive by and sign papers on the bichon frise puppy she was giving her dad for Father's Day. She also needed to fasten some twine on the posts of her earth boxes for the tomatoes and water the flowers. Other than those chores, she actually had nothing to do. She needed to stay away from Garrett. She guessed he wasn't going to try to see her anyway. Maggie and her family were getting ready to leave on an outing over Memorial Day. Andi, Jesse, Matt and Dan were all looking for summer jobs and getting ready for college in the fall. Susan wasn't going to be spending time with them anyway. With nothing else to do, Susan was going to have time to read the book she had started three months before.

Susan was just turning into her parking space when her phone jingled. "Hi, Susan, this is Joycelyn. Do you have a minute?"

"Well, hello. How's it going? Sure I've got more than a minute. I'm just getting home and am walking into my apartment now."

"Get back in the car, come on over—I hope you haven't eaten yet. I'm grilling, and Andi and her friends just took off to the mall. I'm left with chicken, asparagus, a couple of baked potatoes, and oh, I've got something to tell you when you get here."

"Consider me on my way. I was just going to eat a sandwich. Your offer sounds much better. Give me five minutes, and I'll be there before you can take it off the grill." This was a splendid chance for Susan to become better acquainted with Joycelyn.

When Susan drove up, Garrett's car was not in his driveway. Even though every house in the sub division had an attached garage, cars were always parked in the drives. It was amusing to see all the vehicles. The evening was still warm, and the neighborhood was quiet. She wondered what Garrett would think if, when he returned home, he saw her car at Joycelyn's. She was not going to start running away from any contact with him now. With that final thought, she went around Joycelyn's yard to the patio in the back.

After eating, Susan and Joycelyn relaxed over glasses of iced tea.

"This is a truly lovely back yard. I think you must spend hours keeping it manicured. You didn't put the little rock garden fountain in by yourself, did you? If you did, I'm jealous." Susan knew her own proclivity to disastrous results while working on mechanical projects.

"No, Russ, my husband, had made it his pride-and-joy when we first moved in, but I did help. I had to work on it this spring and found it was not as easy as when Russ and I worked together. He was a contractor and a great hands-on person. It seemed effortless then."

"Your effort shows!"

"Listen, Susan, I asked you over to get better acquainted, but I remembered something last night. It may be of no consequence, but it poses a few questions to me now since Andi told us about catching her fish. Earlier, on the same day as the accident, Russ asked me if we had any pretzels left from an enormous jar we purchased at a wholesale house. I remember because we had laughed for the longest time saying our grandchildren might even get a few. The pretzels were in a large, clear plastic container with a snap-on lid. Months after the accident, I found the remaining pretzels in a couple of zip lock bags in the pantry and no jar. When I questioned her, Andi didn't know anything, but now it might make sense." Joycelyn paused to see if Susan understood the implications.

"Pretzels?" It did take a minute, then; "Oh, maybe it was a container for Andi's fish?"

( )

Memorial Day was going to delay the scheduling of the closing on the property. In addition, the title search revealed Mrs. Clara Goldsmith had never had Carol's name removed from the title of the property. Clara, in shock and grieving over Carol's death, appeared not to consider legal financial matters. Iris and Melton were devastated knowing Carol's name was ever on the deed. Iris was in a huff and quickly produced Carol's death certificate. According to Iris, at the time of Carol's death, Carol had no known assets and no will was produced. The bank required proof of clear title before their final approval, so the sale could not be contested. Garrett, then Carol's husband, needed to produce an affidavit stating there were no liens against the property. The sale of the property could be tied up in court if Carol had been engaged in any pending business ventures. The developer might even back out and request return of earnest monies. This was just so much nonsense, but it could not be circumvented. The resolution could depend on Garrett.

How is Iris going to make this all my fault? Not an unrealistic thought. *Just stop the world and let me get off this merry-go-round!*

Ignoring this new development, Susan blocked it out of her mind and made a to-do list for the holiday weekend. She was going to set up her new grill, cook out, brew iced tea, and read her novel. *I just want to stop thinking for a little while.* Actually, what she felt, not thought, was what she wanted to cease. Trying to sidestep trouble with Mr.Wallston, Iris, Clarissa and Garrett reminded her of times as a kid running through the marshy woods

157

when one stumble meant skinned knees and muddy clothes. As an adult, one stumble meant more than bruised knees and dirty clothes, *unless you're out at Floating Bone Lake*. She had to laugh. But she didn't like falling when she was a child, and she would not like it now.

$\backsim$

Susan had her quiet holiday weekend, proud of what she had been able to do with her patio. The sliding glass doors were off of the living/dining room and directly under the second floor sunroom balcony. The roof of the balcony provided a place for three hanging baskets of bright rose begonias. The perimeter of the patio was defined by a low red brick wall ideal for boxes of flowering plants in a rainbow of colors. The patio was roomy enough for her umbrella table and chairs, a reclining lounge chair, her new gas grill, the earth boxes, and people. A hibiscus tree and outdoor carpeting were her additional purchases. What a pleasant time she would have, when weather permitted for her to sit outside. Looking from the inside, as well as out, she would have to describe it as a riot of color. If she had any friends left, she could invite them for a cookout.

$\backsim$

Back at work, Susan smiled pleasantly when Garrett knocked on her office door. A stray lock of hair, always down on his forehead, endeared him to her every time. Her inclination was, as usual, to reach up and brush it back, but she restrained herself as she rose to greet him. "Good morning, Garrett. You're looking well."

"I'm still working at the school: reports to write, files to complete, paper work. I should finish up by the end of the week, but I just stopped by to give you these notarized affidavits. I'm not going to challenge the ownership or sale of the property. Iris and Melton have already agreed Carol's share will go to the boys, and they've put it in writing, so I don't see any need to make a fuss. Carol, you probably know, was a stay-at-home mom. Though we talked about making a will for her, we never got around to it. I'm beginning to go through her papers. I guess it's about time. Furnishing our patio was one item on her to-do list. I came by your apartment and saw what you did with your patio. Susan, when did you find Carol's name on the title to the property?"

Now what did Clarissa say? Susan thought. "When did I know there was a cloud on the title? The sale went so quickly we hadn't gotten the report from the Title and Abstract Company until after the offer was made. I guess I found out when all of the rest of you did. When it surfaced in the title search, a letter was sent to all concerned parties, including the listing agent. Any reason why you ask? Is there anything I should know?"

"No, not really. Well, I've got to go. I've actually got a couple sets of parents coming in to talk about next school-year's placement. Next week I'll be checking for a summer job. The boys miss you."

"Well, I won't keep you. Give the boys a hug for me. I miss them too. I'll make sure these affidavits get to the right parties." She watched as he walked out without a backward glance. Closing on the sale and the destruction of Floating Bone Lake was now a surety.

Susan was sitting quietly at her desk when Iris walked in. "Your little plan didn't work, did it? The commission wasn't going to be enough. Did you think maybe, if contested, I or my brother would be excluded? None of it worked! Oh, you'll get your commission. I can't stop it, this time, but be aware I'm still reporting this to your realtor licensing board. See you at the closing tomorrow."

When Iris stomped out, Susan remained at her desk, her head in her hands. She couldn't stop the tears.

( )

Without-a-hitch described the closing. It was amazing to watch Iris avoid any association with or even recognition of Susan. All was in order and finalized. At least there were five happy parties in the room; Iris Fenton, Melton Goldsmith, Mr.Wallston, and Jerry and Michael of the J.M. Ryan Brothers Construction Company, Inc. The builders were ready with the heavy equipment to grade the land. Within a couple of weeks, they would be marking for the layout of the streets and lots, bringing in drainage pipes, laying sewer lines and erecting temporary poles for electricity; a busy, noisy place. Gone, the quiet and solitude. No more rustling trees talking to each other and God. No more transparent fish. The beautiful wildflowers destroyed. Mama, Brownie, and their puppies would never be seen again, except for Zeke. How would the deer or the indigo snake be able to survive?

Though Susan believed the vegetable house represented some real history of the area, she couldn't bring herself to miss it. She so wanted to be able to label, if nothing else, what it was about Floating Bone Lake making it unique. Why did those bones float? Was it simply warm springs? It might not be the first question on her lips when she was chosen to meet with God, but it would be on her list. *What, Lord, is the secret of Floating Bone Lake? What about the fish?* Was she, alone, concerned?

More than any other reason, she would grieve the loss of the lake because it was where God chose to confront her. She thought of the story of Jacob in Genesis 28:16 -17

> "...*Surely the Lord is in this place, and I wasn't even aware of it....What an awesome place this is! It is none other than the house of God—the gateway to heaven!*"

How could anyone understand? As long as the lake was there, it would be a reminder to her where she found the Presence of God and really began to search for meaning to her life. To be able to see the lake would have refreshed her memory. Now, instead of discovering the mystery of transparent fish and floating bones in the murky, yet still beautiful little Floating Bone Lake, she would soon walk down new streets with street lights, sidewalks, and new houses.

No more floating bones and no dry bones either. Just as in Ezekiel's vision, Susan's dry bones came alive with God's touch. "Did I thank you, Lord, for my Floating Bone Lake experience? I don't know what it all means, but I commit to remembering, even without Floating Bone, how you are leading me with your love." Susan could remember *Ezekiel, huh*, when Garrett pulled her out of the lake. In his arms was the beginning of her healing and as it has developed the creation of more pain. "I leave it with You, Lord."

By Saturday, Susan hadn't talked with Maggie since before the closing and even before Memorial Day. Maggie hadn't called or made any effort to return Susan's calls or leave a message. Between her husband and two children, maybe Maggie was just too busy. Susan tried one more time. Maggie answered.

"Maggie, this is Susan. I've missed you. Hope you had a great trip. How are the children and David?"

Maggie chose not to give Susan a greeting, "Will you answer a question for me?"

"Sure, Maggie, anything."

"Why was the fish so important to you? Did you not really want to sell the property or did you have a plan to delay or stop the sale of Floating Bone

Lake for other reasons? Did you think Garrett would contest? I can imagine several reasons why you were after Garrett, I even helped you." Her words were almost rehearsed.

"Wha-a-at? Maggie… you don't think?" When and how did Clarissa, Iris or maybe Garrett get to her? "Maggie, I wondered why I hadn't heard from you. I'm sorry you think I'm the kind of person who would use friendship to my advantage. I can't really tell you how completely at a loss I am right now. How can this be cleared up? Anytime you want to talk, I would be happy to get with you and listen or explain."

"Right now I don't know."

Susan wanted to cry. "Okay, thank you Maggie. I guess bye for now then." As she hung up, Susan sensed Maggie was going through a difficult time; evidently she felt betrayed by Susan. From what little Maggie said, she thought Susan had used her to get closer to Garrett. What had she been told? If she thought Susan was manipulating her to capture Garrett, Maggie was most likely angry.

Clarissa again? Susan had to admit Clarissa was busy, thorough and effective. God could use people with those attributes *on his side*; Susan was trying to be generous and positive. She could do with some lifting up right about now. What was it Isaiah 40:31 said?

"Those who wait upon the Lord will find new strength. They will fly high on wings like eagles. They will run and not grow weary. They will walk and not faint."

How did anyone make it through rough times without scriptures to quote? Tomorrow was Sunday. She was glad.

Sunday morning Susan decided she needed the exercise, and so she parked at the edge of the church parking lot again. "What is as rare as a day in June, if ever come perfect days, then Heaven tries earth if it be in tune and over it softly her warm ear lays…"[6] That was all she memorized of the poem, but the words were enough for the beginning of a gorgeous June day. This morning she would be sitting alone in the church. She had resolved not to let it bother her.

If she had checked her calendar, Susan would have known it was Children's Day, as it was she had no idea the service was going to be led by the children. As the minister announced the story of the five loaves and two fishes for his sermon, Susan held her breath. She scanned the group

---

6   From "The Vision of Sir Launfal" by James Russell Lowell (1819-1891)

of children sitting on the steps and around the platform, until she found Grant and Gary. She waited.

Grant and Gary would have insisted on *once upon a time*. One day as Jesus was teaching to a crowd of thousands, He turned to his disciples. "The people have been here all day. They are tired, and they have had nothing to eat. Give them something to eat before they faint with hunger."

"What do you mean give them something to eat? How can we feed all these people, it would take much more money than we have?"

"What do we have?" Jesus asked. They brought a young boy with a lunch of five loaves and two fish.

The pastor held up a small lunch basket. "We don't stop and think about the mother who fixed the lunch for her young son. She wanted to be sure he would not go hungry. The pastor addressed the children, "Do you always say thank you for what your mother does for you?"

Susan put her hand to her mouth.

"What if you don't have a mommy to fix your lunch?" Gary asked an honest question.

Susan's heart was aching for Gary as well as for Grant and Garrett.

"A fair question, young man! Some children may not have a mommy. Maybe a daddy or even a neighbor may make your lunch. Do you say thank you to those who take care of you, children? Let's thank God, for *all* those who love and care for us; parents, brothers, sisters, teachers, neighbors, any and all of them. Our young boy here in the story was willing to give his lunch to Jesus. The question is," and the pastor looked directly at Gary and then gestured toward the group of children gathered at his feet, "Would you have given your lunch to Jesus? Jesus loves each of you, and He wants you to love each other enough to share what you have."

Susan breathed a little easier. She thought of several ways, which would add to the drama of the story. She was going to have to see if she could volunteer to help with children's activities. She didn't know what the qualifications were, but she could find out. She realized she might be opening up to the possibility of being accused of trying to reach Garrett again. Maybe she should wait until after the summer.

Sunday afternoon was COR, *cleaning out refrigerator*, as Maggie had told her. Susan had her patio and her grill now. She couldn't ask for better weather, cloudy with a slight breeze, and she was all set. She could call Mom and tell her about Grant and Gary. Her mother would think the way they respond to stories was humorous. Susan took her plate, with a grilled ground beef patty, sweet potato, and zucchini to the table and thanked the

Lord. Her cell phone, as she was getting ready to call her mom, rang as she held it in her hand.

"Susan, I don't like all these hard feelings I'm having. So, can we talk? I need to at least hear your side of the story. By the way, did Angus call about the fish?"

"Angus? Good! I was just thinking about you, Maggie. I'm having COR for lunch! You want to talk now on the phone, or what did you have in mind?"

"COR's not bad, is it? How about the regular Monday night time? Your place? As far as I know David will be here with the children. They got a couple of new videos; one for Trevor's age group and one for Gabi's, so it would be nigh on to impossible to think of talking anywhere around this house."

"Maggie, I would love to have you come over. We can sit on my patio and, of course, since you're the one with the misgivings you would have the freedom to leave any time of your choosing. Don't eat before you come. I'll understand if you're not...."

"I think I plan on feeding my crew before I come, so I will have eaten. Maybe just a snack, okay?"

"Sounds like a plan, Maggie, I'll look forward to tomorrow."

Her dinner was getting cold, but before she could put the phone down and enjoy another bite, it rang again.

"Susan, Susan Walen? Angus McCrae here. Am I interruptin' you? If this is not a reportin'-good time to talk, I'll call ya back. I do have some news."

"Oh, hello Angus. I'm anxious to hear. Maggie said you called her. Were you meaning to talk on the phone or did you want to meet me somewhere?"

"I'm goin' to have to talk to Garrett, but since you have initiated this action, you're involved and deserve to know. Let me just tell you a bit now and more, later. First, I finally got hold of my friend at Columbia University Upstate, and he called me just about an hour ago. He was able to confirm the laboratory at the university has been usin' Casper fish in some of their research for at least two years now. Maggie's information coincides with this timin'."

"See Angus; I'm not losing my mind!"

"It's possible someone who thinks you're a mite bit bird-brained might have to eat crow, Susan. Don't ya just love my description there? Ha, ha. One little remark my friend made has me thinkin' in a direction which will require more investigation. There should be a paper trail if what I am thinkin' is true. A lot will depend on Garrett. I know I'm not makin' any sense, unless you're a step ahead of me, but let me say no more for right now."

"Angus, it gives me hope. A very subdued Garrett came by the office last week, said he had opened up *Carol's room* and was going through some of her projects. You might find him receptive and, at least, non-combative. God is faithful! Thanks, Angus."

"Yes, God is good! I'll be gettin' back with you."

Hot news, cold dinner. An acceptable trade off.

Susan looked forward to having the air cleared between Maggie and herself, but she wasn't sure what was going to happen. Clarissa's insinuations and the misinformation she fed to Maggie were enough to make Susan's blood boil, but she couldn't allow herself to be consumed by anger. "I'm in the middle of a battle!" was all Susan could say to herself.

Another thought came to Susan. If Garrett was serious about Clarissa, she would be Grant and Gary's new mother. Susan needed to be on good terms with Clarissa, then, if she ever wanted to be in touch with the boys and be a friend to them.

∽

Maggie called Susan at the office Monday afternoon: "Susan, Gabi is running a low grade fever and cries when I leave her for a few minutes. I'm sorry, but I feel I ought to stay home this evening."

"Is there anything I can do for you or Gabi?"

"No, there's not much I can do, but Gabi is more relaxed and will go to sleep if I'm here. Mothers are most wanted when a child is sick! We'll talk some other time."

"Let me tell you then; Angus did get in touch with a friend at the University, who in turn talked to another colleague, and confirmed they have been doing studies using the Casper fish. Angus is going to talk to Garrett."

Maggie didn't seem as interested as Susan thought she might, "Okay, well let me know. Talk to you later. Gotta go."

Susan held the phone, staring. Then it dawned on her, duh! The fish! "Maggie thinks I'm using the fish to get to Garrett..." How convoluted! Maggie hadn't seen the actual fish. Maybe she thinks a link to Floating Bone Lake is doubtful. "I guess she could think the fish was just a ploy." Susan couldn't try to change Maggie's mind without discussing Clarissa, but Susan just didn't want any part of it.

Chapter 18

Next day, Susan answered the phone at work; "Susan, we're takin' you to lunch," Angus was a man of a few words, especially over the phone.

"Who?" Susan hoped he meant Angus and Garrett.

"Garrett and I. Have you got the time? We've somethin' to show you."

"I'll take the time. Should I meet you somewhere?"

"No, we'll come get you in about twenty minutes, if you can get away. We want to beat the lunch crowd and make use of the time."

Within *ten* minutes, Angus sauntered into the office. He tipped his hand in an imaginary salute to the office staff, all of whom seemed to have nothing else to do at that precise moment. Susan had planned to wait outside, but she was pleased Angus was considerate enough to come in. He winked and even did a little curtsy for her as he held the door. His smile was big enough for everyone.

At the L & B, Angus and Garrett insisted they order first, talk second. Susan began to be afraid they didn't have anything new and wanted to let her down over lunch, but then Garrett handed her a file. He said nothing. He just handed her the file. As Susan looked at the tab on the file folder, it simply read *fish*.

She took out the top page, and read:

Dear Sirs,

I read with considerable interest in *Science Daily* about current research with stem cells using zebra fish for cancer and other diseases.

Because both my parents died of complications from Cancer, my mother when I was very young, before I was a teenager, and my father, ten years ago, I have annually contributed to support such research.

In addition, my best friend lost twins due to birth defects. On her behalf, also, I have come to feel that I want to become directly involved. I am requesting information, such as the name of an individual with whom I could speak regarding the Casper Fish.

Time is always of the essence, especially cutting edge advances in any field.

Regards,
Mrs. Carol Taylor

Susan took a deep breath. She automatically reached over to Garrett. "Oh, she knew about the Casper Fish. Do you suppose....?" Susan didn't finish her thought. "Do you have any idea about what she might have had in mind?"

Garrett didn't lift his head as he said, "Look at the next page."

Susan slid the letter to the back of the file and read the next page. "Amazing. They responded to her inquiry. The first letter was written to the Journal, but this answer is from the National Institutes of Health, and it looks as if they have referred her to the University of South Carolina Upstate and their current studies. I guess it is all pretty much a matter of public record, but what could these scientists possibly think Carol could do and what did Carol think she could do?"

"There's more...."

"Yes, okay," Susan examined the next letter. "She planned to raise Casper fish in the lake? For how long? It says here per their phone conversation she could pick up the Casper fish embryos. This is dated for June, two years ago. So seeding the lake is how the Casper fish got into Floating Bone Lake. Did Carol receive a grant, and if so, what were the terms of the grant? How and why did Carol keep it a secret from you, Garrett?"

Susan gasped, "Did you know about the large plastic container of pretzels Joycelyn and Russ had purchased at a wholesale club? On the day of the accident, Russ asked her if they still had any of the pretzels."

"What do pretzels have to do with *anything*?" Garrett muttered.

"Not the pretzels Garrett, Joycelyn found the pretzels in baggies later. The container! It was a large, clear heavy plastic container with a snap on lid. Andi had caught a Casper and gave it to her father. He would have needed something to transport it. Does it make you wonder? Oh, Garrett where was the accident? Isn't the University of Columbia Upstate in the same area? Could Carol and Russ have been on their way with the fish?"

"Oh, dear!" Susan just thought of something else, "If her fish figures in any way in the accident, Andi will blame herself, saying if she hadn't caught the fish or shown it to her father, they wouldn't have been on the road; they wouldn't have had an accident, and they would still be alive. I know how she thinks. Be careful Garrett and Angus, when and how you tell Joycelyn and Andi. Of course, there are some big gaps and a lot of questions." Susan covered her mouth with her hands and snapped; unexpected tears coursed down her cheeks and spilled over onto the table.

Garrett sat listening and watching Susan's every move. He had not said a word but looked deep in thought. "Angus, how hard is it going to be to track this down? We do have a name and phone number in the file as well as the letters. If what Iris briefly referred to about Mrs. Goldsmith mentioning a fish is true, then her name could be part of this adventure."

Susan's interest in the fish was born of curiosity, but as Susan let what she had just read soak in, she was a little disappointed there was no longer a mystery. A part of the mystic of Floating Bone Lake just disappeared. In its place, however, could be an end to much pain and a beginning of new life and confidence for Joycelyn and Garrett.

Angus dropped Garrett at his school, and as he drove Susan on to her office, he chatted continuously. "We were up until wee three o'clock this mornin' goin' through Carol's files and boxes. Garrett was beginnin' to come to grips with reality. He's been avoidin' it, you know. Unlockin' Carol's room was probably one of the most difficult decisions he has ever had to make. He was askin' my advice about what to do with her clothing and personal items. Just hang in there Susan. And Susan, Garrett has bottled all his doubts—unable to share them even with me—until today. I had not realized how mistrustin' he had become—not only of his own feelin' and responses, but of everyone around him, too."

Angus insisted on opening the car door for her and escorting her back to the office. He grinned as he turned to leave and whispered again, "Just hang in there, Lassie." He kissed her lightly on the cheek. He gave a friendly wave goodbye to those who were at their desks watching.

Angus was sweet. Now why and how was she supposed to hang in there with Garrett? At first, he didn't seem to be able to keep his hands off her, but now he didn't even want her near his boys. This lunch, in her estimation, had turned the tide, but what effect, if any, might the revelation of Casper Fish in Floating Bone Lake actually have on her relationship with Garrett? She had to smile thinking about Joycelyn and Andi. Laying her questions and emotional exhaustion aside, Susan turned to her afternoon of planning two open houses for the weekend.

"I need help." Though she had done it by herself prior, she didn't want to do it again. This was a marathon open house weekend which meant every available person was scheduled at one of these open houses. In addition to serving at the refreshment table, conducting tours and mingling with prospective buyers, the host/hostess was responsible to answer questions, sign them up for the newsletter, distribute the latest issue of *Homes* and make future appointments at the office. Susan wondered if Andi or if Joycelyn would be interested in helping. She made up her mind to give the Stokes a call.

Susan was too pumped to go home. "I know. I'll go see Danae." Maybe Andi would like to see the puppy. After all, Andi had told her all about the bichon frise breed and suggested it would be neat for her dad. She drove to the Stokes instead of calling and left the car running as went to the door.

"Andi, would you like to see the puppy I got Dad for Father's Day? I signed the papers the other day. She's still at the breeders, but we can go see her. Ask Joycelyn if she'd like to come, too."

"Hey, M-o-om," Andi yelled to Joycelyn, who was in the back of the house. "Wanna go see a puppy?"

Joycelyn came out drying her hands. "A puppy? Whose? Where?"

"Andi suggested a bichon frise for my dad, and I wanted to show her the one I bought. Then, I have a question to ask one or both of you. Do you have about twenty minutes?"

⌒ ͻ

Andi reached for one of the puppies the minute they walked in at the breeders and began discussing the details of bichon frise puppy care with the owners. Susan found Danae and held her out to Joycelyn. You would have thought Joycelyn was holding a baby. "She's so soft!" Joycelyn petted and cooed, scratching the puppy behind the ears. "Oh, Susan, she's beautiful!"

"Where did Andi learn so much about dogs, Joycelyn?"

"I have no idea. You can ask her questions about almost any four legged creature, and she'll be able to fill you in. I'm always thrilled, even if she is my own daughter!"

"I guess I knew she was special with animals when Mama didn't devour us both in the vegetable house!" Susan grimaced at the memory.

"Andi told me about Mama, but I guess I felt as if she were exaggerating about her size and temperament. The puppy seems quite little." Joycelyn shared.

"Joycelyn, about Mama-horse-dog, Andi was not stretching the truth." Because there was no danger of hearing Mama snarl and growl, Susan laughed.

Having completed the tour, Andi came back. "Mom, they need help with all the puppies. I'm going to fill out an application—at least for the rest of the summer."

And so it was, the trip was fruitful—at least for a temporary job for Andi.

On the way back, Susan told Joycelyn she needed help with two open houses over the weekend. "I was wondering if either of you Joycelyn or Andi, would be available and willing to act as hostess for me.

"Maybe I'll be working," Andi called back as she shut the car door and headed up the sidewalk. "I'm going to call some friends, Mom. See ya later, Susan."

Joycelyn sat quietly with Susan in her Malibu.

"Susan, when and where are your open houses? Tell me more. It sounds like a hospitality role, and I miss it. May I tell you something? Do you know what it's like to think people are talking behind your back? I've let it get to me, I confess. Grieve? How when I wasn't sure what I felt? Did he or didn't he? Was I or wasn't I good enough? Did my best friend go behind my back with my husband? I second guess every decision I make and most of the time, I just don't make any decisions. Of course, I do realize when I don't make a decision, it is making a decision. I still don't have any answers, but I'm ready to step out instead of hiding. I don't know if I'll hold up if people start questioning me."

"Oh, then you'll help. Great! Don't worry about questions. I imagine a majority, if not all, of the prospective buyers will be from out of town or at least new to Plaincreek Crossroads."

Since Joycelyn wasn't saying anything about the lake or fish, Susan figured neither Garrett nor Angus had given Joycelyn any kind of an update on the Casper fish yet. Susan couldn't say much. It would be so good to share how Susan, herself, was being misjudged, but she couldn't say anything without mentioning Maggie and Garrett. Susan just wasn't ready, so, for now, she just listened.

That weekend, at both the open houses, Joycelyn was competent, professional, and personable beyond all of Susan's expectations. "Wow, what happened to the quiet, demure, even backward woman I met a couple of weeks ago?" Susan paused, "She has been replaced with a lively, energetic entrepreneur!"

"I love entertaining. I've just had the rug pulled out from under me, I guess. Russ and I talked about starting a small catering business, but talk is as far as it went. This has been life-giving for me. Thank you, Susan."

So, healing had begun. Susan couldn't wait until Joycelyn learned about Carol, Russ and the fish.

Chapter 19

"Hi, Mom, can you talk or is Dad there?"

"He's here, but he's not where he can hear. Is that what you mean?"

"Yeah, are you still expecting me to come on Father's Day? I've got a puppy to bring. Just wait till you see her. Her name is Danae. If it's okay with you, I'll join you and Dad at church. I'll get to your place after you've left for your Headliner's class, and I thought the best place to put the puppy would be in the half bath. Danae is trained, but I don't know how she will react to a strange place. What do you think?"

After a brief silence, Aunt Em answered. "Your father will be surprised, to say the least. Why do I think I'm not getting the total picture? I am pleased you're coming, and I do like the puppy's name."

"I want you to be surprised too, Mom. I've been thinking about bringing friends, Joycelyn Stokes and her daughter, Andi, with me, but I wanted to check with you before I ask them to come. I was also thinking about ordering carry out, so we will be able to relax and talk. We can fill you in on Plaincreek Crossroads."

"Oh, Susan, we would love to meet your friends, and carry-out would give us more time just to sit and visit."

After that affirmation, Susan was sure her brainstorm of taking Andi's memory book was a brilliant idea. Using the book, Mom and Dad would certainly get an idea of what had been going on in the last couple of months.

Both Joycelyn and Andi would get a kick out of showing memories of Floating Bone Lake. The book could be a springboard to share more than what the book had in it. "If I did the talking, the afternoon could become too negative and counterproductive for a celebration." She was getting excited just thinking about her dad's face when he saw the puppy.

◯

As she continued reading her scripture passage in Matthew early Sunday morning, her sense of humor was tickled like a feather against her nose. She snorted. Yes, she snorted as she read,

> "…well then, Jesus said, '…so go down to the lake and throw
> in a line. Open the mouth of the first fish you catch, and you
> will find a coin ….'" (Matthew 17:26)

Now why didn't she know this scripture was in the Bible? What a way to pay taxes. Would Garrett believe a biblical *fish* story? The boys would. Ha! Grant was too practical, just as his father, but Gary would get mileage out of it.

Back to Matthew, Susan marveled at this scripture about becoming as a child and how children, as well as new believers, get individual attention before God. She continued with the words of Jesus;

> "In heaven their angels are always in the presence of my
> heavenly Father." (Matthew 18:10)

Susan still needed to get a volunteer form, so she could start helping out or working with the children in some venue at the church.

Would Maggie be at church? She missed her friendship, but felt she needed to wait until Maggie contacted her.

"I'll sit alone, again," she scowled in the mirror. "I'm not backing out, Lord, I just don't like sitting by myself."

When she entered the sanctuary, Susan was ready to slip into one of the rows of seats in the back. Joycelyn who was sitting a couple of rows ahead turned and motioned to Susan to slide in next to her.

◯

Andi came bounding up after the service, "Oh, hi, Susan. Hey, Mom. Are we going right home? The guys might come over."

"Go ahead to the car if you want, I'll be along in a minute."

"I'll walk with you, Joycelyn. I parked out in the hinterlands for a little exercise. Would you and Andi like to come with me next Sunday, which is Father's Day, to my Mom and Dad's in Columbia, just a little over an hour away? We could go early enough for church, dinner, visiting and then back with plenty of time for any evening activities you might have. I'm taking Danae, the puppy I got for my dad, to him." Susan figured this trip out of town might be a distraction for Joycelyn and Andi on Father's Day, but then it might just be the opposite. Each person is different.

Andi was already in the car when Susan and Joycelyn arrived, "Susan has invited us to go to her parents next Sunday. She's taking the puppy to them."

"Oh, then you'll need some help. A bichon frise can be a good traveler, but they don't like confined spaces, like a carrier, so you need someone to hold her. She could distract you while you're driving. Did we have other plans, Mom? I want to go and help."

"No, no plans, and I would love to go, too. Should I bring anything?"

"No, not a thing. Mom and I agreed to order carry-out would give more time to visit. Don't you think Mom and Dad would enjoy seeing your memory book of Floating Bone Lake? I basically haven't taken the time to tell them anything about Plaincreek Crossroads, and I think it would begin to paint a picture of the town and some of the people. What do you think?" Susan wrinkled her nose.

Andi gave her a thumb up!

Andi and Joycelyn were going with her next Sunday. It wouldn't do to go skipping in high heels down the parking lot, but Susan felt as if she could do just that. The words echoed:

"Susan, you are not alone. You were never alone...."

Bright and early Monday morning, Susan continued her reading about Peter who went to Jesus and asked, "Lord, how often should I forgive someone who sins against me? Seven times?"

"No!" Jesus replied, "seventy times seven!"

Jesus, then, told a story of a servant who owed an astronomical debt to the king. The king, showing mercy, cancelled the debt. Immediately, the same servant went to collect a debt owed to him by a fellow servant. When the fellow servant begged for mercy, the first servant had him thrown in jail. So, when the king found out, he changed his mind and had that first servant thrown in prison also. In relation to the story, Jesus said,

> *"That's what my heavenly Father will do to you if you refuse to forgive your brothers and sisters in your heart."* (Matthew 18:21-35)

Susan had to think long and hard about what would happen if she refused to forgive.

She had only just gotten to her desk at the office when Ronald Keller, her former employer from Columbia, called.

"Morning, Susan! I've been out of the office; otherwise, I would have certainly returned your call before now. Virgie didn't say so, but Jackson said you were upset about the SPOTY, so I've called to explain."

"Yes, Mr. Keller, thank you for returning my call. I called because I had not heard from anyone, except a third party, and it was very negative. You can understand I want to get to the bottom of it. If there is some blight on my record, I cannot refute it if I am not informed. Can you clear up some of the mystery? Was I nominated for the SPOTY? Was my nomination withdrawn? If so, why? If not, why is that story out there?"

"Susan, I think I can explain. I don't think you knew this, but Iris Fenton, her husband and I have been friends for years. When Mrs. Goldsmith was so ill and not expected to live, Iris came to me to handle the sale of the property. You and I both know long-distance sales are done all the time, but it is so much simpler if the business is handled locally. So, I referred them to you because you are such a dedicated, focused salesperson. You have been tremendously successful, and I certainly had no doubts about your ability to get the job done.

Iris came back to me complaining about you overstepping your boundaries and trying to thwart the sale of the property for your benefit. She was going on about her dead niece's husband by saying you were playing up to him, and you had ulterior motives. Until Carol died, both Iris and Melton were afraid she would end up with everything because she had those two boys and, well, Carol's father, I can't remember his name just now, was Mrs. Goldsmith's favorite. Iris wouldn't listen to me at all. It didn't help when her friend, Clarissa, referred to you as—oh, never mind. You get the idea."

"I do Mr. Keller."

"Now, about the SPOTY, I did plan to nominate you. Our office was to send a recommendation form to Franklin and a bio form for you to complete. I wasn't aware of any problem until a red-faced Virgie came in a couple of weeks later with the packet which had never gotten mailed. I called Franklin to explain the delay and personally sent him the form which included the bio for you. After a couple of weeks, when I didn't receive it back, I called Franklin again. He said he'd have to hold off on a recommendation—not because of allegations made directly by Iris, but because he thought you hadn't handled Iris and Clarissa professionally. The SPOTY is a high award and includes client satisfaction and community interaction. Franklin then thought it pointless to give the bio to you at all."

"In my defense Mr. Keller, I didn't know any of this. From the first time we met, Iris was on the offensive with me, but I chalked it up to personality differences. The sale of the property was pretty straight forward until the title search revealed Carol's name on the title. Carol's husband, Garrett, immediately provided her death certificate together with an affidavit stating neither Carol nor her heirs had claims on the property. The closing was scheduled. End of story."

"Susan, Franklin called me last week apologizing for the delay and his initial decision, but it was too late. The deadline was past. In retrospect, I think your move to Plaincreek Crossroads cut off personal communications, or this would have never happened. Maybe next year, Susan."

"Oh, just an aside, Clarissa never was a client. In fact, she may be marrying Garrett. Thanks for taking the time to call. My concern is how these meaningless fabrications became so important, besmirching my character. I would be lying if I said losing the SPOTY didn't mean anything. I do want to be recognized as the best realtor, but the award is not important enough for me to become money grabbing and unethical. Thanks again for calling."

As she hung up, Susan became frightened for Garrett. Did he know what he was getting into with Clarissa?

She was still ruminating over her conversation when Iris walked in. *What a Monday morning.* "Do come in. Could I offer you a cup of coffee; I was just going to get some myself?"

"No, Miss Walen, Susan, I've already had my day's ration, but thank you. I want you to know how well I thought you managed the closing. It went without a hitch and, well, I was afraid. So, a *thank you* is in order. This is hard for me, Susan, but I might have misjudged you. I hear from Ron and Franklin your nomination for the Salesperson of the Year Award fell through. I'm sorry. I just wanted you to know."

Susan sat motionless and then stood, "Iris, perhaps one day we can be friends. Thank you. I did want to win the Salesperson of the Year, but there are other things more important."

For the first time since Susan had met her, Iris smiled. It literally transformed her whole countenance. This time Iris didn't stomp or humph her way to the door, but nodded amicably as she passed each desk. Susan had to chuckle at the bewildered looks the office staff gave each other.

Her third surprise came at lunch time. Angus stuck his head in the door and indicated for her to come out.

"Can we go to the park and eat? I've brought lunch, if you don't mind."

Mind? Susan loved the beautiful weather and the quiet little park across the street from her office. The park was actually just a strip of grass with trees, picnic tables and a spigot of cold spring-fed water. The mountains in the distance were hazy. "We know why they are called the Smoky Mountains, don't we? Perfect timing, Angus. What do you have?"

"Just the typical bachelor fare: cheeseburger, fries, and coke." At Susan's grin and wrinkled nose, he, too, grinned. "You didn't mean food did you? But what do you want first? Here, I can talk while we eat. Garrett's off on his summer job, so he doesn't know this yet. Carol and Mrs. Goldsmith did sign a contract to raise Casper Fish, through a private two-year grant. Carol and Mrs. Goldsmith agreed there would be no payment unless the fish survived. The two years are up at the end of June and monies in this grant will be forfeit unless some fish are delivered. If they thought Andi's fish was a Casper, then, Carol and Russ were most likely on their way to Spartanburg with it. The embryos had been in the lake for about six months by that time."

"They must have been really excited."

"Susan, there's more--this will verify it for everyone, I think. There was a note on a slip of paper in the grant file; a phone memo with an appointment for December 20th, year before last."

"What? An appointment?"

"Yes, and the date of the appointment was the same date as the accident."

"Angus, I knew it! I knew it!"

"They were on the way but never made it. So they had the fish Andi caught, and it was much bigger than expected! Russ must have been involved from the very beginnin'; I'm thinkin' he was not surprised when Andi showed him the fish. Andi said he swore her to secrecy—Russ had a plan, wouldn't it seem? In my personal considered opinion, Carol and Russ were more interested in promotin' research than in the grant money, but I'm sure Joycelyn and Garrett could use whatever is available for furtherin' education for Andi, Grant and Gary. Did you say you caught a large Casper recently? You know the monies will go back into the grant if not claimed by the expiration date."

"I guess when they didn't show, the grant was laid aside until it expires? I don't know how those things work. What should we do, Angus?"

"Want to go afishin', Susan? Can you contact the developer to get permission before they proceed to fill in the lake?"

"Oh, Angus, more than the money or even advancing research, Garrett and Joycelyn will have a new lease on life. Yipes! They're scheduled to fill in the lake. I'll call Jerry and Michael at Ryan Construction Company when I get back inside. Oh, Angus, I could just hug you."

"Well?"

"My pleasure." Susan not only hugged him cheek to cheek but kissed him lightly.

"Okay! Is there any other situation you need help with?" he grinned.

Susan took his arm. "Oh, Angus, I just could not believe Garrett's wife and Joycelyn's husband would cheat on them. Oh, I know it can happen, but what I have learned about Carol and Russ has been the best. Joycelyn has beaten herself up over Russ' death. She said so herself. Now, she can hold her head high knowing he was not running away from her but on a mission to honor her. I don't know if Garrett has *beaten himself up*, but he would certainly feel better knowing he had not failed."

"You have no idea," was Angus' response.

"I wonder if there is more fish. At least we know there is one, the one I caught. I'll call right now. Did you want to wait or should I call you?"

"I'll be awaitin' right here."

Angus had to wait a whole ten minutes. "Angus, we can fish! Serious construction begins July 5th—after the 4th, another fiscal year. They've done a little grading, and some of the trees have been marked for cutting. The office manager at Ryan Construction Company did say, to be on the safe side, they would most likely require a statement exonerating them from any liability for any accidents. We need to go fishing before the heavy equipment arrives. The lake will be one of the first bulldozing sites."

Susan was breathless. "Guess what my devotions were yesterday morning. In Matthew, Jesus told his disciples to go fishing; the first fish would have a coin in its mouth. In more than a Biblical sense, each of our fish will be worth a coin. How are we going to spread the word?"

"We should chart the best time by the moon and the weather and the longitude."

"Angus!"

"Just kiddin', we don't have time to chart the moon or the weather, so let's just start Wednesday afternoon. Some of the men will have nets and poles. I don't want to have to keep the fish alive over a weekend so it's best to start durin' the week, so we can get them to the university the next day. The labs are still functionin' so there's no problem. Let's just try word of mouth. I'll make some calls. Why don't you make sure, if you can, to come?"

"If I can! You couldn't keep me away! Should we have food? Towels? Water? Something else to drink? Is there anything more we need to prepare for the men? What about containers to transport the fish? Who is going to take them?"

"Well we could call the fire and police departments just to be on the safe side...Susan, Susan; we're goin' to go fishin', not on a rescue mission. Well, this certainly could be considered a rescue, I guess. Couldn't it? But food, water, and dry towels will not be needed. We can round up a bunch of fishermen with equipment. This is becomin' a tourist town, and one of the main attractions, aside from a mountain view, is access to great fishin'. Like takin' coins from the mouth of a fish. Ha, ha. I had to add that."

Susan went around the table and gave Angus his second hug of the day. She was glad he had not seen her *fishing clothes* when she went fishing with the teens, because he would have really teased her.

Angus put his arms around Susan and hugged her back. "Look what I was just given this mornin'. It's a message from a woman named Susan who called to say she would meet me at the lake. The date is smudged, but it wasn't recent was it? Care to fill me in?"

"Oh, Angus, never mind. I did leave the message weeks ago, but it was all a misunderstanding. You didn't say anything to Garrett did you?"

"No. It's our little secret if that's the way you want it."

Susan would have punched him lightly on the arm, but he playfully ducked in time.

"I'd better go start spreadin' word-of-mouth. How does this sound? *Attention Fishermen. Take advantage of your opportunity to catch a ghost fish. Fish for Cancer research.* I guess I could put a notice up in the sportin' goods shop with my name and number. I'd better find Garrett, too, to bring him up to date. I'm off Susan."

ᐸ　ᐳ

"Word-of-mouth around here is quite effective," Susan admitted to Joycelyn as fishermen parked in driveways, all along the road and in the cul-de-sac on Wednesday afternoon. The fishermen of Plaincreek Crossroads were going to *take an opportunity to catch a ghost fish for cancer research*, as Angus put it, though Susan didn't know if he put up any notices. Andi, with her pole and bucket, was in the lead heading to the lake.

Susan and Joycelyn waited.

When Casper fish were brought in, Garrett would have to accept her *fish* story. She prayed for closure for Joycelyn and Garrett who could finally know the reason for their spouses' disastrous trip nearly two years ago. She prayed there would be some additional funding for Andi's college. She prayed her beloved Floating Bone Lake would claim a place in medical history.

Two hours later, fishermen from across the field began to return. A pan-faced Andi was in the lead.

Susan and Joycelyn turned to look at each other.

Garrett who had come in from work stood behind watching the approach. As if from a prearranged signal, across the meadow, the fisherman exchanged high fives, all grinning from ear to ear. It must have been the right moon or the right weather because they had fish—maybe 153 fish. Wouldn't 153 fish be just like God? They had the ghost fish. Andi raised a fishing line with a flopping, flashing-hues-of-the-rainbow, transparent ghost fish.

Angus was counting.

Joycelyn began to cry.

Garrett went over to Joycelyn and put his arms around her. He, too, began to cry.

Susan turned away and left them.

Now Joycelyn and Garrett could begin to grieve for lost love. Now there would be no doubts about the faithfulness of either of their spouses. Those spouses were on a mission to bring honor to the families. They were on a mission which, hopefully, would lead to a cure for some life-threatening diseases. Now thanks to the ghost fish of Floating Bone Lake, Garrett and Joycelyn could remove their mantle of shame and self doubt, look the world in the face and move on confidently.

Susan felt some of her own burdens lift.

ᐸ　ᐳ

Sunday morning Susan prepared to pick up Joycelyn, Andi and then puppy Danae for their trip to Columbia for Father's Day. She was fast becoming attached to Community Church and disliked missing a service, but today was noteworthy because she was going to honor the man who had put her ahead of his own interests for the last twenty years. He had earned the right to be called *Dad* and not just *Uncle Owen*. The trip was notable, too, because Joycelyn and Andi were going with Susan; she was going to have an opportunity to deepen their friendship.

Susan had a soft towel for puppy Danae to lie on during the trip. According to Andi, a bichon frise doesn't shed, but Andi would still be dressed a little less casual than usual, and there was no use taking chances. The breeder had the puppies in a fancy little kennel attachment to their house, but the puppies ran free most of the time and were not confined to a small space. Danae had had special treatment so far in her young life and might be difficult to manage in the car. Susan believed Andi could take care of her, though.

Andi claimed Danae when they stopped to pick up the puppy. "Hi, there Danae'" Andi cooed. "Ho, you're curious about my bracelet, aren't you? Here, I brought this for you. Yeah, I thought you would like a toy to chew. Hey, Susan, you know she's old enough; your folks could teach her. This breed is really smart. Did you get some dog food for her? I can tell you what brand would be best for her high metabolism. It will help if she has a tendency toward dry skin, too. Look, well, don't look, but she's sitting very still."

"Yes, they gave me food to get started. They said to feed her twice a day and make sure she had plenty of water. They said these puppies get into everything. She is probably pretty much potty trained and will yap to go outside. Dad's going to love her. Did you see the show dogs at the kennel? I couldn't tell the difference, but a lot of it has to do with papers, I suppose. One of those dogs was in thousands of dollars. Danae has papers, but she was not so expensive, trust me."

"It doesn't make sense for me to get a puppy right now for myself. Someday when I'm settled and have the finances, I want to get one just like Danae. I'm satisfied to wait for now. I've decided, did Mom tell you, I'm going to stay for a year and help her get started in her business? I may take a course or two just to keep motivated, but then I'm thinking I may want to go into medicine. I'll just see. I am excited about possibly working at the kennel even if just part time. Oh, look, I mean, don't look, but Danae is asleep."

"Joycelyn, are you going to start a catering business? You can put a note up on the board at the office. There's also the bulletin board, I noticed, there by the Hospitality Room, at church. Then, too, word-of-mouth in this town is alive and well."

Susan meant word-of-mouth in more than one way, but she wasn't going to think about Clarissa and ruin the day. She had to consider the passage in Matthew about forgiving. What if Clarissa didn't think she needed forgiving or wanted forgiveness? As she thought about it, forgiving Clarissa would have more of an effect on Susan than on Clarissa. Forgiving Clarissa wouldn't necessarily change Clarissa, but it would change Susan's attitude toward Clarissa. Hum? Susan had no doubt there would be an answer when she needed it.

Joycelyn was doing some thinking of her own, "I'm astounded and thrilled at the way my life has changed in the last couple of weeks, Susan. Much of it has been because of you. Andi will tell you that we were not connecting. We're communicating now. The burden of gossip, its innuendos, and scandal plagued my daily existence. I loved Russ so much, and I felt betrayed and the fool. I believed there must have been something deep down, where I didn't recognize it, which caused Russ to turn against me. I didn't feel as if I could trust anyone. I think the memory book is what drew me to you. You took such pains with it.

"Garrett pulled me aside just the night before all the fishing and explained how Carol seeded the Casper fish in Floating Bone Lake, so research on cancer and birth defects could go forward. I've never been as intense as when Andi, of course, and those men and boys all turned thumbs up. I would never have thought a fish could make so much difference in my life. Carol and Russ must have been transporting a Casper fish in the pretzel container to Spartanburg for cancer and birth defect research, not a romantic rendezvous. My heart is broken, but I still have the untarnished memory of the love of my life."

Andi had been sitting quietly, with Danae, listening. "I never was so glad to catch a fish in my life. I think I was the first one to catch one, too."

As planned, Susan, Joycelyn and Andi arrived after Aunt Em and Uncle Owen had gone to church. Danae took a tour of the bathroom while Susan put down the towel, dish of dog food and water. After Susan had tied a bright red bow onto Danae's collar, they headed to the church to surprise Uncle Owen, her dad.

The church Susan's parents attended had grown from a small group of people when Susan was a child, to five or six hundred, but it was still small, compared to Community. When Susan walked in with Joycelyn and Andi, it caused a stir. Susan had gotten used to the natural beauty of the two and did not stop to consider what effect their entry might make. She wanted to chuckle at a couple of teenage boys straining to get a look at Andi. This church had Sunday school and then the church service, so there were youth and children present during the morning worship. Joycelyn and Andi followed Susan in to where Mom had saved room.

$\backsim$

When they got back to the house after church, Susan held her dad back while the others went on in. "Dad, you read Mom's letter on Mother's Day. I spared you, but here, please read this before we go in;

Dear Dad,

Ditto to everything I said to Mom for Mother's Day.

I've come to understand since I was your brother's (my father's) only child, I was a reminder to you of my father every day.

I owe you a hefty apology because I was difficult and distant.

Forgive me; I want you to know, I love you very much.

Your daughter,
Susan

P.S. I know you'll understand when I say I'm not going to ask which round of 7 X 70 you're on with me.

Susan swiped at her tear as her dad finished his Father's Day card, hugged her, and kissed her on the forehead. "Now where are those other beauties? I'll never be the same."

"Neither will some of those boys at church! You'll love Joycelyn and Andi." Susan added.

As soon as Dad and Susan came in the door, Dad went to open the half bathroom door where he kept his slippers. "If I'm gonna be around all you ladies today, and it's my day, right, I'm gonna get comfortable and put on my slippers."

Danae made a beeline for his pant leg.

"Well, what do we have here?"

Susan was awed by the gentle expression on her father's face as he picked up the small puppy with his big hands. "What's your name, little lady?"

"It's Danae. She's a bichon frise," Andi informed him.

"Danae, huh? You remind me of another puppy. You're wearing my favorite color, red," referring to the bow. "I'll bet I could find a red hat or a sparkly gold one with a feather on it for you to play with."

Aunt Em, Susan's mom, punched him playfully on the arm.

Later, Susan sat back listening to Andi show the memory book: "Here's Grant and Gary. They love stories, and this is their father, Mr. Taylor, Garrett, a counselor at the high school. This is Trevor. You should have seen him hose the mud off Susan when she fell in the lake. His mother is Maggie who is an investigator and has camera binoculars." Andi told how the bats dove at them at the vegetable house and how they ran, leaving Susan to find her way home by herself.

"Here's Zeke, this is Grant and Gary's puppy. We called Zeke's mother, Mama, and she was mean. Mama was the biggest dog you ever did see! Susan will tell you. She saw her."

Susan nodded assent.

Mom shook her head in disbelief, "If you only knew. Susan has always been terrified of dogs, and the ones she wasn't afraid of she just hated."

Susan shrugged.

"Mom and Dad, the book is so Andi will have something to remember years from now. Floating Bone Lake is on the Goldsmith property and is scheduled to be filled in for development into a subdivision. We just had a two hour fishing marathon where fishermen from all over town came to catch Casper fish in the lake. These are unique fish used for cancer research. I'll tell you about it later."

While Andi was showing them the book, Susan could almost read their mind, contrasting formal business banquets, business trips, and the drive to be labeled the best salesperson of the year, to a strange little lake, mud baths, bats, and monstrous dogs. Listening, Susan almost didn't know herself. Susan was going to have to tell her mom and dad that she was not even nominated for the SPOTY. She could do that without tears. Today was just the first chapter from Plaincreek Crossroads.

Arriving home after dropping Joycelyn and Andi off, Susan had just leaned back, shoes off, feet propped up on the arm of the sofa, when the phone rang. "Susan, got a minute?" It was Maggie.

Susan sat up. "Sure, just got in from going to see my dad for Father's Day."

"David's out on the front porch with the kids. I said I was going to talk to you for a couple of minutes. He gave me permission to tell you what I'm going to share with you. I think I can trust you not to discuss it with anyone, but David and I have problems. I'm not sure what all is involved, but we've sat down and talked, and we are going to go to counseling. His jobs, our schedules in general, the kids, finances and other problems have driven us apart. He's been extremely paranoid lately about any time I spend outside the family. In fact, his paranoid has fixated on you. He got the idea you were just using me for your benefit, and he heard somewhere you were just after Garrett. Strange, since I was the one who encouraged you to get to know Garrett. I told David I was the one who insisted you wear a *knockout* dress for graduation. I guess he knows some town official who's related to Clarissa and, well, he and Garrett do talk, too.

"Trevor was there when they brought in the fish and, as we only live a couple houses away, I could pretty much see what was happening. I feel good about my research and how it helped solve the mystery of the ghost fish. I wish I had been out there with you that afternoon. After David and I get things sorted out, I really want to be friends."

"Maggie, I was so worried and depressed about the failure of our friendship. Just so you know, I would never take advantage of you or use you to my own benefit. Let me know when you're ready, and we'll get together and talk this out. I'll wait to hear from you."

"David, the kids, and I went to church this morning. We used to go years ago before Gabi was born and before we moved here. It was an inspiring service, and the sermon, of course, was geared toward the family and the pivotal role of the father as the head of the household. It was a miracle we went as a family on Father's Day. They showed a couple of clips from a marriage/family DVD. Oh, and before I forget, I have a message for you. It doesn't make any sense to me, but it evidently will to you. Garrett said to tell you, and I quote; *'Tell Susan I didn't have to take off my socks or shoes.'* You may have to seek out the Wizard of Oz to understand, but I have delivered it!"

Yes, Susan figured she understood—Garrett didn't have to make an un-proposal, in other words take back his proposal to Clarissa. He must have meant it, and she must have said 'yes'. Grant and Gary will finally be getting a mother. Hearing about it this way was easier. Not too long ago, Susan would have judged herself capable of putting on a happy face no matter what, at least regarding business. Now—not so!

"Thanks Maggie, you can tell Garrett message delivered." She said more magnanimously than she felt.

The pieces of the puzzle were falling in place. Falling might be the right word.

Chapter 20

The Goldsmith property had been sold. After this transaction, the real estate market would have other properties to show and sell, houses built on the very streets over what had been Floating Bone Lake. The builders on the Goldsmith land would soon be marking to pave roads, curbs and sidewalks. Streetlights would be installed, and the darkness would be no more; Floating Bone Lake would be no more.

A forlorn Susan watched as the bulldozers pushed and scraped the hunks of rocks—pretty sure it was what remained of the ledge she and Andi had enjoyed—into the ravine. Already the lake was disappearing inch by inch. Only a line of smaller trees remained. The brook still flowed through the field, as promised. Gone were the whispering tree tops, the comforting rustling of the meadow grasses. The lake had been her standing stone, a reminder of God's unchanging presence in her life. She prayed the remembrance would not fade, though Floating Bone Lake would disappear.

The tears came uninvited but were a welcome release. She turned to leave only to face Garrett.

"Damsel in distress?" He handed her his handkerchief. Susan nodded, stepped into his arms and allowed herself to feel the sadness. After a long moment, she silently turned from Garrett and walked away to her Malibu parked on the cul-de-sac.

Garrett watched her go.

Next morning, when Susan was perfunctorily opening her mail to begin the day, she was taken by surprise:

Dear Family, Friends and Neighbors,
    You are invited to a cookout and patio party to celebrate the birthdays of Gary Taylor, 6, and Andrea Stokes, 18, Saturday July 23rd[th] at 5:00 pm at 1430 Bone Lake Circle RSVP--by Monday, July 18th[th], to Mrs. Joycelyn Stokes, 864-997-5307.

Susan's gift juices began to flow; she was going to enjoy this. She would have a tee shirt printed with a photo of Gary making a silly face as the center of a huge sunflower. She would get him two puppets, so Grant could be a part, and hopefully she would be allowed to give them a demonstration.

Susan called Joycelyn, "I'm not going to miss this party. I'm offering my help to set up and to clean up if you would like. Oh, and give me some ideas of what Andi would like."

At Joycelyn's suggestion, Susan chose a dresser set with mirror, brush, and comb for Andi. She found the perfect book for her, too: a book of antidotes entitled the *Mishaps: Animal Fun, Fact & Fiction*, with the sub title *How not to do what shouldn't be done.*

Except for her brief contact with Garrett out on the property, Susan had not seen or spoken to him since the fishing. She had tried to put him out of her mind since Maggie gave her the message about his proposal to Clarissa. She still wanted to be a friend to Grant and Gary, so she was going to be as natural as possible.

As soon as Andi opened her package, she began leafing through the book at some of the cartoons and read from the joke section: How can you tell a cat from an elephant? Answer: It doesn't pay to drink and go to the zoo! Cats are whiners because they say *me Ow*! Dogs are winners because they say *bow Wow*! Andi had the three musketeers offering some of their own jokes and ideas. Could be someday Andi would write her own book.

"Dad, can I put my new shirt on now?" Gary asked at the same time he was taking off his party shirt and putting on his sunflower shirt. He strutted around the patio in front of Susan, repeating "Once upon a time…." He ran off the patio in the direction of the garage.

Angus arrived just as Susan was sitting down to relax with a plate of food, and just in time to see Gary run onto the patio and dive under the table where Garrett was sitting with his legs sprawled out. No one could see what Gary was doing, but it was curious to see Garrett purse his lips and frown.

Gary came out from under the table smiling about whatever he had accomplished. Garrett looked down and scratched his head. He stood. Blue masking tape crisscrossed his shoes and socks. He looked questioningly at Gary.

"Dad, you know what you said about making sure you wouldn't take off your shoes and socks. So, I taped them up!"

Susan looked at Garrett wondering what kind of conversation he had with his youngest son. In that moment, all she wanted to do was brush the stray lock of his hair back in place. Why was she always wanting to do that?

Garrett stared.

Gary had the wrong person. Everyone was unusually quiet.

Susan had been expecting to see Clarissa and was braced for her arrival. "I must. I must be cordial. Clarissa will be the one who will or will not allow me to see the boys," Susan whispered to herself. Clarissa, however, had not yet made an appearance.

"Miss Susan will you…."

Garrett interrupted Gary, "I'll take over Gary, you go get Grant and go play with your friends. Susan? W-W-Would you? Do you think you could?" Garrett couldn't seem to say what he needed to say.

Clarissa stood at the patio gate.

Susan couldn't handle this one. "Joycelyn, if you're not too tired, and you think you can finish the clean up, I think I'll go on home." Clarissa had arrived; Susan came face to face with the reality of Clarissa's relationship to Garrett. Susan felt she was a traitor to Gary who had made his wishes known weeks and weeks before. It was sad, but the blue masking tape was quite original and funny. She was sure no one else there except herself, Gary and Garrett understood. Clarissa didn't give any indication of understanding. Had Garrett shared with Clarissa about the *un-proposals?* "He had better turn father/counselor," Susan muttered, as she drove home slowly, through blurred vision, head pounding and heart aching.

The next morning Susan wasn't sure how she would handle it if she saw Garrett, Grant, Gary and Clarissa at church, but Community was so huge it was unlikely she would see them. She needn't have worried, because she didn't see anyone she knew. After the service, she turned her volunteer form in at the hospitality room desk and chatted with an usher. One of the pastors introduced himself and welcomed her. Other than those two, she spoke to no one and went on her way, which was a field track away, as had become her habit when parking.

What was this *plan* God had for her? She wasn't seeing it, and she didn't know what else she could do.

Susan went out to her newly decorated patio and leaned back with a glass of iced tea. Little rivulets of condensation ran down the outside of the glass as she turned it slowly in her hand. Her tomatoes looked healthy, growing nicely, but there were no tomatoes ready to pick. She watered them every day through a tube at one end of the box. Water and wait. Water and wait. What else was there to do?

Monday morning, Susan's devotions included the story of the talents from Matthew 25:14-30:

She envisioned one child acting as the owner of a company handing out bags of gold. She could see the first child going into business with a popular product to sell, the second child setting up a lemonade stand, and the third child playing hide and go seek with the money. They could write a short chant, one or two or three notes on the scale would do. I've got five bags of gold, what will I do? It has to make my boss happy. Ho, oh, oh. What fun it could be. Then they could talk about how God, the owner, gives each person resources, gold, and instructs each person to do his/her best. They could give examples of doing their best and not doing their best, such as hiding and not using what God has given. Of course, seeing the story through Gary's eyes would be hilarious. She could only imagine.

"How's that for devotions, Lord?" Suddenly, it wasn't fun anymore.

"What have I been doing with my talents?" Suddenly it was clear she had hidden them under a portfolio of listings and closings. She was using her talents, but she wasn't using them for God. She had been using them for her own personal gratification and advancement. On her job, creative possibilities abounded; meeting with prospective sellers, pointing out areas and details needed to make their property more marketable and even laying out strategies to leaders for desirable community traits to attract buyers and new homeowners. Imagination was the limit. How, Susan wondered, would God want to use her talents for His purposes? She didn't want to think of the cost if she chose not to live for God's glory.

Angus called midmorning, "Susan, this is Angus. I'm comin' to kidnap you for dinner tonight at the L & B. How about 6:30 pm? It's a late dinner, I know, but, it will be quiet."

"Nice to hear from you. I don't mind the time. Is there something more to discuss? Is this strictly a business meeting or is it social?"

"For one thing, it will be great to see you again. It's been a couple of weeks. Just be casual. Is that enough?"

"I'm guessing since you seem insistent, something is brewing. Right? Let me guess, you're not going to tell me over the phone, are you?"

"Absolutely right, Susan!"

"Okay, I can meet you there."

"No, no I'll pick you up. Will ya be at home or at your office?"

"I'll plan to get home and at least freshen up. Since it's just around the corner, 6:30 pm it is."

"Perfect, Susan. See ya at six thirty."

( )

Angus led her back to the same corner booth Susan and Garrett had shared. "Do you guys know the owners or something? Each time I come with you or Garrett, always it's this same booth; *Memoirs of Our L & B Booth.* Angus why won't you tell me what this is about?"

"Sit, Susan. I need to go do somethin'."

She was scanning the menu when Garrett walked up. "Hi, Garrett, are you looking for someone in particular?"

"Angus called and left a message for me to come. He asked Joycelyn to watch the boys, so I came from work. I quit my summer job because our new office computers at school are in and training on our new systems starts right away. I had some details to clear up and stayed late, so I haven't gone home yet this evening." Garrett sat down, "Where's Angus?"

"I don't know. He said there was something he needed to do."

"He told me not to wait on him when I got here and to go ahead and order. Wait a minute." Garrett flipped out his phone. "Joycelyn, where is Angus? He's where? You're doing what?" Garrett closed his phone.

"Well?"

"Well! Let's order, Susan. Angus won't be coming back. He is with Andi, Joycelyn and my boys. They're eating popcorn and trying to teach Zeke to beg. He said something about us getting the blue tape straightened out." As Garrett slipped his phone back in his jacket pocket, he slapped the partially used roll of blue masking tape on the table. "Speaking of blue tape, believe it or not, this has been in my pocket since Gary's birthday. I just never took it out."

Remembering the tape on his shoes and socks, Susan laughed. "You're lucky Gary didn't tape your feet together. I can see you stumbling and off balance."

"Yeah, I was lucky. Well, trouble is I think I was already stumbling and off balance. Susan, I'm so sorry about all this. Let me explain, please."

"Garrett, where's Clarissa in all this?"

"Clarissa. Yes, Clarissa. Well, where do I start? I think I felt as if I owed her something. We didn't date, just a couple of dinners. As I told you, Clarissa and I met at a bereavement support group."

" ..and she made the move from Columbia to your high school to get near you?"

"I, oh Susan, this is going to take all night."

"I guess you are my transportation home so go on."

"Okay, here goes. Iris and Clarissa are friends with your former employer, Ron Keller. He said he thought you were a successful salesperson. He said to make a sale you'd stop at nothing. Since you had moved to Plaincreek Crossroads, you would be a suitable agent for the Goldsmith property. From the first mention of the pending sale of the lake, Clarissa warned Iris and me about possible deceitful and unscrupulous tactics. Looking back, you sure became a threat early on. I thought she was acquainted with you because of the way she dropped remarks about you all along. The night of the banquet Clarissa began to *point out* the possible extra ways that could be used to make a sale. She even predicted you would knock yourself out to show everyone up by wearing a designer outfit to the graduation. She also said you wouldn't get some award, because Franklin Wallston wouldn't recommend you. After graduation, all Clarissa could say was something like: 'I told you so.'"

"Oh!" Now Susan understood about the dress.

The waitress brought their salads. Garrett continued between bites. "It's just… Clarissa seemed to have an explanation for everything you did. I even thought your fish was just an excuse to be involved. What Clarissa was saying made sense. I didn't think you could be doing what you were doing because you meant it, but because you just wanted to make a sale. David and I talked about it, too, and we both thought Maggie had become just too much taken in."

"Do you still think so?"

"Wow, at your girls' night out when I took Clarissa home, she let you have it. I should be grateful she became so adamant, because then I began to see what she was doing."

"Clarissa?"

"I still had doubts about you, but I thought I made her understand, though I valued her friendship, there could be nothing more. I was surprised when she showed up at the birthday party."

"But, I thought... From your message, I understood you had proposed to her, and the un-proposal was not necessary; you didn't have to take off your shoes or socks."

"Is that what you thought? Oh, my! I took it for granted you would understand." Garrett pushed the lock from his forehead. "I didn't have to take off my socks or shoes, because I had not proposed to anyone, silly, no proposal, no un-proposal."

"Now I know where Gary gets *silly*. So you didn't ask Clarissa to marry you?"

"Look, for now, I am fully shoed, but I have an unanswered question. What about Jackson? Not exactly a disinterested party."

"Oh, Jackson? After six months of no contact, I saw him in a different light."

"Hum, then you're not involved with him at all."

"Right. I still don't know why he really came. He seemed to be looking for something or someone. If I know Jackson at all, he doesn't do anything without a reason; he didn't give me one when he was here or when we talked on the phone later. I still don't know how they found me."

"Well since Clarissa and Iris know Ron Keller who is Jackson's boss, isn't it possible they know Jackson, too. If Clarissa and Iris know Jackson, they could have told him about the graduation. Maybe he wanted to see Clarissa or Iris?"

"You don't suppose? Well, it is old news. Now, I have to know about this *Ezekiel* thing."

"Ezekiel, huh?"

Susan brushed at his shoulder.

As usual he ducked, "Susan, I hadn't planned to get married ever again. How do you think I felt? How could Carol have run away with my best friend? Then Grant and Gary, especially, began hounding me about a mother, and like I told you, he starting picking out ladies to be his mother. It got rather embarrassing. I couldn't get you off my mind. When you were standing there at Maggie's, you were absolutely lovely. You stood there in your immaculate suit with muddy, bare feet. I had to leave to keep from hugging you then and there. I fought the attraction, but you needed me to rescue you time and time again."

"Yes, you and your rope. And the freezing water!"

"It's a wonder you didn't deck me a couple of times. I didn't realize it, but I had begun to look for someone who knew God personally. Do you remember when I pulled you out of the lake you were the first to mention Ezekiel? Then I saw you at church. I admit I was confused with Clarissa. The tongue is a sharp weapon. As far as Ezekiel goes, Gary and Grant are still begging to hear it again. You have no idea. Do you know what happens if I innocently say shake-a-leg guys?"

Susan didn't need too much of an imagination to visualize the boys hooking up dry bones. She snickered and then laughed. "Gary, huh?"

"Yeah. Susan, if it hadn't been for Floating Bone Lake, I may never have met you. If you hadn't insisted on getting to the bottom of the transparent fish, I may never have found the truth and been free to love again."

"So, you didn't know I was a real estate agent until the day you walked into my office?"

"No, there was no face to Clarissa's remarks until that morning. Iris was on the offensive already. With all that had been said behind your back, I was surprised Iris didn't ask for another realtor, but she wanted her property sold pronto. After the night at the L & B when Clarissa showed up, and we laughed about the Promethean Board, Clarissa became even more personal. I'll say you had both Iris and Clarissa going during the graduation activities. Then, there was Jackson and well, it all sort of fit. I know now I was an idiot for listening to any of it."

"It's about time we learned about each other first hand. Come to think about it, I don't know much about you at all. Well, when you said you were a school counselor, I understood your attention to me was just natural. Then I sensed a change and just decided to leave it all in God's hands. My attempt to be pretty and fit in at graduation blew up in my face."

"Oh, Susan, only temporarily."

"Garrett, I ignored God from age ten. You met my mom and dad, Aunt Em and Uncle Owen. They brought me up in the church, but I wasn't satisfied with any of it."

"Would you describe yourself as a little *brat*? I'm learning about *you*." Garrett looked up at the ceiling and grinned.

"Yes, I guess so...." Susan hated to admit it. She grinned, too, and then continued on, "My move to Plaincreek Crossroads was supposed to be an answer for me, but after six months, I was going nowhere. I was strangely drawn to the lake. Oh, by the way, don't ask Angus about meeting me there. I'll explain, but for now let's just say it was a misunderstanding. God was there, Garrett. I sensed his presence more real than if He had been physically standing next to me in the lake."

"I guess we're beginning to have our little talk, but we can continue this later. Let's get out of here for now, would you like to go…?"

(   )

It was nearly dark by the time they made their way to the silent, still site.

Remembering her first trip to look at the property, Susan addressed and stared down at the rusty barbed wire. "There you are, at least you're still here." As Susan and Garrett stood, daylight fading fast, the night sky began to sprinkle stars, but there were no longer sentinel pines whispering of the invading darkness to all the lake dwellers. No longer did bones ripple and disturb the surface of Floating Bone Lake. Any secrets were claimed by the machines, and lay under the foundations of what would be built. If Susan closed her eyes, she could imagine the ghost fish keeping watch.

Bulldozers were parked for the night. Lights on makeshift poles illuminated the red clay which was ever present, now heaped in clumps or graded so there was no longer even a shadow of a fishes' habitat. How incredibly erased!

"God was here, in person, Garrett. He spoke to me. He showed me what I was, and I didn't like it. His Word gave me instructions and a promise. This place, as it was then, is no more. I can't experience the solitude and the breathlessness of His presence in the same way. I know, though, He was preparing me for this time of change and even for homes and families who will come to live here, Garrett. Isn't God good? He never gives a snake when we ask for a fish."

"A snake for a fish?" Garrett rolled his eyes.

"What am I going to do, Garrett? Floating Bone Lake was my standing stone. Just as people of the Old Testament used to mark events with stones, standing stones as a reminder, so the lake would have been a memory refresher of my experience with God."

Garrett took Susan's hand. "We can remember it together. Susan, how could I not love you? Let me count the ways, from the muddy, fishy waters of Floating Bone Lake…."

Susan put her finger on his lips.

I know the plans I have for you, plans for the future and a hope….

"Susan, I think Angus is waiting to hear about the blue masking tape," he whispered, "and a little boy is waiting for you. I guess if Gary thinks he needs the masking tape, I have the rest of the roll…."

There beneath the star-scattered heaven, the mirage of a rippling surface pulsating with floating bones and biting fish, whispered hope to Susan as it began to fade. She began to envision street after street lined with homes, one right after another. She saw children running and laughing, riding their bicycles, and people with the ankle bone connected to the leg bone waiting for a breath of life. They would need to hear and know The Source of true happiness and life. If Susan would do her part, and she *was* ready and willing, they could learn the lesson of Floating Bone Lake: God, through Jesus Christ, has a perfect plan for each and every one.

Garrett gently traced the outline of Susan's upturned face, brushing her moist, sweet lips as he gathered her closer. She surrendered to his arms and brushed the stray strand of his hair back into place.

"I'm going to burst with joy," she whispered as his lips claimed hers.

God indeed did give Susan a fish.